Resolutions Embraced

Ardor Creek, Book 4

By

AYLA ASHER

Contents

Cover Design: Angela Haddon Book Cover Design

Because we all need a sweet, steamy story with some sizzling banter to close out this crazy year...

A Note from the Author

♥

Well, dear readers, Chad's book is finally here...and this one was really fun to write. I thoroughly enjoyed the banter between Chad and Abby and hope you do too! I've always wanted to write a frenemies to lovers book—one where the main characters want to dislike each other but have a tough time because they really enjoy hanging together. Chad is very likeable so I mulled for a bit about what could make someone dislike him (or *try* to) and came up with the idea of him accidentally bequeathing Abby's terrible nickname.

There are things in our past that we remember our entire lives, even if the memories dull a bit as we age. I loved that Abby evolved into this strong, badass woman during her time in D.C. but still struggled with lingering self-doubt from a transgression she experienced so long ago. It just seemed really human to me, and I hope you connect with her as I did.

In the end, I found this book to be fun, sweet, and steamy (and cracked myself up a few times at Chad and Abby's hilarious teasing and banter!). As always, thanks for taking the journey to Ardor Creek with me, and don't worry—I'm not done yet! We still need Justine and Gary's story (and maybe a few more??). I have quite a few stories in my head and I can't wait to write them down for you. Thanks so much for reading and enjoy!

Chapter 1

C had Hanson had one true love: being mayor of Ardor Creek, Pennsylvania. It was almost as if he were born for it. First, there were his looks. Not movie-star status, because that would be cliché. No, he was more a cross between a CW superhero and an Instagram model—like the ones that graced the steamy romance novel covers his buddy Mark's fiancée liked to read.

Stephen Amell meets sexy, adorable, shirtless guy on cover...yep, that was Chad in a nutshell, in his humble opinion, at least.

Which led to point number two: Chad was nice. He might have been a bit cocky here and there—a side effect of his innate self-confidence—but it was really important to him that he was kind. Because the world was a dumpster fire sometimes and the least you could do was treat your fellow human with compassion and empathy.

He often joked that his personality was a cross between Dolly Parton and Tom Hanks. A little bit small-town with a dash of everyman humor. On his journey through life, he'd rarely made an enemy. In fact, he only held one regret from his four decades on the planet. Something that happened long ago in high school that he wished he could change. Unfortunately, the past was written, but he'd certainly learned a valuable lesson from that harrowing incident: don't hurt someone else to further your own agenda. Even if you prevailed, the win would be hollow.

It was a mantra Chad embraced as he got his bachelor's degree in history at a local college in Scranton and entered adulthood. He'd worked for his dad at the town hardware store during the years he'd prepared to run for office until, eventually, he secured the job that fulfilled every part of his soul. He was basically a self-taught politician who always had a book in his hand about Churchill, Kennedy, Lincoln, or some other well-known leader.

In his mid-twenties, Chad ran for town council and enjoyed his tenure as a council member. A few years after that, he ran for mayor on a platform that heralded modernizing Ardor Creek while retaining its small-town charm. No easy feat, but being an Ardor Creek lifer who was still so young had perfectly represented that aspiration and he was elected in a landslide. He'd run against the previous mayor, Mike Bass, who was extremely unpopular due to a nasty little habit of cheating on his wife with multiple women. Now, after two four-year terms, Chad was ready to run for his third term. It was exciting since he loved campaigning, and he was pretty sure he would run unopposed in both the primary in May and the overall election in November.

"What's the goofy grin for?" Mark asked, sitting beside him at the local Main Street pub. "You deciding which girl to date on Tinder since you ended things with Maria?"

"Nah," Chad said, sipping his beer. "I'm kinda digging being solo at the moment."

Mark arched a brow. "You?"

"Look, I know you were always the solo dude while I was the player with a revolving door of girlfriends but maybe we're both evolving. If you can settle down with Teresa maybe I can be single for a while so I can focus on the campaign and my duties as mayor of this charming little town."

He scoffed. "No way. I think I remember you telling me once that you found it physically impossible to go for more than a week without getting laid."

Chad squinted before rubbing his chin. "That *does* sound like something I'd say..."

"You and Maria broke up last week. That gives you three days to find someone else before you turn into a pumpkin from lack of sex."

"Funny." Rolling his eyes, he sighed. "The thought of going on the apps again and finding someone else is just...exhausting. All the messages back and forth. What do you do? What do *you* do? What's your favorite color? How many siblings? Uggh, I'm already bored."

Mark pursed his lips. "Are there even any women left you haven't met on the apps yet?"

"I know you're joking but, honestly, I'm not sure. I might have to expand my range."

"Age or mileage?"

"Both."

His lips twerked. "How old are you on the apps?"

Chad contemplated. "Thirty-eight on Tinder and thirty-seven on Bumble, I think."

"You're forty-one," Mark said in an acerbic tone.

"Uh, yeah, *you* know that because you've known me all my life. *They* don't know that. And, besides, I don't look a day over thirty-five."

Mark stayed silent, sipping his Heineken.

"Dude, I'm looking for some affirmation here."

"I know."

Chad shot him a glare. "You're an ass."

Chuckling, Mark set his beer on the bar and tossed a twenty beside it. "That should cover us with a hefty tip for Terry. Teresa should be home from brunch soon so I've got to head out. You gonna be okay here alone on a Sunday afternoon with no date in sight?"

"You know, I liked you a lot better before you decided to leave me in the cold like the rest of the crew. You, Scott, and Peter totally left me hanging. You're all attached and old while I'm young and hot."

Patting his shoulder, Mark grinned. "We're all married or engaged to smart, gorgeous women and having way more sex than you at the moment. I'd be careful who I call old. Pretty soon, you'll end up like Smitty over there," he said, gesturing with his head to the white-haired man sitting at the end of the bar. "Although, I do hear he and Edna have been seen together around town. Even *he* might be getting laid more than you."

"He probably is," Chad muttered. "Never underestimate Smitty."

Laughing, Mark nodded. "He's one of Ardor Creek's best. Sorry to run, man. Next week's going to be crazier than last week now that I'm sworn in, and I want to spend some time with Teresa. She's got three episodes of Real Housewives DVR'd that I'm absolutely *not* interested in."

"Worst liar ever," Chad said, saluting him with his beer. "But that's what makes you such a damn good D.A. I enjoyed your swearing-in last week, although I have no idea why you decided to do it outside on the steps of the courthouse the first week of January."

"It seemed symbolic," he said, shrugging, "and it was a quick ceremony. Thanks for coming, by the way. It was nice to have the mayor of Ardor Creek there."

"I knew you only wanted me for my political skills."

Mark grinned. "You know I'm kidding. I appreciate your support, Chad. Your advice along the way was invaluable. I hope I can repay the favor one day."

Chad's brows lifted. "I mean, if Teresa has any hot single friends, I wouldn't turn down an introduction."

"Uh, yeah. I just proposed two weeks ago, buddy. Let me settle in a little before you begin the love 'em and leave 'em campaign on her friends."

"Fine," he said, waving him away. "Go home and bang your amazing fiancée. I'm not jealous at all."

Laughing, Mark shrugged on his coat. "Text me your picks later," he said, referring to their fantasy football league. "See ya."

The cold breeze from his departure through the front door wafted over Chad as he swished the beer in his pint glass, resuming his earlier musings. Where had he left off? Oh, right. Number one: he was born to be mayor. Number two: he was kind and compassionate. Number three? Well, number three was what it was: Chad Hanson was a bit of a man-whore.

It wasn't as if he'd *tried* to become a player. It had just sort of happened along the way. Who could blame him when there were so many amazing, gorgeous women in the world? Of course, Chad respected women immensely. His headstrong mother had ingrained that in him. His respect had turned to adoration, which had led to a need to get close to as many women as possible. A feat at which he'd excelled.

His friend Carrie had warned him that, one day, the act of dating so many women would lose its luster. He'd never believed her. Not until she'd married Peter, and his buddy Scott had married his amazing wife, Ashlyn. And now, Mark was engaged to Teresa, who was pretty much perfect for him. They were all settled into happily committed bliss, which naturally prompted Chad to reconsider his serial dater status.

He wasn't opposed to settling down or being monogamous—he'd had multiple exclusive relationships that had lasted several months. Rather, he'd never dated someone whom he felt compelled to settle down with. Someone who elicited the same deep-rooted feelings and connection his buddies had with their partners.

Sighing, Chad contemplated his beer. Damn, Carrie had been right. After forty-one years of amazing sex with some really great women, he was over it. The thought of getting back in the ring just made him...tired. Fuck. Glancing down at his crotch, he arched a brow. *Well, buddy, might be you and your hand for a while. Get ready.*

Chuckling at the inner musings, he smiled at Terry as she approached behind the bar.

"Watcha smiling at over here, Mr. Mayor?"

"Just 'Chad' is fine since I'm pretty sure I'm the only person who's seen you naked besides Brian."

"Don't say that out loud," she whispered, waving her hand. "And it was only because you walked into the locker room while I was changing in eleventh grade. So creepy."

"Uh, it was the *men's* locker room, Terry. I still fail to see how it was my fault."

"The janitor was cleaning the women's locker room and I needed to change for cheerleading practice. And it will always be your fault, Chad. Just get used to it."

"Fine. I'll agree if you give me one more beer on the house."

Grinning, she nodded. "That I can do. Be right back."

Once the fresh beer was in front of him, Chad took a sip, wondering if he looked pathetic sitting alone at the bar on a Sunday afternoon. Glancing around, he noticed the woman sitting a few seats away. She was watching football on the screen above the bar, face rapt with attention. There was something familiar about her button-nose and apple-ripe cheeks, causing him to wonder if he'd met her before. Long, black eyelashes extended from her eyes, and blue strands of hair intermingled with the brown locks that ran down her back. Feeling his eyes narrow, he realized he was interested.

She wore a green sweatshirt and dark jeans which encircled her ass and thighs like a glove. Her body was curvy in all the right places, and he suddenly wondered what it would feel like to squeeze the flesh under those tight jeans. Clearing his throat, he took another sip, trying to ease his suddenly parched mouth.

"You a Jets fan?" he asked before he even realized the words left his mouth.

She slowly turned her head and brown, almond-shaped eyes assessed him.

"Excuse me?"

"Jets?" he asked, pointing. "You're wearing a green sweatshirt and they're playing on the TV you're watching."

She scowled. "I'm not sure you can call what they're doing *playing*. They suck."

Chuckling, he nodded. "Yep. I'm an Eagles fan. They're not the greatest but everyone is better than the Jets."

"I know. My college roommate in D.C. was a Jets fan so I jumped on board. Should've gone with the Ravens. Now, they've got me in their clutches and I'm loyal. The second I shun them, they'll win the damn Superbowl."

"So true. I admire your loyalty."

"Thanks."

Reaching into her purse, she pulled out some cash and set the bills on the bar before standing.

"Thanks, Terry," she said, placing the purse strap on her shoulder. "Big day tomorrow. I'm heading out. Keep the change."

"You got it, sweetie. So good to see you."

She started to walk past him and Chad had the insane urge to grab her arm. Instead, he said, "Hey, I didn't get your name. I'm Chad."

She halted and stared at him like he had four heads.

"Um, yeah, I know. See ya."

Resuming her brisk pace, she exited the pub as a waft of cold air rushed behind her.

"Well, that was rude," he muttered to himself. "She could've at least told me her name."

Terry sauntered over, holding a wet cloth in her hand.

"You know her name, Chad," she said as if he were an idiot.

"I do? She seemed familiar but I couldn't place her. Who is it? Someone from Ardor Creek High?"

"Chad," she said, resting her palms on the bar and leaning forward. "I can't believe you didn't recognize her. That was Abby Miller."

His eyes grew wide as he studied his friend.

"No," he whispered.

"Yes, sir. That was the woman you decimated all those years ago in high school. I'm surprised she didn't throw her drink in your face."

"Holy shit." Running his hands over his face, he shook his head. "She looks...different."

"Seems like she's lost a fair bit of weight but she still looks the same to me. She always did have a pretty face."

"She did," he murmured as remorse began to simmer in his bones. Why? Well, that thing he really regretted in high school? It revolved around one person. One super-nice, super-sweet person who hadn't deserved what he'd done to her.

"She's been back in town for a while from what I hear but I haven't seen her at the pub until today."

"I feel terrible I didn't recognize her."

"Well, she might not care since she's probably not your biggest fan. She may be the only person in Ardor Creek who doesn't like Chad Hanson."

"I don't blame her," he said, running his fingers through his hair. "Should I go after her and...apologize?"

"Uh, you're about twenty years too late, I think. And besides, how do you atone for giving someone a nickname that basically ruined their senior year? Not even sure where you'd start."

"I have no idea. Do you think people will still remember after all this time?"

"That you called her Flabby Abby in front of the entire school and cemented her status as an outcast? Um, yeah, I think people will remember. It's Ardor Creek, Chad. There are no secrets here."

"Fuck," he whispered, shaking his head. "That was the worst day of my damn life. I felt so awful afterward. People called her that until she moved away the week after we graduated. I destroyed her. Man, I'm going to burn in hell."

"You were intent on winning student body president at all costs. Seemed it cost you a lot."

"Too much. I learned a huge lesson that day. The victory was hollow and I promised myself I'd never hurt someone like that again."

"Well, you've done a lot of great things as mayor. The community center has a ton of activities for seniors and kids, you've rebuilt every park in town, and you run the holiday festivals like a champ. Hopefully, you've built back up some good karma."

"I have to apologize to her," he said, standing and grabbing his coat. Pulling some cash from his wallet, he threw it on the bar and gave her a salute. "See you later, Terry."

"I'm not sure you'll catch her," she called after him, "but good luck!"

Waving, he stalked out the door and searched the street for Abigail Miller—the person he'd hurt more than any other in his entire life.

Chapter 2

♥

Abby Miller drove into her apartment complex, proud her hands were only slightly shaking. Seeing Chad Hanson again after so many years had dredged up every ounce of self-doubt she held deep within. God, she detested him. That was the logical emotion one felt for the person who ruined their life. Still, she knew the vitriol wasn't healthy so she let it fester for a moment before inhaling a calming breath.

"He can't hurt you now, Abby," she said, parking in her designated spot and gripping the wheel. "You're a successful D.C. political advisor who's moved back home to make a positive impact and foster constructive change. He has no power over you."

Nodding, she exited the car and drew the cold air into her lungs, loving the crisp chill. Closing her eyes under the blue toboggan she wore, the memories surfaced before she could stop them.

"Good luck today, Abby," Chad said as they stood in front of the row of lockers. "I thought I was going to run for student body president unopposed but you surprised me by jumping in. I'm excited to see your speech during the assembly."

Swallowing, Abby took a moment to comprehend that Chad Hanson was actually speaking to her. After all, he was the hottest guy in school and he usually dated cheerleaders or athletes...and girls in the chorus...and girls from the drama club...well, anyway, he dated a lot of girls, none of whom looked like her. But he was standing in front of her, giving one of his million-dollar smiles, and she rubbed her damp palms on her thighs.

"Thanks," she said shyly. "I really want to get into Georgetown. Mom says I have the grades but need more extracurricular activities. I looked at their admissions history and forty-two percent of the students were student body president so I decided to run. Of course, I don't expect to beat you—I mean, you're so popular—" she hesitated, feeling like a huge dweeb, "but it's a good experience and helps me with my fear of public speaking so, there's that."

"I didn't know you were afraid of public speaking," he said, crossing his arms as he leaned against the locker. "Want some pointers?"

"Sure," she said, grinning.

"Obviously, everyone knows the whole 'imagine everybody naked' thing," he made quotation marks with his fingers. "But what you might not know is it helps to imagine them, uh, experiencing pleasure, if you know what I mean."

Abby felt her face turn a hundred shades of red. "You mean, like, an...orgasm?" she whispered.

"Yep," he said, chuckling. "I know it's super-gross and I sound like a perv—hell, I probably am—but no one is intimidating when they're getting off. The facial expressions alone are hilarious. So, if you imagine everyone with goofy expressions like that on their faces, they won't seem intimidating at all."

Pursing her lips, she contemplated. It was kind of creepy but also weirdly made sense. Shrugging, she decided it was worth a shot. "Thanks...I think. Sounds like a strange but interesting way to take the focus off your own nerves. I'll give it a shot...maybe."

Straightening, he cupped her shoulder. "Don't tell anyone what a weirdo I am, okay? Only my closest friends know." He winked.

Abby's legs threatened to collapse at his touch. Clearing her throat, she nodded. "Okay."

Squeezing her shoulder, he tilted his head before drawing back. "See you at the assembly, Abbs. Can't wait." With one last gorgeous smile, he pivoted and headed down the hallway.

"Abbs," she whispered, loving the sound of the nickname on her tongue. No one had ever called her that. It was Chad Hanson's special nickname for her. Sighing, she turned to her locker to grab the books she needed for the next class.

"Hello, dear," her neighbor called, jolting her from the memory. "Have you seen Tubs? I swear, I thought he'd come back after doing his business since it's so cold."

"I just got home, Martha," she said, glancing around. "If I see him at my window, I'll certainly let you know."

"Thank you, dear. He loves coming to your place and playing with Kitana."

Abby wasn't so sure about that since Kitana outweighed the cat by seventy pounds and barked incessantly when he was near, but who was she to argue?

"Speaking of, I need to walk her. I'll keep an eye out, Martha. Take care!" Stepping inside her apartment, she was greeted by an overjoyed Bernese Mountain Dog who was ready for her afternoon walk. Grabbing the leash, she attached it to Kitana's collar and headed back into the cold.

Abby had always loved the cold for some reason. There was something clean and fresh about it, as there was to Ardor Creek. She'd grown up there and, although she should probably hate the town where she'd been "Flabby Abby" to everyone, she couldn't shake her affection for it. She'd returned home a year ago, all part of the master plan she'd set in motion, and now her roots were firmly established. Her parents had left Ardor Creek years ago for a retirement community in Florida, and her older sister lived in Oregon, but Abby had always known she'd return. One day when she'd armed herself with fortitude and ammunition to take down her greatest foe.

And now, she was ready. Years of planning and strategy had led her here. After she'd graduated from Georgetown, she earned her master's in Political Science and became an advisor to one of the most prominent senators in Washington D.C. It afforded her the experience and the opportunity to learn everything about the political system and how campaigns functioned. When the senator retired, it had been perfect timing because it just so happened the mayor's term in Ardor Creek was almost finished.

Perfect because Abby had moved back to Ardor Creek for one sole purpose: to become mayor. Not only was she going to infuse the town with some new energy that was sorely needed, but she was going to take away the thing Chad Hanson loved most. Both goals would be accomplished in her laser-focused way, allowing her to add to her impressive political resume and show her long-ago enemy that being a jerk had consequences.

Walking alongside Kitana, she contemplated the breadth of her actions. Tomorrow, she would file the paperwork to run against Chad in the primary. They were the same political party so she had to beat him there first. Then, she'd run as the party's candidate for mayor. And on the day she was sworn in on the steps of Ardor Creek Town Hall, she would stare deep into Chad Hanson's gorgeous green eyes and revel in the misery on his handsome face.

Flabby Abby had come home and she was ready to defeat Chad Hanson.

Chapter 3

C had spent a good ten minutes trolling the sidewalks looking for Abby after he left the pub on Sunday. Unfortunately, his efforts were in vain and he headed to his apartment feeling like an ass. Once inside, he sat down with a beer to watch the rest of the game but his thoughts were on the woman he'd met in the pub.

Of course, he'd *met* her before, but the woman he'd spoken to looked nothing like the Abigail Miller he recalled from high school. She'd been heavy in school, leading to the stupid nickname, but she'd also had a killer smile. For some reason, Chad remembered that quite well. The image of a smiling Abby flitted through his brain causing his lips to twitch. She'd always been so nice, and a bit shy, and certainly didn't deserve what he'd done to her.

After a while, Chad whipped up some stir fry before heading to bed to study the proposal Rydell Industries had filed at town hall the previous week. They were a huge developer who wanted to modernize Ardor Creek with fancy malls, luxury condos, and corporate box stores, which Chad vehemently opposed. He'd encouraged some modernization in Ardor Creek because it was good for the local economy but felt it imperative the town retain its homey feel. It led to some pretty fantastic tourism that kept the town thriving.

Eventually, the words on his laptop all ran together and he removed his reading glasses before rubbing his tired eyes. "You can read the rest tomorrow, old man," he muttered. "Time to get some sleep."

Unfortunately, sleep never came. After tossing and turning all night while Abby's sweet face flashed in his mind, he got up with the sun and donned his standard work clothing: khakis, a button-down collared shirt, tie, and loafers. He wore a suit when the occasion called for it, which thankfully wasn't that often. Chad enjoyed the perks of being a small-town mayor, and he preferred to keep things casual and laid-back.

Arriving at town hall, he parked in his dedicated spot before heading inside. Breezing into the office, he waved to his administrative assistant, Shelly, before sitting down at his desk in the back room. Pulling up the proposal, he munched on his everything bagel and picked up where he'd left off.

Two minutes later, he was thinking about Abby again. Frustrated he couldn't concentrate, he finished the bagel and wiped his hands. Sitting back in his chair, he let the memories wash over him, even though he hated thinking about that fateful day.

"Okay, guys, calm down," Principal Rucker said, giving a stern look to the crowd of a hundred and twenty kids that sat in the bleachers of the school gym. "I'm prepared to dismiss you all for the day as soon as we've heard the speeches."

Those magical words did the trick and the throng grew quiet and attentive.

Chuckling, he spoke into the podium microphone. "Figured that would do it. As you all know, we have two very qualified candidates running for student body president this year. Let's give them both our undivided attention as they try to win your vote. First up, Abigail Miller."

Lethargic claps sounded from the crowd as Abby stood and walked toward the podium. She was wearing a pretty dress and her long brown hair was styled and full. Glancing down, Chad regarded his jeans and t-shirt. Hmmm. Maybe he should've dressed nicer? Lifting his gaze, he watched her tap the microphone.

"Heh...hello?"

A chuckle ran through the bleachers.

"Whew, I'm really nervous. Okay, don't blow this, Abby." Smiling, she shrugged. "That wasn't in the speech but, oh, well."

Chad saw several of his friends smile and his heart began to pound. He'd run for class president multiple times, always unopposed. Anxiety rushed through him at the thought of losing. What would he do if he wasn't student body president? That was his thing, after all. Super-popular, well-liked, Chad Hanson. The image was important to him and he longed to maintain it. What if Abby actually won?

Impossible. She wasn't nearly as popular as he was and the other students often took shots at her weight—albeit, behind her back. Although he thought they were asshats for making fun of her, it cemented his belief he would win the election in a landslide. There was no way in hell she'd beat him...right? Sitting back in his folding chair, he listened to her speak.

She detailed several platforms like implementing feedback surveys for the teachers so the students could anonymously pass on what they found helpful and what needed improvement. It was a good idea and Chad was annoyed he hadn't thought of it. She also detailed the need for outside lunch seating and an excellent idea about having local businesses "adopt" each class so they could help fund student government objectives. Chad's platform was more about trivial things like funding the homecoming dance and securing a float in the Christmas parade.

Scanning the crowd, he noticed how they listened to Abby with rapt attention and saw his dream of winning slowly fade. Holy crap. He'd be known as a huge-ass loser if he lost the election to Abby Miller. Wheels churned in his brain as he wondered what the hell to do.

"In conclusion, I want to be your president because I think I can foster change," she said, knuckles white as they clenched the podium but otherwise appearing confident and concise. "Together, we can create a school environment that encourages positivity and team-work, and determine our future as smart, creative young adults who will become model citizens once we go into the big, bad world."

The students laughed, thoroughly engrossed in her words.

"With that, I thank you all for listening and wish you the best. Go Spartans!"

Chad watched in disbelief as the student body leaped to their feet and began clapping and cheering for Abby as if she'd announced they'd all won a million dollars. Terrified he'd lost before his speech even began, he stood as Mr. Rucker introduced him.

"I did what you said," Abby whispered as she passed him. "Super helpful. Thanks, Chad."

He stared at her, unable to speak, sure that he was going to go down in history as the biggest loser in the world. Approaching the podium, he gazed at his classmates, suddenly nervous that he hadn't written anything down.

"So, uh, nice speech, Abby," he said into the microphone. "As you all know, I was class president freshman, sophomore, and junior year. It only makes sense I would make the leap to student body president senior year. I have years of experience and will do the job better than anyone."

Wide eyes stared at him from the bleachers as silence blanketed the room.

"This year, it's important we have the biggest homecoming dance ever, so I'll be asking Principal Rucker for an extra thousand dollars for decorations."

"Not happening, son, but you can try," Mr. Rucker called behind him as the crowd laughed.

Well, there went one platform. Okaaaaaay. Rubbing his neck, Chad continued.

"I'll also ensure we get the premier float in the Christmas parade this year. It will allow more people on board so we can collect donations from the crowd and buy the new basketball uniforms the team has needed for years."

The students gazed ahead, many of them appearing bored, and Chad felt everything slipping away. Holy shit, he'd blown it. He was going to lose the election to Abby. Searching for something, anything, he could try, he glanced her way. Gesturing to her, he spoke before he realized the words left his mouth.

"I mean, come on, Abby's really nice, guys, but do we want Flabby Abby as our president? She never attends the school dances or football games, and doesn't really care about anything important."

Audible gasps filtered through the room as Chad realized what he'd said. He'd heard other kids call her that before and it must've stuck in his brain. Turning to look at Abby, his heart plummeted to his knees.

Fingers covered her mouth as she stared at him with tear-filled eyes. Wanting to melt into the floor, he opened his mouth to take it back.

"Flab-by Ab-by!" a voice called from the stands. Whipping his head around, he noticed it was Butch Connors, football kicker and most likely the dumbest person Chad had ever met. Also, he was a huge dick.

"Flab-by Ab-by! Flab-by Ab-by!" Butch began to chant and within seconds, the entire football team had joined in. The other students joined, succumbing to peer pressure, and before Chad knew it, half the crowd was chanting along.

Pivoting, his first thought was to rush to Abby's side. To draw her into his body and protect her from the terrible chant while profusely apologizing. Unfortunately, that ship had sailed. Bolting from her chair, she ran out of the gym and disappeared.

"Okay, okay!" Principal Rucker called into the mic. "That's enough." Glaring at Chad, he shook his head. "I expected more from you, young man."

"I'm sorry," Chad whispered, realizing he'd just morphed into the worst person in the world. Like, maybe worse than Jeffrey Dahmer, if that was possible. Okay, maybe not **that** bad, but certainly pretty shitty. "I have to go find her."

"Go on, son," he said with a tilt of his head. "I'll wrap this up. It's certainly been one of the more memorable assemblies in recent memory. That's for sure."

Chad sprinted from the gym, through the cafeteria, and found her outside, leaning against the wall as she cried.

"Abby," he said, approaching. "I'm so sorry—"

"Go away!" she yelled, lifting her tear-stained face to his. "How could you?"

"I..." he lifted his hands, "it just came out, Abbs. I'm so damn sorry. I'll fix it. I promise."

"I know I'm fat and ugly to someone like you but I thought we were at least friends. I never expected that from you. From Butch and half the others, maybe, but never from you."

His first thought was that she wasn't ugly. Not by a long shot. Yes, she was overweight but so were half the kids in their school, and she certainly wasn't ugly. In fact, as she gazed at him with those big brown eyes surrounded by long, thick lashes, he felt something stir in his chest. Abby Miller was actually very pretty. Stunning if you took into account those full lips—cherry red even though she didn't appear to be wearing any gloss or lipstick.

"Stop staring at me like I'm some freak," she said, shoving his chest. "God, I hate you. I swear, Chad Hanson, I'll make you pay for this. I don't know how and I don't know when, but I'll make you pay. Screw you!" Huffing, she began to march away.

He grabbed her arm and she whirled around, furious.

"Abby—"

"Don't ever speak to me again. Do you know what you've done? Everyone will call me that now. Everyone! Oh, god." Lowering her face to her hands, she began to cry again.

"Please, Abbs, let me fix it. I'll go back in and make an announcement. I'll tell them I was joking and just being an idiot. A huge idiot. God, I'm so dense. Please—"

"Leave. Me. Alone!" Wrenching her arm from his grasp, she stomped away, shoulders set in a fury.

"Fuck!" Chad exclaimed, burying his head in his hands. "What the hell is wrong with you, Hanson?"

"You talking to yourself over here, dude?" his friend Peter Stratford asked as he approached. "Also, way to go in there. You just destroyed the nicest person in school. Carrie's trying to talk to her but she's beelining it to the parking lot. Not sure if we'll ever see Abby in school again. What the hell, man?"

"It just came out, Peter," Chad said, shaking his head. "Her speech was so good and all I could think was that I was going to lose and...it just came out. Damn it!"

"Her speech was awesome. Hell, I'd vote for her. You might have cemented your loss there, dude. People don't like dicks from what I've heard."

"No shit," he said, rubbing the back of his neck. "Honestly, I deserve to lose. I feel awful."

"Come on." Peter slid his arm over Chad's shoulders. "You'll find a way to make it right. The previous half-hour excluded, you might be the second nicest person in school. You'll figure it out. For now,

the girls' soccer team is getting ready to stretch. Can't miss that."
He waggled his brows.

Chad followed his friend, even though he wanted nothing more than to find Abby and beg for her forgiveness. Vowing to make things right, he entered the school and began thinking of ways to make that happen.

"Knock, knock!" a voice called from the doorway, dragging Chad from the memory. "Got a few minutes?"

"Sure," he said, gesturing to the chair in front of his desk. "What's the good word, Rachel?"

"As town clerk, I'm here to inform you that you'll have some competition in this year's election, Mr. Mayor." Her tone was teasing but alarm ran down his spine.

"Competition? Who filed to run against me?"

"Two candidates, actually. One from your party and one from the opposition."

His eyebrows drew together. "I know everyone in my party in Ardor Creek. No one wants to run for mayor that I'm aware of."

Glancing at the papers in her hand, she searched with her finger before landing on a spot. "Oh, yes, here it is. Abigail Miller. Does the name ring a bell?"

Chad swallowed, unsure he'd heard correctly.

"Abigail Miller?"

"Yep," Rachel said with a nod. "She has the appropriate number of signatures on her petition and everything was filed correctly. You have some competition, Chad."

"Wow." Puffing out a breath, he sat back in his seat. "She's got some balls."

"Okay, you're doing that goofy smile thing you do when you meet a new woman on Tinder."

"Ha. Ha," he droned, wondering why everyone was suddenly trolling his Tinder habits. Rachel had been the town clerk for years and Chad considered her a friend. She was also married, which probably worked out well since he totally would've tried to date her if she was single. "I know Abby, although I didn't realize she was interested in politics."

"Well, she worked for Senator Robert Dawkins," Rachel said, reading from the paper. "She seems to have a well-cultivated history of federal politics under her belt. Wonder why she chose to move here and run for mayor."

"I can venture a guess," he muttered.

"Okay. Go for it."

Sighing, he told Rachel the story about what happened in high school. She listened intently, her mouth slightly agape.

"Wow," she said, shaking her head. "I thought you were such a nice guy." Her tone was teasing but it jolted something in Chad's solar plexus.

"I am a nice guy, okay? I felt terrible afterward and did my best to make it up to her but I'm pretty sure I failed miserably."

"Who won the election?"

"I did," he said, grimacing. "She dropped out the day after the assembly. I didn't see her around much after that. Carrie told me she would wait in the girls' bathroom and walk to class after the bell so she didn't have to see anyone...or hear anyone call her Flabby Abby."

"Good lord. You relegated her to outcast with one terrible nickname."

"I know. There's no excuse. It's probably the only thing I truly regret in my life. After the assembly, I did my best to become a better person. I figured if I couldn't fix things for her, at least I could for other people. That's when I started volunteering at the soup kitchen and visiting the seniors at the nursing home."

"And you still volunteer at the soup kitchen every Saturday," she said, beaming. "It's pretty rad. Okay, you're not a terrible person. Maybe just sort of awful."

"Thanks," he muttered. "Anyway, I don't blame her for wanting to run and beat me fair and square. I denied her the chance and she deserves a fair election."

"Said like someone who thinks they're going to win."

"Come on, Rachel. I work really hard as mayor and people know that. I've cultivated a lot of goodwill in this town. While I admire Abby's gall, there's no way she'll beat me."

"The confidence is good but don't count out someone with her credentials," she said, lifting the stack of papers. "Which brings me to the second candidate."

"Who's running for the opposition? I thought I knew every possible person in town who would mull a run on their side and ruled out anyone having the nerve to run against me."

"Okay, before your head gets any bigger, let me see..." Trailing her finger over the paper, she tapped it. "Sterling Rydell."

Chad's mouth fell open. "You can't be serious."

"Says so right here."

"He's Charles Rydell's idiot son. Holy crap. Rydell must've ginned up his candidacy in the hopes he would win and implement the contracts for Rydell's developments."

Rachel's nose wrinkled. "Shady."

"It sure is. Rydell is loaded. Running against him will be difficult just due to the sheer amount of dollars he has at his disposal."

"You'll need to raise a lot of money to get that Chad Hanson smile on more TV commercials than Rydell."

"No shit." Running his hand through his hair, he huffed. "Damn."

"Well," she said, standing and clutching the stack of papers. "My damage here is done. Sorry to ruin your day, Mr. Mayor. Being a politician isn't easy."

"Never said it was. I'm ready to fight to keep my job, Rachel. It's the only thing I truly love."

Her head tilted as she studied him.

"What?"

"As a happily married woman with a husband I adore, it makes me sad to hear you say that, Chad. I want you to find someone to love instead of something."

"You sound like my cheerfully domesticated friends. I appreciate the sentiment but it's not easy to find the connection you all have in this modern dating world. But who knows? Maybe one day I'll meet the woman of my dreams. Until then, I'm very happy running our charming little town as its dashing, single mayor."

"It should be annoying when you say stuff like that but it's just endearing," she said, grinning. "Don't know how you do it but keep it up. And I know you'll find your person one day, Chad. You deserve love and I can't wait to see you find it. In the meantime, I've got to get back to work. Have a good day being dashing!" Waving, she exited the office.

Chad relaxed in the chair, digesting the news. The situation with Abby was...weird. No way around that. The situation with Rydell was...well, it was dangerous, in Chad's opinion. Welcoming developers like Rydell would only lead to the desecration of the town he loved so dearly. Chad would move heaven and earth to ensure that never happened.

Pulling up the web browser on his desktop, he spent a few minutes researching Sterling and Charles Rydell. Then, he spent two full hours researching Abby Miller. For some reason, she was a lot more interesting—and a lot prettier—than Sterling Rydell.

Chapter 4

♥

Abby knew it was only a matter of time before Chad searched her out. She'd done a pretty great job of avoiding him and most of the other people from high school who still lived in Ardor Creek but that could only last so long. She'd become a master at hiding after the disastrous fall-out from the Flabby Abby nickname and often avoided people her senior year of high school. That skill had come in handy when she'd moved to Ardor Creek last year.

She'd rented an apartment in a nondescript complex—modern but affordable. To run for mayor, one had to live in Ardor Creek for at least a year so her lease had begun January 1st of last year. Between then and now, she'd surreptitiously observed Chad and assessed his weaknesses.

First, there was his overconfidence. He carried himself with the swagger of someone who felt he deserved to be mayor. Perhaps some found his confidence reassuring but Abby resented his sense of entitlement. It was the same sentiment he'd projected when he announced to the school that he deserved to be student body president just because he was Chad Hanson.

"I don't think so, buddy," she muttered as she sat at the diner on Main Street, making notes on a pad that detailed her schedule over the next few months.

Second, there were Chad's friends. The group consisted of all the popular kids Chad hung out with in high school. Peter Stratford and Carrie Longwood, Scott Grillo and his new wife, Ashlyn, Mark Lancaster and his fiancée, Teresa. Abby counted them as one of Chad's weaknesses because of one glaring fact: Ardor Creek had never elected a woman for mayor.

It was ridiculous and antiquated, and Abby had observed and researched the three women in Chad's friend group enough to know they were all feminists who shunned the patriarchy. Abby planned to garner their support for her female-led ticket at all costs. She didn't need their votes—she understood they'd still probably vote for Chad—but if she had their support, it could go a long way to convincing other residents to vote for her.

The last weakness she'd identified was that Chad was a serial dater. Abby had mulled for months to discern a way that could help her. If she wanted to play dirty politics, she could contact his exes, find ones that were bitter and willing to talk, and get them to go on the record against him. Eventually, she'd decided against employing that strategy. She didn't want to make the campaign personally nasty, although she would certainly attack Chad's lack of experience. Even though he'd been mayor for two terms, she'd worked in Washington for years and was vastly more qualified, in her humble opinion.

Armed with her plan, she stuffed her notebook and laptop in her bag and headed out into the brisk, sunny day. As she approached her car, she heard the deep voice behind her.

"Hello, Abby."

Emotion jolted through her body as her spine straightened. Turning, she faced him as he stood on the sidewalk a few feet away.

"Hello, Chad."

His green eyes were clear, laced with the dark flecks she'd noticed so long ago when he would talk to her by the lockers. Light brown hair sat atop handsome features that formed an expression she couldn't quite read.

"I'm, uh," he ran his fingers through his hair, appearing nervous. "I'm sorry I didn't recognize you the other day."

"Didn't expect you to," she said, shrugging. "I've lost about a hundred pounds since high school." Eighty-seven, actually, but who was counting?

His brows lifted. "Well, you look great. It's nice to see you back in town. I didn't realize you'd moved back over a year ago."

"Yes, well, I became very good at hiding and blending in. Circumstances dictated I had to so people wouldn't call me names or make fun of me."

Sighing, he shook his head. "I'm sorry—"

"No," she said, holding up a hand. "I've worked hard to let go of that painful time in my life and you do *not* get to stand here and bring it up while feeling sorry for yourself."

His brows drew together. "I don't feel sorry for myself. I'm sorry that I hurt you so badly."

"I don't want to discuss it. It was a lifetime ago. That girl died when I decided to grow a spine and build a new life for myself. And that's exactly what I'm doing."

"Yeah. I saw the filing. Welcome to the race."

Her eyes narrowed. "I think you actually mean that."

"I do. It's time we had a fair race between us since I fucked up the last one so badly."

"Hmmm. We'll see." Her fingers were now clenching the strap of her bag so tightly, she was restricting blood flow. Telling herself to calm down, she lifted her chin and relaxed her grip. "I'm not going to go easy on you, Chad. You've had it easy your entire life. This election won't be a cakewalk like your other ones. There's never been a female mayor of Ardor Creek and I intend to be the first."

Pursing his lips, he gave a slight nod. "I was wondering what platform you'd use. First female mayor is a good one."

"I'm using that and others. My platforms are deeper than yours and Ardor Creek deserves a fresh outlook. I can't believe they haven't imposed mayoral term limits. If I didn't come along, you would've probably been elected in perpetuity."

He smiled, transforming his features into something so handsome, her heart slammed in her chest. "I want what's best for Ardor Creek, Abby. If they decide it's you, I'll be okay with that. The most important thing is that Rydell doesn't win."

"He's a threat, for sure," she said, nodding. "I'm confident I can beat him but I have to beat you first. One race at a time."

His smile grew deeper. "This confidence thing you have going on is really attractive, Abbs."

"Oh, please," she said, rolling her eyes. "Let's get one thing straight. I'm not interested in being one of your conquests, Chad. I wondered if you might try to 'charm' me or whatever," she made quotation marks with her fingers, "since I had a huge crush on you in high school but, believe me, any attraction I felt toward you ended the day you ruined my life. You might be a player but it won't work on me, so save your energy. You're going to need it for the campaign."

Something flared in his eyes and it looked a hell of a lot like desire. Huh. While she'd entertained the prospect of Chad attempting to charm her so he could manipulate her to withdraw, she never imagined he might actually be interested. Guys who looked like Chad were not attracted to women who looked like Abby. It was a fundamental belief she'd held for decades and one that had served her well.

She'd dated guys in D.C., most of them in her political circles who were attracted to smart women. While she was about a five on the attractiveness scale, she was a nine and a half on the intelligence scale, which meant she was a solid seven overall. Abby could live with being a seven.

"Why are you giving me that stupid grin? You look like an idiot."

Chuckling, he shrugged. "I just had no idea you had a crush on me in high school."

Damn. She thought everyone had known of her unrequited crush on Chad.

"Well, I did until you decimated me. Of course, now, I loathe you."

"Of course," he said, his tone indicating he didn't believe her in the slightest.

"I don't have time for this," she said, stomping to her car. "Nice job tracking me down. I knew it was only a matter of time. Best of luck with your campaign. You're going to need it!"

Giving him one last acerbic smile, she folded into the car and started it. When she tried to turn the wheel, it was jammed, as it had often been lately. She'd needed to take it to the shop forever but had been putting it off. Damn it. Attempting to turn the wheel, she elicited a frustrated groan when Chad stepped to the window and knocked on it with his knuckle.

Rolling down the window, she snapped, "Can you please leave me alone? The wheel sticks sometimes, okay? I'll get it to move eventually."

He rested his arm on the roof and gave her a lazy grin as if he had all the time in the world.

"You need to turn off the ignition and then turn the wheel clockwise. Hold it there while starting the car and it will unlock."

"I don't need help from you, thank you very much," she said, struggling to turn the wheel. "I've gotten it unstuck before. It just takes a minute."

She struggled for a good thirty seconds before slapping the wheel and groaning. "Piece of crap car!"

"Abby," his amused voice said above her ear. "Turn off the car and follow my instructions. I swear it will work. My dad makes car keys in the hardware store and showed me this trick ages ago when the new keys would lock the wheel."

Glaring up at him, she gritted her teeth. "I hate you right now."

Arching a brow, he asked, "Only right now?"

Glowering, she shut off the car, tilted the wheel, and started it again. Testing the wheel, it turned like magic. Annoyed, she glanced up at him.

"Thank you."

"You're welcome. Happy to help. If you need any pointers on how to run a winning campaign, I can give those to you too. You're going to lose, Abby, but I'm *really* looking forward to running against you. This is going to be fun."

"Don't choke on your ego before I beat you," she called, rolling up the window while batting her eyelashes. Tearing her gaze from his gorgeous smile, she backed out of the spot and headed home.

Well, that had been a disaster. Chad Hanson now knew she had a piece of shit car, he could ruffle her feathers, and that she'd had a huge crush on him in high school. Pulling into her parking spot, she slapped her forehead.

"Way to go, Abby. One conversation and you almost blew it. Do better next time."

Determined to listen to her own advice, she headed inside to prepare her speech for the local Kiwanis meeting later that evening. It was her first official campaign appearance and she couldn't wait.

C had realized sometime around mid-afternoon that he'd been wearing a perma-grin all day. It had formed when he'd had the interesting conversation... argument... discussion... whatever it was, with Abby that morning, and it was now permanently affixed to his face. Figuring he was fine with that, he replayed the interaction over and over in his head.

She'd been fierce, her cheeks reddened by the cold as her eyes shot daggers at him. The blue strands in her hair were cute as hell and he wondered if she'd ever tried other colors. And that body...holy shit, her body. No one would ever call Abby Miller flabby again. Her hips were perfectly flared in tight jeans that led to knee-high boots. Even though she'd been wearing a coat, he could tell she had large breasts. Closing his eyes, Chad imagined sliding that coat off her shoulders and peeking under her shirt to see what was beneath.

"Boss?"

"Huh?" he asked, lids flying open as he dropped his feet from their resting place atop his desk. "Sorry. I was daydreaming." Was he ever. About Abby Miller. Who would've thought?

"No problem," Shelly said, placing a stack of papers on his desk. "I'm leaving early today to take Jeremy to the pediatrician. These need signatures and then you're done for the day."

"Right," Chad said, saluting her. "I'll get on these. Hope everything's okay with Jeremy."

"Oh, it's just a check-up," she said, waving. "See you tomorrow."

Chad signed the documents and stacked them before deciding to clear out the emails in his queue. There were several, and when he was done, he noticed it was dark outside. Hearing his phone chime, he lifted it to his ear.

"Hey, Scott," he said, rubbing his eyes. "What's up?"

"Just thought you'd like to know that Abby Miller is giving a speech at the Kiwanis dinner tonight. I wasn't going to attend but I think I will now to see what she has to say."

"Wow," Chad said, feeling his eyes narrow. "She's coming in hot. Good for her. Thanks for doing recon. Let me know what she says."

"Will do. Heard you two had a nice talk on Main Street this morning."

"Of course, you did," he said, sighing. "It's Ardor Creek. Did they also tell you whether I'm wearing boxers or briefs?"

Scott chuckled. "Even the locals aren't that detailed. Carrie told me and she heard about it from Donna. Anyway, Carrie's all aflutter because the way Donna tells it, some serious sparks were flying between you two."

"Maybe they were. She's pretty damn hot, man. I didn't see that coming."

"I imagine she's not returning the sentiment."

"If that's a nice way of asking if she hates my guts, the answer is yes. But many women have hated me before. I'm not scared of her. She let it slip that she had a huge crush on me in high school."

"Oh, I know. She used to stare at you from afar and we'd all feel sorry for her."

"Why didn't you guys tell me? I had no idea."

"Would you have dated her? I got the impression she wasn't your type."

Chad pondered, unsure of the answer. "I don't know. I guess it doesn't matter now since she's vowed to hate me forever. I've thought about her a lot today."

"Oh, man. This could get interesting."

"It could. You know I love a challenge. Let me know what she says at the meeting. I want to know her platforms so I can come up with alternatives."

"Will do. You ready for this, Chad? You haven't had to fight for mayor, well, ever."

"I'm ready, Scott. In fact, I'm looking forward to it. Call me tomorrow."

Clicking off the phone, Chad swiveled in his chair as he contemplated. Oh, yes, things were about to get *very* interesting in Ardor Creek and he, for one, couldn't wait.

Chapter 5

♥

T he speech at the Kiwanis dinner went well and Abby was thrilled to officially kick off her campaign. The primary would be held the first week of May, so she had roughly three months to win over the residents of Ardor Creek. A huge feat but not impossible.

She'd thought about hiring a campaign manager, but Ardor Creek was small and Abby felt she had enough experience to organize the campaign herself. The first step was forming a team of people who believed in her platforms and would help her canvass. She put up ads on social media, local restaurant bulletin boards, and even telephone poles asking for volunteers who were interested in helping elect the first female mayor of Ardor Creek.

On Saturday morning, she walked into the meeting room of the town library, which the librarian had allowed her to use for free. Abby was stunned to see at least thirty people milling around the room.

"Uh, hello, everyone," she called, holding up the bags in her hands. "Thanks so much for coming. I got doughnut holes and coffee. Let's dig in and then we'll get to work."

After setting up the refreshments on the table, she set up the room, placing a long table up front and several rows of chairs facing it. She called for everyone to be seated and sat on the table as she addressed the room.

"I hope you all don't mind the informality," she said, gesturing to her outfit. "I'm a jeans and sweater kind of girl. It's best to be comfortable when you're trying to take over the world."

Laughter circled through the room.

"I'm Abigail Miller and I'm running for mayor for a lot of reasons. I'm going to go over my various platforms in detail this morning in the hopes that you'll connect with them and help me win. But, first, I'd like to get to know you all. Let's go around the room so you can introduce yourselves."

They started with the front row, which consisted of an elderly couple who was retired, a grandmother and her two teenage granddaughters, and an elderly gentleman named Smitty whom she recognized from the pub.

"Thank you for volunteering, Smitty. I wasn't sure I'd poll well with single senior white males. I can definitely use your help."

"Oh, he's not single, honey," a woman called from the seat behind him.

"Shut your trap, Edna!" Smitty whispered over his shoulder. "No one knows we're together."

"Oh, boy," Abby said as chuckles filtered through the room. "I have a feeling we might have our first newsworthy moment of the campaign. Either way, your secret is safe with me." She drew her fingers across her lips. "Okay, let's continue with introductions."

They continued down the rows until two women stood up in the back of the room. Abby recognized one of them immediately.

"Carrie Longwood," Abby said, smiling as she swished her legs back and forth under the table. "I never thought I'd see you here in a million years."

"It's so good to see you, Abby," Carrie said with a brilliant grin. "I have to go on record and state that I'm still voting for Chad, but Ashlyn and I are very excited to help you spread the word."

"Oh, yes, we're *very* excited," a dark-haired woman said beside her, eyes sparkling with mirth. "Carrie and I think it's time to shake things up in Ardor Creek and we're reporting for duty." She gave a salute.

"Well, thank you, ladies. Carrie, you always were one of the nicest people in high school and I appreciate your support, even if I don't have your vote. To address that very fact, I want you all to know I understand how difficult it will be to beat Chad Hanson. He's a fixture in this town and a very good mayor. But even good mayors get complacent and I don't think it will hurt anyone to consider some new blood."

The volunteers clapped and Abby felt pride surge within. Humbled that so many people wanted to help her, she began to lay out the details of the various activities the volunteers would employ over the next few months to help her win.

Afterward, Abby approached Carrie, noticing her distended abdomen.

"You're a kind soul to help me out, Carrie," she said, extending her hand.

"Can I hug you?" Carrie asked, arms open.

"Sure," Abby said, giving her a warm embrace. "I didn't know you were pregnant. Congrats."

"Yep," Carrie said, pulling back and rubbing her stomach. "I'm pretty sure it's Peter's although our new mailman is *really* cute," she teased, winking.

Chuckling, Abby beamed. "Tell him to come to my neighborhood, will ya? Anyway, thanks so much for your support. I'm grateful. How pissed is Chad that you're here?"

"Honestly?" Carrie shrugged. "He seemed kind of...giddy about it, or something. I think this campaign is igniting his competitive spirit. Like you said up there, he's been kind of complacent for a while and I feel like this is exactly what he needs."

"Ashlyn Rivers-Grillo," the woman beside Carrie said, extending a hand. "Thrilled to meet you, Abby."

"The pleasure is mine. I was hoping you ladies would want to help me. The lack of female political representation in Ardor Creek is appalling."

"Sure is," Ashlyn said. "I can't believe all the council members are men. We need to drag this town into the twenty-first century. And to be clear, I haven't made up my mind about who I'm voting for. I told Chad he'd have to convince me, as you will. He was super helpful when I applied for my food truck permits, so that's a point in his favor, but I'm still a newbie and I want to hear all ideas with an open mind."

"She's not a newbie," Carrie whispered, holding her hand to the side of her mouth. "We love her to pieces."

Laughing, Abby nodded. "Well, I'm kind of a newbie all over again so we'll navigate this together."

"Oh, and our friend Teresa wanted to come but she's volunteering at a health fair today. She's part of this female entrepreneurs' club that meets once a month on Sundays and definitely wants you to speak at one of their brunches."

"Awesome," Abby said, overwhelmed by their support. "I'd love to."

"On that note, I'm going to grab one...or several...more doughnut holes before we head out to canvass. Be right back!"

Ashlyn scurried away and Carrie smiled. "How are you really, Abby? Returning to Ardor Creek must bring back memories of high school. If you ever need to talk, I'm here."

"Thank you, Carrie," she said, her voice slightly laced with emotion. "It is tough sometimes but I remind myself of the ultimate goal."

She arched a brow. "To become mayor or to get revenge against Chad?"

Blowing out a breath, she lifted her hands. "If I say both, will you think I'm crazy?"

"Not in the least. That was a difficult experience for you. I don't blame you for wanting to claim justice."

"Yeah." She kicked the carpet with the toe of her boot. "Don't tell anyone, okay? I left that nickname behind years ago, although it will always be a trigger. Settling back in Ardor Creek as D.C. political advisor Abby Miller is pretty cool, though. I guess there's something to be said for reinventing yourself."

"There sure is, sweetie." Her green eyes swam with compassion. "Now, come on. Let's get on the road. I'm so excited we're starting with Northern Ardor Creek. We'll introduce you to every house on the map. Let's do it."

Thankful for her support, Abby gathered up her things and led the throng of volunteers to begin the first of many days of canvassing.

I t didn't take long for Chad to realize he was losing. The realization washed over him about two weeks after his sidewalk chat with Abby. She'd amassed a massive team of volunteers, many of whom Chad had known for years, and to say it hurt was an understatement. Where was everyone's loyalty? Didn't they understand he'd worked his tail off for two terms to make things better in Ardor Creek?

Perhaps people didn't realize how hard he worked because of his laid-back attitude. Chad was pretty chill and usually tackled things at his own pace. Did that mean Edna over at Parks and Rec was pissed because he didn't approve her budget in the requested timeframe last year? Sure, but he'd eventually allocated more than she'd requested and they'd built lovely new tennis courts by the lake.

And Bob Vance repeatedly told Chad he hated the new ordinance that required all businesses on Main Street to have the same colors and fonts for their signage. But every other business owner had loved the idea and rapidly complied, especially with the grant Chad approved to help them cover the costs. Of course, Bob had a big mouth, and one squeaky wheel was always louder than a thousand happy residents.

And then there were Carrie, Ashlyn, and Teresa. Chad found it endearing when Carrie told him they were going to help Abby canvass. After all, he didn't see her as a threat and what would it hurt for Carrie to show her some goodwill? Chad assumed it was going to be a one-time thing and they'd move on. Now, several weeks later, his friends' wives were regularly canvassing for his opponent and it was starting to piss him off.

One Sunday in mid-February, as he sat with the guys in Peter's house, Chad decided to make his displeasure known.

"Look, guys, I don't want to be a downer here, but what's up with your women?" he asked, making eye contact with each of them as they sat sprawled on the couch and chairs. "The three of them are at Teresa's brunch today where Abby is probably winning every single voter to her side. Where's the loyalty?"

Peter looked at Scott. "Do you want to explain to our oblivious friend how marriage works, or should I?"

Scott lifted his cup. "Go for it, dude."

Facing Chad, Peter lifted his brows. "Chad, let me explain a very simple concept to you about our wives. We have absolutely no say in anything they do. In fact, they wear the pants and make every decision while we keep our mouths shut. This ensures they let us touch them in very naughty places when we're alone together and that's all we really care about."

"Here, here," Mark said, saluting with his beer.

Chad scowled. "You guys are dicks."

Laughing, Peter straightened on the couch. "Seriously, man, the ladies want to help Abby. Carrie has a soft spot for her because of what happened in high school, which was your fault in case you've forgotten."

"Yes, I know. I'm a terrible person."

"The thing is, you're not, Chad. We all know that. But what I can't figure out is why you're here with us and not out there fighting for your job. Abby seems to really want this and she's expending a lot of energy to run an engaged and informed campaign. The women love that she would be the first female mayor, and her platforms are great."

Peter began ticking things off on his fingers. "Replacing the parking meters with an app-based system? Check. Allowing wineries to buy property on the outskirts of town? Love it. Building an app that houses all the community events and volunteer opportunities in Ardor Creek? We've needed that for a long time."

"I'm working on something like that," Chad said, hating his petulant tone.

"Well, you've had two terms and it hasn't materialized yet. People are impatient, Chad. If they believe she's going to do the job better, they'll vote for her no matter how much they like you."

"Fuck," Chad said, sitting up and sliding a hand through his hair. "I have to campaign harder."

"You really do, buddy," Scott said. "Understandably, you'd need time to figure it out because you got elected so easily before but, to be frank, she's kicking your ass."

Standing, Chad grabbed his jacket from the chair in the corner and slipped it on. "Thanks, guys. Although I hate the tough love, I need it. I've got to sit down and figure this out. Mark, I'll text you later about next week's fantasy basketball picks."

Giving them a nod, Chad exited Peter's home, determined to jump-start his flailing campaign.

Chapter 6

C had jumped into high gear, amassing his own team of volunteers to canvass and putting together several events around the community. He didn't feel the need to hire a campaign manager since he was the incumbent and felt that proved he knew *something* about getting elected. Abby hadn't hired one either, which appealed to Chad's sense of fair play. It was a modern sort of hand-to-hand combat which Chad really enjoyed.

One Friday morning in late-February, he was walking down Main Street and spotted Abby buzzing around the local diner. It looked like she was...waiting tables? She had a pot of coffee in her hand, which she took around to several tables before returning it to the back counter. Then, she headed to one of the booths, pad in hand, and began taking the table's order. Curious, Chad stepped inside.

"Two eggs sunny side up with toast and home fries, and an order of French toast. Got it, Mr. and Mrs. Johnson. Be right back." She stuck the pen behind her ear and trailed to the back counter.

Approaching, Chad noticed how cute she looked in the checkered apron over her jeans and t-shirt, and felt himself grin. "Uh, are you waiting tables?"

Pivoting, she glared at him. "Yes, Chad, I'm waiting tables. Don't you have somewhere to be? I heard you're copying all my canvassing ideas. Glad you find them effective."

The words hurt and he rubbed his chest. "I'm not copying you, Abby. You stole all my friends so I had to do something. I've never had to canvass before since I ran against Mike Bass the first time and ran unopposed the second time. Give me a break, okay?"

"Whatever. I'm busy. See ya later." Turning, she began preparing two coffees.

"The diner is packed today, Abby," the owner, Nick, said, appearing from the kitchen. "This is just fantastic. Thank you for the wonderful idea."

"Thank you for having me, Mr. Dombalis," she said, beaming. "I want to show the residents of Ardor Creek I'm serious about helping them grow with new and creative ideas."

"Uh, I'm lost here," Chad said, inserting himself in the conversation. "What are you two cooking up?"

"Chad," Nick said, his tone warm as he extended his hand. "Good to see you, my friend. Want a cup of coffee on the house? Happy to support our esteemed mayor."

"Not today, Nick, but thank you. I'm heading to the store. But I didn't realize you'd hired Abby."

"He didn't hire me, okay? It's a campaign event. Mr. Dombalis—"

"Nick, please," he interrupted.

Abby smiled and nodded. "Nick agreed to let me wait tables to raise money for the new computers the library needs. They've been using the same desktops forever and they need an upgrade. I came up with this cool idea that I'd wait tables for the day and all the proceeds from my tips would go toward new computers. Nick is matching what I earn and the patrons can choose to donate the cost of their meal toward the cause. I think it will be enough to buy three new computers at least."

"And it allows our lovely Abby to meet and chat with the residents while drawing some new patrons into the diner," Nick said, cupping her shoulder. "Win-win in my book."

"Yeah," Chad said, feeling defeated. It was a great idea and one he should've thought of. Man, he was rusty at finding creative ways to engage the residents. After almost eight years, he was bogged down by the bureaucracy of being mayor. He missed all the fun community engagement activities he used to plan. "Well, I wish you luck. The library always requests a yearly grant for new computers but I've never been able to find the money in the budget. Glad you're helping out."

Nick stood silent, his always affable smile on his face, as Abby studied Chad with those luminous eyes.

"You can help if you want," she said softly. "I can always scrounge up another apron."

Chad smiled at the kind offer. Damn, he couldn't even be mad at her when she was gazing at him with that adorable face. Why was she so pretty? It made it really hard for him to want to crush her. He wished things were different and they could run together. Co-mayors or something. With her experience and creativity, and his connections and knowledge of the town, they'd be unstoppable.

"I would but I have to work at the store today. Dad's got a doctor's appointment."

Concern laced her features. "Is he okay?"

"Yeah, he's just had killer heartburn lately. They're going to run some tests on his heart to make sure he's okay. I'm sure he will be and then they'll tell him to stop eating steak for every other meal. He's needed to eat healthier for a while so it's probably a blessing in disguise."

"Well, I hope he's okay. Give him my best."

"Will do," he said, waving to them before heading back out into the cold, cloudy day. Pulling his coat tight, he walked the two blocks that separated the diner from his dad's store. Arriving at Hanson Hardware, he stepped inside, the bell chiming above his head.

"Hey, Dad," he said to his father who stood behind the counter. "The bell is making that weird noise. When are you going to install the mechanical system we talked about? It has cameras and all sorts of fancy stuff."

"I like the bell," his dad said.

"I know, but you've had it for almost twenty years I think." Removing his coat, he hung it on the hook behind the counter. "At least get a new bell then. Geez."

"I don't know why it's a big deal, son. I'll get around to it one day."

"Donald..." a feminine voice called between two of the aisles. "I still can't find the right lightbulb."

"Let me help you, Claire," his dad called, striding toward the voice. Chad heard them chatting about the different bulb options until they both walked to the counter and she placed a few on top.

"Hi, Mrs. Connaughton," Chad said to the retired middle school music teacher who was beloved by everyone in town.

"Hello, Chad," she said with a tilt of her white head. "How's the campaigning going?"

Donald rang up the bulbs as they chatted. "Honestly, I think Abby's kicking my ass, Mrs. C."

"Well, it might have to do with that fresh mouth you have, young man."

"Oh, right, well...she's kicking my butt. How's that?"

"Better," she said with a wink. "I remember Abby from school. She was sweet and so smart. If I remember, she was valedictorian, right?"

"Yeah, although she chose not to make a speech."

Mrs. Connaughton arched a brow. "Perhaps because someone assigned her a very mean and undeserved nickname?"

Feeling chastised, he rubbed the back of his neck. "I'm going to pay for that mistake forever, aren't I, Mrs. C?"

"You're a good boy, Chad. Donald did a great job raising you," she said, glancing at his dad, "and it seems you learned your lesson. I trust the experience made you a better person which is a very positive outcome from a regrettable mistake." Chad noticed his dad's cheeks flush as he loaded the bulbs in a bag.

"Karen and I did our best. She was so proud when Chad became mayor. She got to see him implement a lot of positive changes before she passed."

"That she did," Mrs. C. said. Taking the bag, she handed Donald two twenty-dollar bills. "Just keep the change, Donald, because I might not be able to figure out how to install these newfangled environmentally friendly bulbs. I might call you to come over and help me."

"Anytime, Claire."

With a wave, she exited the store, the bell making the strange sound above.

"Thanks for manning the store today, son," Donald said, shrugging on his coat. "I hope I'm not dragging you away from any important mayoral business."

"Nope. I processed all of today's paperwork earlier and am here as long as you need me. I still wish you'd let me go to the doctor with you."

"I'm just going to walk on a treadmill while they hook up a bunch of wires to my chest. I think I can accomplish that on my own."

Chuckling, Chad nodded. "Okay. When's Logan coming in?" he asked, referencing the high school student who worked afternoons at the store.

"Around three o'clock, I reckon. I should be back by then but, if not, you can leave the store in his hands. He's a good kid."

"How are the numbers looking this month? I know February isn't always great."

"Scott was nice enough to place a bulk order for some of the houses he's finishing up over by Cyprus Street so that was a nice bump. It will begin to pick up once the weather gets warmer. Always does." Sliding on his cap, he waved. "See you later, son."

"Bye, Dad."

Left alone in the store, Chad pulled out his laptop and began researching creative ways to help one's local community. Abby had inspired him—along with sending a jolt of fear down his spine that she was going to win—and he wanted to reclaim the zeal he'd lost somewhere along the way.

Being mayor had been so exciting in the beginning. Everything was fresh and new, and he'd vowed to make a difference. But as the years wore on, the luster began to wane, as all shiny new things did. At this point, he'd certainly taken his lumps. He'd learned no matter how hard you tried, you couldn't make everyone happy. If you assigned a grant to the parks department, the waste management department would blacklist you because they needed the funds. If you signed an ordinance that ninety-five percent of the local business owners liked, the other five percent would drag you for it. If you hired a local to work at town hall, you weren't encouraging fresh blood...but if you hired an outsider, you weren't loyal. Honestly, it was exhausting.

Even with all those flaws, the job was Chad's dream. Although it was a grind, he still loved it with every fiber of his being and wanted to do a good job. Hell, he wanted to win so he could keep doing a good job. Determined to figure out new methods to engage the residents, he took meticulous notes between customers, adding to his strategy.

Chapter 7

M arch arrived with slightly warmer days and the thrill of a fully thriving campaign. Abby loved the various activities and slowly felt she was morphing back into a local. Ardor Creek certainly hadn't been a place where she'd experienced a ton of joy, but the town was embracing her and it was extremely meaningful to the once-maligned girl who'd left all those years ago.

The breakneck pace didn't leave much time for a social life but who needed one of those anyway? Abby hadn't dated anyone in two years. Her last boyfriend, Michael, had been a D.C. lobbyist who barely put down his phone long enough to use his fingers anywhere near her vagina. But he'd been hot, and Abby was always attracted to hot men. They never lasted long—in her life or during sex—she thought, chuckling at her joke. For some reason, the majority of hot guys she'd dated were really bad at sex. Maybe because they could get any girl they wanted and, therefore, didn't have to be great between the sheets? Who the hell knew?

One day, she'd settle down with a nice, moderately attractive man and have a baby. Maybe two babies. Once she won the election, she really needed to get on that because she was forty-one and not getting any younger. Many of her D.C. girlfriends had babies in their forties, as career-minded women often did these days, and she was fine with being a slightly older mom. Older mothers had experience and Abby could raise a little girl—if she had one of those—to be prepared for anything. No way would her child experience the anguish and vitriol she did in high school. Over her dead fucking body.

At the end of another long week, Abby took note of her sore shoulders and lack of energy. Realizing she needed a break from campaigning and her consulting projects, she vowed to remember to take some time to breathe. Since leaving D.C., she'd become a per diem consultant for other players in Washington who wanted to benefit from her experience. Her clients ranged from lobbyists to potential candidates to political aides, and she enjoyed it. Still, being mayor would be a whole new venture and she would cut back on her consulting business if she won. She might consider taking appointments here and there but wanted to dedicate her time to running Ardor Creek.

Closing her laptop, she decided she'd earned an afternoon off. Puffy clouds hung in the bright March sky as she drove toward the main square, craving a hamburger, fries, and a beer. She found an open parking spot outside and waved to several passersby as she approached the pub. Stepping inside, her heart fell to her knees when she saw Chad Hanson sitting at the bar, reading a book. He glanced toward the door and smiled as she walked over.

"Hey there, worthy opponent," he said, closing the book. "Here for lunch?"

"Yeah," she said, noticing the only open seat was beside him. How utterly annoying.

"Have a seat," he said, pulling out the stool before she slid over it. "I just ordered a burger. They have a special where you get two sides on Fridays. I chose a side salad and fries. Figured I'd do both healthy and fattening." He patted his stomach.

She shot him a caustic glare, noting he probably had a six-pack underneath his button-down shirt and tie. Chad was extremely toned and must work out several times per week. On the other hand, Abby used the treadmill and elliptical at her apartment complex gym five times a week, cursing the stupid machines the entire time. She absolutely hated working out but it was a necessary evil if she wanted to stay at her current weight. Not that she was skinny—that ship had sailed long ago.

For the past few years, she'd balanced on the line between normal and overweight on the BMI chart. That was acceptable since she loved food and absolutely refused to go on a diet. Life was short and she wouldn't waste it eating like a damn rabbit. She did practice portion control, which was effective, but every once in a while, she allowed herself a cheat day. Today was that day. She was going to devour a burger. And fries. And a damn salad since it was free.

"Fattening and healthy sounds great. That's probably what I'll have too." Glancing at the book, she read the title aloud. **"Destiny and Power: The American Odyssey of George Herbert Walker Bush."** Impressed, she lifted her brows. "Wow, I didn't realize you read Jon Meacham. He's one of my favorite historians."

"Me too," he said, tapping the cover. "It's a really interesting read. Bush was one of the few one-term presidents. Figured it might do me some good to read about an incumbent getting annihilated by his opponent."

"Why, Chad," she said, brushing her hair from her shoulder, "are you admitting I might beat you?"

"Honestly, hon, I began accepting you might beat me weeks ago. You're running a killer race."

Annoyed her heart was racing from the silly endearment said in his smooth, deep voice, she cleared her throat. "Well, you've stepped up over these past few weeks. I think it's going to be really close."

"It is." His eyes roved over her, making her feel uncomfortable.

"What?" she asked, touching her cheek. "Do I have something on my face?"

"No, I just...well, I was just wondering something."

"Yes?"

"I like the blue streaks in your hair," he said, picking up a strand and rubbing it with his fingers. "I was wondering if you've ever dyed it any other color."

Abby's entire body slammed with desire and she told herself not to hyperventilate that Chad Hanson was touching her. Who cared that he was the hottest guy who'd ever lived? He was an ass who'd made her an outcast. Struggling to remember that as he gazed at her, she felt her nostrils flare.

"Thanks. I figured out a long time ago it was futile to try and look like everyone else since I never would. I'll never be traditionally pretty," she said, shrugging. "So, I began to dye my hair. I had pink streaks last year but I went with blue this year. I like it."

His fingers moved along the strand as he contemplated her.

"You're staring."

"Sorry," he said, straightening and dropping the lock of hair. Bummer. "I think you're really pretty, Abbs. I don't know why you'd want to look like anyone else."

Her responding glare was skeptical. "You expect me to believe the person responsible for ensuring everyone called me ugly in high school thinks I'm pretty?"

He huffed a breath through puffed cheeks. "Right. Because I'm an asshole. I get it."

Well, damn. She didn't expect him to admit it so freely. Of course, he was an asshole but she expected him to deny it, at least. Now she felt bad, which was ridiculous since he was the transgressor.

"Okay, sorry. God, I can't believe I'm apologizing to you. You really are good at this political thing. You somehow manipulated *me* into feeling bad for *you*." Picking up the menu on the counter, she looked it over before Terry appeared.

"Hey, Abby, good to see you. What can I get you?"

"The burger special, medium, the side salad with honey mustard on the side, and fries, please. And a Guinness."

"You got it, honey. Chad, need another beer?"

"Sure," he said, sliding his empty glass toward her. "Maybe if I'm drunk, I won't piss off Abby like I'm doing now. I'm pretty charming when I'm drunk."

"You sure are, sweetie," Terry said, winking. "I'll grab that beer and be right back."

Abby watched him stuff the book in his bag before facing her and resting his elbow on the bar. Balancing his face on his hand, he regarded her.

"Sooo, if you're going to stare at me through lunch, I'm going to go sit on Smitty's lap at the end of the bar. Somehow, that's less creepy than how you're looking at me now."

His lips curved as those green eyes sparkled and Abby felt a rush of wetness at her core. Holy shit. Her body was ready to drag

Chad Hanson to the nearest booth and bang him senseless. Since the chances of that happening were zero to none, she clenched her teeth.

"Okay," she said, pushing away from the bar. "I'm done—"

"Wait," he said, grabbing her arm. "Why are you so jumpy around me? Sit down, Abbs, geez." Feeling like an idiot, she slid back on the stool. "I was smiling because I never thought you were ugly in high school. Sure, you had some baby weight—"

"That's a nice way of saying I was a whale," she muttered, picking up the Guinness Terry dropped off and taking a sip.

"I never cared or really noticed your weight, hon. I remember other things."

"Like what? The huge zit that appeared in tenth grade and resided on the side of my nose for several months?"

Snickering, he shook his head. "Nope, but that sounds traumatic."

"It was. I named him Bob. He was persistent."

"Well, I don't remember Bob." His gaze fell to her lips, hooded and full of desire, and she clenched the bar, needing a stronghold. "I remember those full, gorgeous lips, and your eyelashes. You have such long eyelashes, Abbs."

"Yeah, I always have," she said, lifting a shoulder. "Mom does too so I guess I got them from her."

"They're really pretty."

"Thanks."

Terry appeared with their salads, ending the awkward moment. As they ate, Abby began to relax a little and enjoy the conversation with her handsome lunch companion. Chad was funny and charming, as he'd always been, and her desire to hate him waned with every passing moment. Frustrated he could charm her so easily, she finished her beer and asked for the remaining half of her burger and salad to go.

"You're leaving?" he asked, looking so cute as he pouted. It annoyed the ever-loving hell out of her and her tone was brisk.

"Yes, Chad, I'm leaving," she said, standing and grabbing some cash to throw on the bar.

"I'll buy lunch," he said, encircling her wrist.

"This isn't a date," she said, yanking her arm away. Furious she couldn't control her emotions or her body's reaction to him, she wanted to run away and hide like she'd done all those years ago in high school. Hating that he'd dredged up the painful memories, she grabbed the to-go container and left without saying goodbye.

Once in her car, she berated herself for acting like a raging idiot. How stupid she must look to Chad, losing her crap like that. Tears welled as she struggled to wrangle the emotions and they began to stream down her face.

Arriving at her apartment, she jogged inside, wanting to close out the rest of the world. Kitana rushed toward her and nudged her thigh, her brown eyes filled with joy she was home.

"At least you love me, girl," she said, bending down to pet her best friend in the whole world. "As long as I feed you."

Kitana barked and Abby laughed, wiping away the tears. She'd adopted Kitana from a shelter a few years ago and it had been the best decision of Abby's life. There was just something so comforting about the unconditional love from a pet.

"Okay, let me put this burger in the fridge and we'll take a walk. Sound good?"

Kitana barked and Abby inhaled a deep breath, feeling more solid by the second. "We had a freak-out there, girl, but Mom's gonna be okay. We're always okay, right?"

The dog sat, tongue hanging from her mouth as she panted.

"Exactly," Abby said, heading to the kitchen. "You've got the zen down pat, girl. We'll both be zen together."

Placing the leftovers in the fridge, she headed back to the foyer and leashed Kitana before heading back outside. She'd messed up today, but she was human and humans made mistakes. For a few moments, she'd let her guard down with Chad, and the results were disastrous. As someone who always learned from her mistakes, Abby vowed not to make the same one twice.

Chad Hanson didn't deserve her sympathy or forgiveness, and he certainly wasn't her friend...no matter how genuine he'd sounded when he'd said such sweet things to her. No, she wasn't falling for that crap again. He'd also been nice in high school before he'd decimated her. No matter how gracious he appeared, Chad was a jerk, and she'd do well to remember that.

Chapter 8

♥

As March wound down, Chad focused on two major goals: beating Abby Miller and studying the proposal Rydell Industries had filed with town hall. When Sterling Rydell had moved to Ardor Creek two years ago, Chad had thought nothing of it. He was known as the lazy heir to the Rydell empire—a puppet for his father who'd famously vowed in several local interviews to remain CEO of Rydell Industries until he was six feet under.

It was a bit dramatic for Chad, but he understood that Charles Rydell was ruthless in his conquest to build properties across all of small-town Pennsylvania, no matter the damage done in his wake. Tales of his cost-saving measures and ability to bypass regulations meant any properties built in Ardor Creek wouldn't be up to the standards the residents deserved, which was unacceptable to Chad. Ardor Creek was his home and he would protect it, even from itself.

Many business owners had grumbled their displeasure that Chad was fighting Rydell so vehemently. They saw his ideas as modern and able to create a new influx of customers for their small businesses. While Chad agreed with modernization, he understood it had to be done in a meticulous way that wouldn't harm the town. Unfortunately, it was hard to explain that to the owners who longed for change in the stable town.

After compiling a plethora of notes on the proposal Rydell had filed, Chad felt an urge to see the site he wanted to build upon. It used to house an old tar factory that had been abandoned decades ago and was heavily polluted. Still, he knew it well since he'd hung

out there quite a bit in high school. Abandoned properties were
the perfect place for kids to hide from their parents and sneak
some beers after school dances.

After tidying up his desk, he passed Shelly, informing her he was
heading to the site and would be back by four to finish up for
the day. Folding into his gray sedan, he drove to the outskirts of
Ardor Creek, surprised to find another car. Abby Miller's car. He
recognized it from the day she'd had the epic fail with her steering
wheel. Parking beside it, he zipped his coat and headed out into
the brisk day.

She stood at the top of the embankment that surrounded the
site, hands in the pockets of her coat. A cute forest green beanie
covered her long brown and blue curls. Striding up the small,
grassy hill, he stood beside her as she gazed at the abandoned
warehouse.

"It's kind of creepy," she said, acknowledging his presence.

"Yeah." He kicked the long grass with the toe of his shoe. "It
always was. We used to have bonfires here in high school and
Carrie and Tina were convinced this place was haunted."

"I remember," she said with a nod. "And who knows? Maybe it
is haunted. It's definitely got a weird vibe."

Studying her profile, he said, "I don't remember seeing you at the
bonfires but there were always so many of us, maybe I missed you."

"I never joined," she said, shrugging. "Sometimes, when it was
warm, I'd drive over and stand behind that tree," she pointed to
a thicket where the forest began. "I'd watch you guys and hear
you laughing and...it sounded so fun, but I was too shy to join.
And then, well, after the whole assembly debacle I didn't really go
anywhere."

"Bummer," he said, guilt consuming him as it always did when he
thought about his part in her past. "I would've hung out with you.
I think Drunk Abby would be fun."

Her lips twerked. "Drunk Flabby Abby. I think it would've only
taken minutes for people to find ways to decimate me if I was
incapacitated. Probably better I didn't join."

"Yeah." Struggling to find the right words, he longed to reach
for her. To draw her into his arms and hold her while explaining

that he'd been a stupid kid with a big mouth. He'd never meant to hurt her but his careless words had done so much damage. "Peter always ended up barfing everywhere anyway. It was pretty gross. You probably dodged a bullet."

Chuckling, she glanced at the ground. "Maybe so."

"What are you doing here anyway? I came to check out the site because I've been studying Rydell's proposal like a madman."

"I need to sit down and study it too. I've just been so busy trying to kick your ass, I haven't found the time to dedicate to it yet." She finally glanced up at him and smiled, and he felt himself drowning in those deep brown eyes.

"I'll share my notes with you. I might not even make you pay me back. We'll see."

Laughing, she turned to face him. "That's a terrible offer which I will gracefully decline, thank you very much. I'm capable of doing my own research after I beat you. One thing at a time."

"I'm still digging the confidence thing you have going on, Abbs. It's hot."

Rolling her eyes, she gave a frustrated little huff that went straight to his dick. "I came here to see the site. I just wanted to familiarize myself with it, and I needed some fresh air after a morning stuck in Zoom hell."

"I came to check it out too." Extending his hand, he shook it. "Come on, let's go together."

After glaring at his outstretched hand, she pivoted and began walking to the site. Chad jogged behind her, making sure to keep up but also keep enough distance to see her luscious thighs in her tight jeans. Her legs were long and sexy as hell, and he wanted them wrapped around his body. Any part of his body would do just fine.

"Don't stare at my ass," she said, stomping ahead as they approached the warehouse.

"I'm not, Abbs. Geez." It was true since her ass was mostly covered by her coat, but he wouldn't tell her he was staring at her legs. Nope, he'd keep that little tidbit to himself.

"This place has seen better days," she said, stepping over some of the crumbled cinderblocks into what was left of the building. "Wow, it's really run down."

"The old tar company was supposed to remediate it, but they went bankrupt and dissolved before they could."

"And now Rydell wants to bypass the regulations that would require him to pay for the remediation."

"Bingo," Chad said, following her around the dirty warehouse. "He's not going to get away with it. Not on my watch."

"Or mine," she said, lifting a finger.

"Or yours." He grinned, loving her competitive nature. It was good for him since Chad hadn't competed in so long. Although he hated how well she was doing in the race, she'd also reignited a passion in him that had fizzled out. For that, he was grateful for her return to Ardor Creek.

They approached the back of the warehouse, coming to a stop at the knee-high wall of mangled concrete. Chad stepped over it before turning and placing his hands on her waist. Holding tight, he picked her up and set her on the other side.

"Chad!"

"What?" he asked, releasing her and wiping his hands. "It was dangerous. I didn't want you to fall."

Her eyes narrowed. "I'm perfectly capable of climbing over a dilapidated wall."

"Well, I was trying to be a gentleman. Sorry."

"Gentlemen don't grab women without asking them."

Expelling an annoyed breath, he shot her an exasperated glare. "Excuse me for trying to be nice. I forgot that I'm the personification of evil to you for one mistake I made in high school. *One* mistake, Abby. I've apologized to you a thousand times. I don't know what else you want me to do." Running a hand through his hair, he studied her, cheeks flushed with anger as she crossed her arms.

"I don't want you to do anything. I'm going to beat you and become mayor and then we'll be even. That's all, so just drop it."

"You know, if you'd let yourself take one second to stop hating me, I think we could actually have fun together. I had fun with you at the pub the other day until you ran out like your car was on fire. What the hell?"

"I had an appointment. I have other things to do besides hang at the pub, Chad."

"And I don't? I'm starting to get really tired of this narrative you've created that I don't work hard as mayor. I might have a different style than you. I'm certainly not as uptight—"

"I am *not* uptight!"

"Uh, okay," he said with a disbelieving grimace. "I care deeply about this town and run it the best way I see fit. If you have a problem with that, I don't know what to tell you. We can't all be hardened D.C. operatives. Some of us are just simple, small-town people who like to chill and have fun...while *still* working hard in jobs we love."

Her expression fell as she studied him. "I think you're a good mayor, Chad," she finally said. "I didn't mean to relay otherwise."

"You do?"

"Yes," she said, breathing a laugh. "You've done a great job for many years. But I also think change is good and, in this instance, it's warranted. Ardor Creek deserves a change—not because you're bad at being mayor but because it's time. That's all."

He mulled her words, elated she saw him as competent, at least. For some reason, her opinion had become extremely important to him.

Chad's phone buzzed, interrupting the moment, and he lifted it to his ear.

"What's up, Shelly?"

"There's a huge fire on South Main Street. The fire squad is all over it but I thought you might like to head there too."

"Damn it. The row of businesses with the jewelry store and Bob Vance's place?"

"That's the one."

"Okay, I'll be right there. Thanks." Clicking off the phone, he cupped Abby's shoulder. "Fire on Main Street. I've got to go."

"Okay." She nodded and licked her lips, causing Chad to ache with yearning. God, he wished they were friends, and maybe more, if only so he could kiss those full lips. Squeezing her shoulder, he tilted his head.

"It was nice hanging out with you until I ruined it."

Laughing, she bit her lip. "You didn't ruin it. I might have overreacted a bit."

"A bit?"

"Get out of here," she said, gesturing with her head. "See ya around."

"See ya."

Jogging through the warehouse, Chad rushed back to town to help his constituents in any way he could.

Chapter 9

♥

The last Saturday in March, Abby's phone rang as she was lounging on the couch after yet another vicious session on the elliptical. She was coming to loathe the machine but did relish the endorphins that now coursed through her sweaty body. Glancing at the caller ID, she smiled.

"Hi, Ashlyn," she said, thankful she'd plugged all the canvass volunteers' numbers into her contacts. "How are you?"

"I'm great, sweetie. How are you?"

"Oh, you know. Living the dream."

"Aren't we all?" she asked, chuckling. "So, I know this is super last minute but I've decided to throw a little sip and see for Carrie tomorrow so she can introduce Emily to everyone."

"Oh, how sweet. I heard she had the baby a few weeks ago."

"Yep! It will just be a few of us girls—me, Carrie, Teresa, Terry, Justine...well, you get the gist. We'd love to have you. You can show up any time after two o'clock and stay until the wine runs out. I'll text you my address."

Laughing, Abby was overcome with excitement at being included. "I'd love to, Ashlyn. What can I bring?"

"Booze, obviously. I'll take care of everything else. I've relegated Scott to hang out with the guys at Peter's house so we can gossip like it's 1999."

"Perfect. Thank you so much for inviting me, Ashlyn."

"Of course. We're all so excited to see you...and maybe discuss how smitten our lovely mayor is with you. He denies it but we're not blind. See you tomorrow. Text me with any questions."

"Sure will. Thanks, Ashlyn."

The phone went dead and Abby squealed. As someone who'd been a pariah in high school, getting an invite from the coolest ladies in town was pretty damn awesome.

On Sunday, she donned a silky purple top, jeans, and ankle boots and took a rideshare to Ashlyn's. Since they were going to be drinking, she didn't want to take any chances. After climbing the porch stairs, she lifted her hand to knock before the door was swung open by a smiling Ashlyn.

"Oh, get in here, you," she said, pulling her inside and giving her a smothering hug. "We're so excited to host the first female mayor of Ardor Creek." Drawing back, she grimaced. "Don't tell Chad I said that. He still might win. I love him, Abby, but we desperately need fresh blood in this town."

"I won't say a word," she said, smiling at the praise. "He's really stepped it up over the past few weeks. It's turned into a great campaign."

"Oh, I know," she said, leading her into the living room. "We've seen him everywhere in town at various events and he's been canvassing a lot too. We help him as much as we help you. I'm not sure if that's counterproductive but I have fun campaigning for both of you."

"Hi, Carrie," Abby said, waving to her as she sat on the couch. "Wow, you look stunning. If this is how someone looks after having a baby, I'm in."

"Aw, thanks, Abby," Carrie said, standing. "Want to meet Emily?"

Abby peeked at the baby in her arms and felt her heart melt. She had tiny wisps of red hair and was sleeping soundly in Carrie's arms.

"Hey, there, little angel," Abby whispered, gently brushing her cheek. "Oh, my god, Carrie. She's adorable."

"Here," Carrie said, handing her over. "I need to use the restroom anyway...and grab some wine. I already told Peter he would be on bottle duty later because Mama's drinking today."

Taking Emily in her arms, Abby softly rocked her, wondering if she would wake up at any moment and begin to wail. Abby loved babies but they did seem to scream a lot around her. When her sister, Sherilyn, had her two babies, they'd laughed at how much they wailed when Aunt Abby held them.

Sure enough, Emily's blue eyes opened and she stared straight at Abby before beginning to cry.

"There, there, little sweetheart," Abby cooed, attempting to soothe her. "Is it really that bad?"

Emily calmed down a bit, inhaling tiny gasps as she regarded Abby. "Okay, my uterus just kicked into high gear. Help."

The ladies laughed and Abby settled on the couch with Emily until Mark's sister, Justine, asked to hold her. Since her hands were free, Abby figured it was time to dig into the wine. Once settled in the comfortable chair by Ashlyn's fireplace, she regarded the women in the room, curious to learn more about them.

"How are you doing after the divorce, Justine? I hope that's not too forward of me to ask but I saw the stories when Mark was running for D.A. last year."

"Better than ever," Justine said, grinning. "I should've left him years ago, Abby. Avery and I are thriving in our awesome little twosome. Mark's watching her at Peter's today and she loves hanging with Carrie's boys."

"Although their twosome is fabulous, Aunt Teresa loves to visit a lot. I think I drive Justine crazy," Teresa said, grinning.

"No way. We love you, Teresa, and the free babysitting is gold. Don't ever stop coming around. If you'd rather live with us than Mark, that's totally fine. He's kind of annoying anyway," she teased.

"Well, I sort of love him so I'll have to decline but thanks for the generous offer."

"Have you two set a wedding date yet?" Abby asked.

"Saturday, August 6th. You'll be getting an invite, Abby, and I really hope you'll come."

"Maybe Chad will bring her as his plus-one," Ashlyn said, waggling her brows.

"Okay, you guys seem to have this idea that Chad is into me, and let me assure you, he most certainly is not. If anything, I think he sees me as yet another woman in his long line of conquests he can charm into doing his bidding. It ain't gonna happen, ladies."

"Well, the goofy expression he gets every time he talks about you would indicate otherwise, but whatever you say," Ashlyn said, shrugging.

"Chad's always been kind of goofy," Abby said, laughing. "Like, sexy-goofy. Is that a thing?"

"It totally is," Teresa said, lifting her glass. "If Mark can be sexy-geeky and Scott can be sexy-grumpy, Chad can totally be sexy-goofy." They all concurred before drinking.

"What about Peter?" Abby asked Carrie. "Not sure how to categorize him."

"Oh, honey, we don't tell Peter he's sexy. He has a big enough ego all on his own. We'll just let that one lie." She winked.

"Fair enough." Sipping, she regarded Teresa. "Are you and Mark going to have kids, Teresa? Again, please tell me if that's too forward of a question."

"Not at all," she said, shaking her head. "I'm a few years older than you lovely ladies and can't have biological kids, unfortunately."

"Oh, I'm sorry," Abby said, covering her heart. "I didn't mean to bring up something painful—"

"It's not painful...or, well, not as painful as it used to be. Mark and I have discussed a bunch of different options, and once we're married, we're going to register with several adoption agencies in the hopes of adopting a child. If that goes well, we might adopt another one. We'll see." She lifted her hands, her smile broad under her thick, black curls.

"I didn't realize you'd decided to adopt," Carrie said. "That's wonderful, Teresa. Congratulations."

The room buzzed with cheers and well wishes, and Abby had a fantastic time getting to know everyone. Eventually, the ladies started heading home and Abby knew it was time to call a rideshare.

"Thanks so much for having me," she said to Ashlyn in the foyer. "It's so nice to get out of the house. I'm kind of a loner who hangs out with my dog a lot."

"You have a dog?" Ashlyn exclaimed, excitement in her eyes. "Grant will love that. What kind?"

"She's a Bernese Mountain Dog and about eighty pounds of awesomeness. Her name's Kitana. She's pretty good with kids although not so great with adults sometimes. Especially men but that's another story. I'd love for her to meet Grant."

"I made Scott take him to Peter's today because I wanted to focus on wine time, but we'll totally make that happen."

"My boys would love that too," Carrie said, stepping into the foyer. "Once it gets warm, you'll have to come to some of our cookouts, Abby. We usually have them here or at our house and they're very relaxed and fun."

"I'd love to." Her phone chimed indicating her rideshare had arrived. Thankful for both Carrie and Ashlyn, she gave them both huge hugs before heading home. After walking Kitana, she prepped for bed and threw on her sweats. Nestling under the sheets, she snuggled with Kitana once she crawled on the bed, and turned on the wall-mounted TV. As it droned in the background, she grinned as a wet tongue placed several kisses on her face.

"You want to meet Carrie's boys, Kit?" she asked, ruffling the hair at her neck. "I bet they're really cute."

Kitana panted and stared at her.

"What's that? Not as cute as Chad? He is pretty cute, isn't he? I'll only admit that to you since you can't speak English. We can't tell anyone, okay? I've decided to hate him forever."

Kitana gave her a look that indicated she knew Abby was full of shit.

"Okay, we don't hate him. *Severely dislike.* How's that?"

She barked, spurring Abby to laugh. Flipping off the bedside lamp, she threw her arm over her companion and fell into slumber.

Chapter 10

♥

As the weeks wore on, Chad continued to bust his ass campaigning. Still, the town was abuzz with tales of Abby Miller and her fantastic platforms, and he wondered if his time was running out. Maybe Ardor Creek was ready for something new. After all, he'd been mayor for almost eight years. Perhaps people wanted a change.

The thought made him incredibly sad since his entire identity revolved around being mayor. What the hell would he do if he lost? Of course, he'd always known he couldn't be mayor forever, but he figured he had a least another term or two left in the tank. The idea that he'd go back and work in the hardware store with his dad held zero appeal.

One Saturday in mid-April, he headed to volunteer at the soup kitchen located off the highway between Ardor Creek and Battle Falls. He'd been volunteering there forever and was surprised to see Abby behind the carving station when he entered the community center.

"Hello, Chad," Mrs. Connaughton said, approaching. She ran the soup kitchen for the community now that she was retired—just one more reason why everyone loved Mrs. C. "I ran into Abby Miller the other day and invited her to volunteer. You don't mind, do you? I know you're technically competing but every volunteer counts."

Chad gave her a droll look. "Did you happen to 'run into her' at your house when she was canvassing?"

Patting his cheek, she smiled, a sparkle in her eye. "You were always so smart, Chad, and so good at reading people. I'm sure you can tell I'm smitten with the idea of having a female mayor. I never thought I'd see the day."

"Is this your way of telling me I've lost your vote, Mrs. C?"

"I haven't decided yet, young man, and I don't like your tone. Now, the station beside Abby is open and I've assigned you to work there today."

"Yes, ma'am," he said, feeling chastised. "I hope you'll still consider voting for me. I love being mayor, Mrs. C. I'm not quite sure what I'll do if I lose."

"Oh, sweet boy, you'll do just fine. I remember when your darling mother passed away and left you and your dad with two broken hearts. You were sad but picked up the pieces and Donald seems to be doing fine now. You'll be fine too. Sometimes the paths we're forced to take lead to the best destinations."

"You were a good friend to Mom," Chad said, noting the glint in her eye when she'd spoken his dad's name. Did Mrs. C. have a thing for his dad? He hadn't dated since Chad's mom passed away years ago but the thought was...interesting. Remembering his dad's flushed cheeks when he was ringing her up a few weeks ago, Chad smiled. "I haven't had dinner with Dad in a while now. Maybe you can come over one day and the three of us can have dinner together."

"Oh, I'd love that, dear. I miss having family dinner since the kids are gone and Mr. C. passed away. Let's plan that one day soon. Now, go on and man the pasta station. People are starting to line up." With one last firm pat on his cheek, she sauntered away.

Approaching the station of long tables, Chad shrugged off his coat and placed it on the chair behind the pasta station. Abby was to his left, doing a terrible job of ignoring him as she held her chin high.

"Hello, Abby."

"Hello, Chad," she said, sparing him a glance. "Mrs. Connaughton asked me to volunteer today so don't blame me that I'm here."

"I think it's great that you're volunteering. Don't have a problem with it at all." Plus, she was wearing those tight-as-sin jeans which afforded him the opportunity to stare at her gorgeous ass for the next two hours.

"Please stop leering at me," she said, shooting him a glare. "It makes me uncomfortable."

"Was I leering?" he asked, rubbing his chin. "Sorry, sweetheart, but it's hard not to notice you in those jeans."

Her head snapped and those almond-shaped eyes latched onto his. "And what, pray tell, is wrong with my jeans?"

"Nothing," he said, showing her his palms. "They look good. That's all, Abbs. Sheesh. Why are you being hostile? I thought we made progress at the abandoned site. You didn't look like you wanted to punch me when I left, which is a huge accomplishment in my book."

"Oh, I don't know, maybe it has something to do with the fact that I saw Butch Connors on the way here."

Chad's eyes grew wide. "Shit."

"Shit is right," she snapped. "*Oh, hey, it's Flabby Abby. I heard you were back in town. You look way better than you did in high school,*" she said, mimicking his voice.

"He was always such a dick," Chad said, rubbing his forehead. "I haven't seen him around town in a while, ever since his divorce from Heather Combs."

"She was no picnic either. She and the other cheerleaders were vicious. I detested them. Except for Terry. She was the one exception who was actually nice to me."

"Well, Heather cheated on Butch, which is common knowledge, and she had a terrible boob job that made one of her boobs lop-sided. That has to make you feel a little better, right?"

"I don't feel better when other people suffer, Chad."

Blowing a breath through his lips, he shook his head. "Obviously, there's nothing I can say here that won't be disastrous so I'm just going to keep my mouth shut. Sorry you had to deal with that, Abbs. It's beyond annoying but they're idiots. You're way too awesome to let Butch ruin your day. Okay, I'm seriously shutting up now."

She scowled before turning to carve a piece of turkey for the man extending his plate in front of her. Feeling like an ass, Chad wondered when he'd lost the ability to speak to women. He'd always been rather smooth and an excellent flirt but with Abby, he was the king of epic failures. Every time he took one step forward, he took about a million steps back.

"Sir?"

"Oh, sorry," Chad said, smiling at the man in front of him. "Looks like we've got penne vodka or spaghetti. What will it be?"

The man chose spaghetti and Chad loaded it on his plate, not even pretending he was concentrating on anything other than Abby's ass in those amazing jeans. The two hours dragged by with minimal conversation from her, and Chad felt the urge to make things right.

"Hey," he said, facing her as they wiped down the tables. "Want to grab a drink after this? I definitely owe you one for the annoying Butch encounter."

"Thanks, but I'm heading home to prepare for a speech I'm giving to the Ardor Creek book club tomorrow."

"No way," Chad said, almost dropping his cloth. "I tried like hell to get into one of their meetings. I offered to buy them wine, a month's worth of books, and a hundred other things. How the hell did you get in?"

"Mrs. Robertson likes me," she said, shrugging.

Realization washed over him as his mouth dropped open. "You little tease. Mrs. Robertson has been trying to marry her son off for years. You went on a date with him so she'd let you attend one of their meetings."

"No, I didn't," she mumbled.

"Holy shit, you totally did. Well, how was it? I hear most women are enamored with Larry's facial mole, with the cute black hairs that grow out of it. Did they tickle you when you guys kissed?"

She threw her rag at him, belting him in the chest and he recoiled.

"Ouch! She's physically assaulting her opponent. Help!"

Rushing toward him, she hissed, "Shut up, Chad! You're so annoying."

"Holy crap, Abbs. You totally pimped yourself out. Did he use a lot of tongue? No, wait, don't tell me. I want to imagine it all for myself."

Huffing a breath, she crossed her arms over her breasts, pushing them high. Lust racked his frame as she stared up at him. "He took me to dinner in Battle Falls, okay? That was the only way I'd agree to it since I didn't want to set tongues in Ardor Creek wagging. It was nice. Then, we both went to our cars and drove home."

"Together?" he asked, waggling his brows.

"No!" she whispered, agitated. "Unlike you, I actually like to know someone for more than an hour before I bang them. We don't all have an endless stream of sexual partners lined up."

Recoiling, his features drew together. "Actually, I haven't had sex in a while now," he said, realizing he'd barely noticed. "I've been busy with the campaign. Seems my opponent is kicking my ass and I had to step up."

"Well, I'm glad someone made you realize that holding public office is important."

Swallowing, he stared down at her, longing to touch the vein pulsing at her neck. The skin looked so smooth and it led to the mounds that now jutted from the neckline of her sweater. Feeling himself harden, he took a step closer.

"Will you still hate me?"

Confusion laced her features. "Huh?"

"If I lose," he said, unable to stop himself from tucking a strand of hair behind her ear. "Will you forgive me if you beat me? I wish you didn't hate me, Abby."

"I don't hate you," she said, her tone gravelly.

"Yes, you do, and I deserve it. But maybe if I lose, you'll just mildly detest me? I really hope so because I'm pretty damn impressed with you and would really like to win your forgiveness. Perhaps even be friends one day."

"Why would you want to be friends with me? You have a ton of friends."

Something about the question splintered his heart. "Because you're amazing, Abbs. You do know that, right?"

Her brows drew together. "Why are you saying this stuff? I told you, I'm not interested."

His lips twerked at that little lie because if there was one thing Chad understood, it was the signs of desire. The pulse at her neck, her flushed cheeks, the slight hitch in her breathing—oh, yeah, Abby Miller was attracted to him. It made sense she would fight it, but it was obvious.

"There are three weeks until the primary. During that time, I want you to think about what's going to happen afterward. No matter who wins, I want to bury the hatchet, Abbs. That's a lot for me to ask, but I have faith we can do it."

White teeth toyed with her lip as she contemplated. "It does take a lot of energy to loathe you so much."

Laughing, he nodded. "Sure does. Just think about it, okay? In the meantime, I'm heading to the pub after this. You can meet me for a drink or not. Your call." Stepping back, he wiped down the remaining corner of the table before grabbing his coat. "See ya."

Afterward, Chad sat at the pub for hours, pining for her like a lovesick sap before accepting she wasn't going to show. Eventually, Terry cut him off and called him a rideshare. Once home, he collapsed in his bed and grabbed the pillow, holding it tight. Surrounded by the darkness, he acknowledged three truths: he was enthralled by Abby Miller, she was going to win the primary, and his life was all but over.

Chapter 11

Primary day arrived with record turnout. After heading to town and casting her vote, Abby nervously waited for the results to come in, biting off her fingernails in rapid succession as she tried to focus on her video consultations. After the sun set, she poured a glass of wine and devoured the pasta she ordered from Uber Eats, choosing to forego portion control on one of the most important days of her life.

She'd decided to spend the night alone, although many volunteers from her campaign had invited her over, including Ashlyn and Carrie. But she wasn't sure if Chad would be there and didn't want to make anyone uncomfortable, so she politely declined, content to hear the results with Kitana by her side.

At nine o'clock that evening, she received a call from the town clerk, explaining she'd won the primary with fifty-five percent of the vote while Chad received forty-five percent. Sterling Rydell had run unopposed in his primary, so he would be her challenger for the rest of the race. No longer would she have to run against Chad.

The thought made her...*sad* for some reason. Did that mean she wouldn't see him around town as she had during the campaign? Would he revert to hanging with his friends since he wouldn't be campaigning? Although Carrie, Ashlyn, and Teresa had been extremely supportive of her campaign, they were Chad's friends, not hers. Did winning the primary mean they'd pull back so they wouldn't make Chad feel uncomfortable about the loss?

The questions were maddening so she poured herself a glass of champagne, determined to celebrate her victory. Holding the bubbly high, she toasted herself. Wanting to share the news, she video chatted with her sister and parents. After thirty minutes of virtual celebrating, she noticed her Dad's eyes drooping and let them go.

Relaxing on the couch, she did her best to savor the moment. "You did it, Abby. You beat Chad Hanson. Phase one complete. Well done." Sipping the champagne, it tasted dry on her tongue—definitely not as sweet as she'd anticipated.

Kitana whimpered below, relaying her displeasure at being left out of the celebration. Patting the couch, she laughed as the pooch jumped and nestled into her side. Grateful for the comfort of her sweet girl, she pondered the victory. She'd always thought she'd feel a sense of peace and fulfillment when she beat Chad. Instead, she felt...empty. Sighing, she trailed her finger over the glass, wondering how he was handling it.

He was probably distraught, and her heart squeezed in her chest. He loved being mayor and had given it his all before she'd come in and ripped it away. Remorse blanketed her until she reminded herself that she was feeling sorry for Chad Hanson, the person who had callously denigrated her years ago.

"He deserved this outcome," she said, trying to convince herself. "He reaped what he sowed. Now drink your damn champagne and savor your victory, Abby."

She managed to finish the glass, even though she couldn't find the will to celebrate. Although she'd accomplished her goal, the victory felt cold and hollow.

Abby awoke the next day, ready to tackle the next phase of her campaign. Running against someone with deep pockets like Rydell would be tough, and she needed to revamp her entire strategy. As she was sitting in her tiny home office sipping coffee in front of her laptop, she heard a knock on the door. Figuring it was probably Martha looking for Tubs, she relegated a barking Kitana to her bedroom before opening the door.

Chad Hanson stood on her doorstep, contrite and as handsome as ever.

"Uh, hi," she said, glancing down at her gray sweatpants—with no less than seven holes—and white t-shirt. "I wasn't expecting company."

"Sorry to just show up. I figured if I called, you might tell me I couldn't stop by."

Squinting, she pondered. "Maybe. Depends on what you want to talk about. If you're here to tell me I ruined your life, my reply would be that I learned it by watching you."

His lips curved. "Nice '80s drug prevention commercial reference but, no, I'm not here to blame you for ruining my life. I did that all on my own. I learned a lot over the past few months and I'll need to digest it one day. For now, I'm here to help you."

"Help me?"

"Uh, yeah. It might be better if you invite me inside? Offer me a cup of coffee? Let me meet your dog who sounds like a beast?"

"So, um, no, no, and no. I have things to do today, Chad. I don't have time to invite you in. How did you get my address anyway?"

"Uh, I'm the mayor," he said, waving. "For a few more months, at least."

"I'm not even going to comment on how creepy it is that you're using your public office to track down my address."

"Geez, Abby. Chill. You're always so wound up. I figured you'd be ecstatic that you kicked my ass. The least you could do is invite me inside."

Martha chose that moment to step onto her stoop, obviously curious about what was happening.

"Abby?" she called. "Is everything okay, dear?"

Before she could speak, Chad answered.

"Everything's fine, Martha. Nice to see you, by the way. Abby and I had a one night stand last night and I'm about to take the walk of shame."

Abby's mouth fell open as Martha's eyes grew wide. "Oh, my, I...well, good for you, Mr. Mayor."

"Get inside," Abby gritted, grabbing his shirt and pulling him over the threshold. "You're such an ass." Shoving him into the foyer, she waved at Martha. "Everything's fine here, Martha. And don't worry, I'm still a virgin. Have a good day."

Slamming the door behind her, she pivoted to find a snickering Chad Hanson.

"You son of a bitch."

"What?" he asked, lifting his hands. "That was so funny. Come on, Abbs. We gave ol' Martha the best thrill she's had in months. Trust me."

"Martha is nosy as hell and will tell the entire complex we're banging," she said, crossing her arms over her chest.

"How exciting. Wonder if she'll pass on how great I am in bed."

Rolling her eyes, she sighed. "What do you want to talk about?"

"Can we at least go into the living room?"

"Fine. Come on." Leading the way, she sat on one side of the couch while he sat on the other. "Okay, give it to me. What's so important that you have to show up at," she glanced at the wall clock, "eight thirty-five in the morning?"

Sitting back, he rested his ankle on the opposite knee. "So, no coffee, then?"

Giving a frustrating groan, she fisted her hands. "Spit it out, Chad."

He regarded her for a moment before shifting and resting his forearms on his thighs. "Have you thought about what running against Rydell will entail?"

"I'm not even going to honor that question with a reply."

"Look, I'm not trying to be an ass, but it's going to be tough, Abby."

"I know it's going to be tough, Chad. Beating you was tough but I did it, didn't I?"

He nodded, staring at his hands laced between his legs. "You sure did."

Empathy welled in her chest and she wanted to push it away but it was thick and heavy.

"I'm sorry. Is that what you want to hear? I wanted to beat you but didn't realize it would feel so hollow. It kind of sucks, actually. I expected to be doing backflips right now."

His gaze lifted to hers. "That's how I felt all those years ago when you dropped out. I realized that winning at the expense of others sucks."

"Well, I didn't win at your expense," she said, feeling the annoyance flare. "I won fair and square."

"You did. I'm not sure I've accepted it here yet," he tapped his temple, "but I know it here." Lowering his hand, he covered his heart. "You deserved to win and I'm really proud of you, Abby."

Something about his heartfelt words and earnest tone shifted something deep within. "Thank you, Chad," she whispered. "That means a lot."

"You're welcome." Circling his thumbs, he seemed to be contemplating his next words. "Charles Rydell is dead-set on building in Ardor Creek. The abandoned tar factory is just one of a multitude of sites he's expressed interest in. He's chosen to use his son as a pawn in his exploits. I'm intimately familiar with Rydell's current proposal and future plans, and would like to help you beat him."

"Okay," she said, surprised by his offer. "I'm going to be putting together a new team for this phase of the campaign. I'd be happy for you to join."

"Not as a volunteer on your campaign," he said, shaking his head. "That's not what I'm offering. I want to be your campaign manager, Abby. I think I have a lot to offer and, honestly, I'm not sure you can win if I don't help you."

"Well, thanks for the vote of confidence."

He held up a hand. "I'm not saying that to knock you down. Rydell's going to bring in the big guns and there are a lot of nuances in Ardor Creek you just don't understand. You've been away for a long time. Some demographics will be swayed by Rydell's fancy new offerings. Half of the locals are already enamored with his ideas and we have to explain the far-reaching implications they'll have on the environment, taxes, small businesses, and all sorts of other things."

Abby chewed her lip as she mulled. "I see your point, and you definitely understand Ardor Creek, but are you allowed to be my campaign manager while you're mayor?"

"I looked over all the statutes last night. It's perfectly legal as long as you don't pay me."

She stared at him as if he were daft. "So, you're offering to be my campaign manager—for free—the day after I creamed you?"

Grimacing, he said, "*Creamed* is a bit excessive since there was only a ten-point spread but, yeah, that's what I'm offering. Sterling Rydell will be mayor over my dead body, Abby. That means, I'm committed to helping his opponent, which happens to be you."

She gnawed her lip as various feelings swirled inside. Suspicion. Gratitude. Confusion. Squinting, she asked, "Why do you want to help me?"

His brows drew together. "I just told you."

"Is this some weird strategy to infiltrate my campaign and ensure I lose so you can get revenge?"

"Man, D.C. really fucked you up, Abby," he said, leaning back on the couch and rubbing his eyes. "Not everyone has a super-secret ulterior motive. I love Ardor Creek and I detest Rydell Industries. Therefore, I want to help you. It's pretty fucking simple."

Huffing out a breath, she nodded. "Okay. If you really want to help, and you're offering to be my campaign manager for free, I'm smart enough to understand I'd be an idiot to turn that down. Can you balance being my campaign manager while still being mayor?"

"Sure can," he said with a nod. "I'd be campaigning for myself if I'd won, so I'll just dedicate that time to your campaign."

Abby regarded his open, honest expression. "Are you doing this so I won't hate you anymore?"

"That might have a tiny bit to do with it," he said, holding his thumb and index finger an inch apart. "I'm on good terms with everyone in Ardor Creek, Abby, and I don't want to end that streak with you. I really want us to be friends."

"Let's start with campaign manager and candidate and see how we do with that," she muttered.

"Challenge accepted." He waggled his brows. "So, we have a deal?" He extended his hand.

Abby slid her palm over his, ignoring the tingles that shot through her body.

"We have a deal," she said, shaking.

"Awesome," he said, releasing her hand and breaking into one of his million-dollar smiles. Pointing toward the hallway, he asked, "Can I meet your dog now? I love dogs."

"Of course, you do," she said, rolling her eyes. "And grandmas and babies. It's part of the mayoral package."

Laughing, he nodded. "It kind of is."

"She's not great with strangers. She weighs eighty pounds and jumps a lot. Also, she's kind of jealous and usually hates every guy I bring home."

"You mean you lied to Martha about being a virgin?" he teased, making a *tsk, tsk, tsk* sound as he covered his heart with his hand. "Lying to your constituents is the first cardinal rule a mayor cannot break, Ms. Miller."

"Funny," she muttered, standing. "Okay, I'll let her out but she might be pissed you're here. Like I said, she doesn't like men. She's better with women and kids."

"Bring it on."

Padding down the hall, she opened the door and Kitana bounded from the room. Following her, she observed her run straight to Chad and crawl on his lap. He laughed with glee as she licked his face. Hell, he could've been a damn model in one of those stupid dog food commercials that always popped up on her internet browser.

"Traitor," she said, glaring at Kitana.

"Oh, yes, you're such a good girl," he said, petting her with zeal as Kitana ate up the attention. "Yeah, she really seems to hate me. What's her name?"

"Kitana."

"No way," he said, eyes wide as he stared at her with awe.

"Yeah. So?"

"That's a killer Mortal Kombat reference, Abby. Damn, I think I just fell halfway in love with you."

Abby almost collapsed in a heap on the floor at the words and quickly told herself to get a damn grip. Obviously, he was joking.

Mentally scolding herself, she sat on the couch and pet Kitana as she licked Chad's neck. *Lucky dog.*

"She's awesome, Abbs, but that makes sense since she's yours."

Unable to digest the praise from the person who should be somewhat pissed at her, she lifted her brows. "Okay, well, this has been fun but I've got a consultation at ten that I need to prepare for, and the Scranton paper wants to interview me tomorrow. Let's meet on Friday if you have time and we'll form a plan. That's always my lightest day."

"Sounds good. I've got to get to town hall anyway," he said, placing a kiss on Kitana's nose. Abby's heart absolutely did *not* melt at the sweet gesture. Nope. Not at all. Gently urging her off his lap, he rose. She followed behind him, holding the door open as he exited. Once outside, he turned to face her from the stoop.

"Should I break the news to Martha on the way out? She's going to be really disappointed in you."

"Goodbye, Chad," she droned, closing the door in his face.

After a few seconds, a knock sounded.

Opening the door, she scowled. "Yes?"

"Thanks for being open to the idea, Abby. Rydell is going down. I think you'll be a really good mayor. See ya." With a salute, he turned and headed to his car.

Sighing, Abby closed the door and rested her forehead against it.

"What did you just do, Abby?" she whispered, gently banging her head against the door. "You signed up for close proximity with the sexist man in the entire world whom you've vowed to hate forever. What the hell is *wrong* with you?"

Kitana whimpered below and Abby shot her a glare.

"Don't even get me started with you, young lady. You were supposed to hate him on sight."

Kitana gave her a look that said, *Come on, Mom, he's hot and not even remotely as terrible as you thought.*

"I know, okay?" she said, striding toward the kitchen to grab a fresh cup of coffee. "He's actually a really nice guy. Damn it."

Pouring the coffee, she pushed the musings aside, determined to focus on her consultations for the day. Of course, her thoughts were consumed by Chad Hanson and the weird but beneficial arrangement they'd agreed upon.

C had was racked with relief as he drove home from Abby's. He hadn't slept all night and was thankful she'd agreed to his plan so he could get some sleep. Although he'd mentioned heading to town hall, his first meeting wasn't until one o'clock and he was definitely going to take a nap before heading in.

Why hadn't he slept? Well, it had to do with the fact that his life had inexorably changed last night and he'd had a shit ton of realizations. Carrie and Peter had offered to host a small watch party as the primary reviews came in but Chad had declined, knowing he was going to lose. Although he'd run a good campaign, Abby had run a better one. More efficient with better platforms and tons of energy. In effect, she'd kicked his ass.

Chad had never been a sore loser. One of his favorite subjects to read about were people who'd experienced great failures in the past and gone on to create huge success. Many of them learned lessons from the blows and implemented them in their next ventures. Chad was determined to do the same.

As he'd sat on his couch last night after the results were announced, he'd opened his laptop and typed out an exhaustive plan for the next few months.

Step one was ensuring Abby beat Sterling Rydell. Everything he'd said to her was true: he would protect Ardor Creek against shady corporate businesses like Rydell Industries until his dying breath. Chad loved Ardor Creek, even if the residents had voted him out, and he knew Abby would do a fantastic job as mayor.

Step two was burying the hatchet with Abby. It was important to Chad they become friends, especially with the transition that would need to occur once she won the election in November. He also wanted to remain involved in local government, even if he wasn't mayor, and being friendly with Abby was the best way to accomplish that.

Step three was the most daunting of all: Chad wanted to date Abby Miller. He'd realized it last night as he'd sat in the dark with his laptop on his knees, that stupid perma-grin on his face as he longed for her. He wanted her. Like, head thrown back, moaning his name, wanted her. Somewhere along the way, he'd become enamored with her whip-smart sense of humor, snappy comebacks to his playful teasing, and those ultra-long eyelashes and sexy lips. Oh, and the tight jeans didn't hurt either. Yep, he was toast, and if there was one thing Chad never denied himself, it was the opportunity to pursue a woman he was interested in.

Understanding she would fight the idea tooth and nail, Chad racked his brain for a way he could make it happen. Then, in a stroke of brilliance, the lightbulb illuminated. He searched all the local, county, and state statues online before heading to town hall like some criminal in the dead of night just to confirm the statutes in the physical books housed there. The documentation was clear: it was perfectly legal for him to volunteer as Abby's campaign manager.

Armed with that knowledge, he headed home to formulate his plan. Abby was smart and practical, and wouldn't turn down an opportunity to align with him if he presented the idea in clear, forthright terms detailing the advantages. In the wee hours of the night, he practiced what he would say to her until the sun finally rose and he headed to her apartment. Thankfully, she'd agreed to his slightly insane plan.

Now, arriving home after their conversation, Chad ditched his clothes and crawled into bed, exhausted but elated. Abby was on board, which was pretty much the only thing that had gone right in the past twenty-four hours. He was going to align with her to beat Rydell and hopefully get her into bed, where he could worship every inch of her gorgeous body. In the meantime, he had an excuse to spend tons of time with her. If he had it his way, he'd spend every hour of the damn day with her. To say he was smitten was the understatement of the century.

"Well done, Hanson. Don't blow this. She's fucking special."

Silence surrounded him as he contemplated the effort he'd expended to procure her acceptance of the plan he'd concocted.

Chad had never worked so hard to find a way to spend time with a woman. Unable to discern or admit what that ultimately meant, he finally allowed himself to sleep.

Chapter 12

A bby waited at the diner on Friday, absently kicking her leg as she sat in the booth. Chad had texted her he was running a few minutes late, which gave her extra time to focus on her nerves. *Great.*

"Hey, hon," he said, sliding into the booth. "Sorry, I'm late. The budget meeting ran over. How are you?"

Her nostrils flared—at the endearment, obviously, not the fact that he looked sexy as hell in his red tie and checkered collared shirt. "Okay, let's get something straight. I'm going to be the next mayor of Ardor Creek, hopefully, so it's probably best you don't address me as 'hon' in our business meetings."

His lips curved into that lazy, sexy grin as he rested his arm over the back of the booth.

"Chad?" she asked, waving her hand in front of his face. "You're doing the weird staring thing."

"Sorry," he said, straightening. "You're absolutely right. I won't call you that in our business meetings. Can't promise it won't slip during other times but I'll try my best." Leaning forward, he grinned. "And you *are* going to be the next mayor. We're going to make that happen, hon—" He halted and pursed his lips. "Abby. We're going to make that happen, Abby."

Sighing, she pretended to be annoyed, even though the endearments sent jolts of pleasure through every cell in her body. In truth, she loved them. Waaaaaay too much, in her opinion. Picking up the menu, she pointed.

"I'm getting the egg special. Have you eaten?"

"I ate a bagel earlier so I'll just get coffee."

The waitress came to take their order and they settled in, each opening their laptops.

"Okay, I think we need to go over the development plan Rydell submitted first so I have a detailed idea of what he wants to build in Ardor Creek. Once I know what he plans to do, I can develop a strategy to fight it."

"I've read the official submission a thousand times at this point," Chad said, slipping on reading glasses before clicking to find the documents. Abby all but lost the ability to breathe as she regarded him in the black-rimmed glasses. He looked like a damn Pearle Vision model, and suddenly her brain was clouded with images of steaming up those glasses as he stared deep into her eyes while pounding her senseless.

"Abbs?"

"Uh, yeah," she said, thankful she could still actually speak. "Show me what you've got. I'm going to take notes."

Two hours later, Abby knew everything that existed on Rydell Industries, what they planned to build in Ardor Creek, and how it would impact the town.

"I can't believe he wants to build over the old warehouse sites without properly remediating them," she said, lifting her hands. "The old tar factory is bad enough, but the former petroleum storage terminal on the west side of town and the abandoned phonebook factory are also extremely polluted. Anyone who lived on any of those sites would be vulnerable to all kinds of cancer and other diseases without proper decontamination."

Chad nodded. "State, county and local laws require remediation but a company can get some regulations waived if they know the proper channels. A company as wealthy as Rydell Industries can hire fancy lawyers to fight the state and county regulations."

"And if Sterling Rydell is elected mayor, he can waive the local ones."

"Bingo," Chad said, sitting back in the booth. Removing the glasses, he rubbed his eyes. "That's one of about a million other reasons we can't let him win."

"What do you see as the biggest hurdles?"

Squinting, he contemplated. "Ardor Creek has seen a shift in demographics lately. We still have the local lifers but there's been a new influx of young adults with kids, and millennials. People are excited for change and modernization—which I understand—but in their haste to modernize, I don't think they understand the downside of letting big industry build here."

"Besides the environmental impact, there's the economic one," Abby said, pulling up some research she'd compiled on Rydell Industries. "Rydell has contracts with certain corporate stores and only grants office space to them."

"Exactly," Chad said, nodding. "If he's allowed to build his huge development, the stores that comprise the ground floor will only be given to those Fortune 500 companies. I have no problem with big box stores, but they have enough of them in Scranton. Ardor Creek has always restricted how many large corporations can set up shop here but they'll be grandfathered in if Rydell wins his bid."

"And small businesses on Main Street will lose out."

"Hell, half of them will probably close." He gestured around the diner. "Nick told me the other day he was excited about Rydell's proposal because it would bring new customers to town. But do you think millennials are going to want to eat Nick's homemade hummus platter for lunch or go to the fancy new restaurant in Rydell's development?"

"Hey," Abby said, "I love Nick's hummus platter."

"I do too." He held up his hands, showing his palms. "But I'm just trying to be realistic. Homey, small-town restaurants like this won't stand a chance if we let a ton of corporate restaurants in. I want to manage the influx so guys like Nick stand a chance."

"And maybe so Hanson Hardware won't have to compete against Home Depot and Lowes?" she asked, grinning.

"Maybe," he said, chuckling. "Small businesses are the backbone of this town, Abby. I don't want to see them die."

"Me neither. We have to educate the residents so they can modernize without inadvertently hurting themselves in the process."

"Exactly."

"I can imagine several business owners who are in favor of modernization don't get why you're fighting Rydell."

"They don't," he said, clenching his laced fingers atop the table. "I should've done a better job educating them and explaining it to them. Fortunately, I'm here to ensure you don't make the same mistake. Let's learn from my terrible failure."

Laughing, she sat back in the booth and bit her lip. "Man, you might have lost the election because you were trying to help them. That's brutal."

"Thanks," he muttered. "Keep twisting the knife."

Resting her chin on her fist, she gave him a sympathetic smile. "How are you doing? Are you okay, Chad? I feel so weird about this whole thing. I expected you'd hate me when I beat you but you're being so nice. Like, really nice. I'm wondering if you have some sort of ulterior motive I still haven't figured out."

Something flashed in his eyes before it disappeared. "Can't a guy just be nice to the person he hurt in the past? I never really got the opportunity to make it up to you, Abbs. Maybe I can now."

She searched his eyes, looking for any signs of malice but finding them clear and guileless. "I guess so. It's kind of weird, but okay."

"Eh, I've never minded being a little weird," he said, shrugging. "Over the next two weeks, I think we should formulate a talk track we can use to educate the residents. Several succinct points we can both echo at the various campaign events we'll have over the next few months."

"Good plan. Do you want to keep meeting at the diner or should we meet somewhere else?"

"We can meet at my place or yours," he said, lifting a shoulder. "I'm a big flip chart kind of guy so we can set one of those up in each of our living rooms and work off that."

"Love it. I'm a sucker for a flip chart myself."

"We both love flip charts and Mortal Kombat," he said, ticking the items off on his fingers. "I'm wondering what else we have in common. If we discover a few more things, we might have enough common ground to be friends."

Abby wrinkled her nose. "Probably not but I guess there's always a sliver of hope," she teased.

He breathed a laugh. "How did you get into Mortal Kombat anyway? I used to play all the time as a kid."

"Me too." Her gaze lowered to the table. "I spent a lot of time playing video games. It was just easier than...well, than trying to make friends."

His hand covered hers and he squeezed. Lifting her gaze, she found his expression remorseful. "I'm sorry, Abbs. I know some of that was my fault."

"It's fine," she said, pulling her hand away. "It was a long time ago." Closing her laptop, she stuffed it in her bag and checked her phone. "I've got to get home for an afternoon consult," she lied. Actually, her day was free but she suddenly felt the need to be alone. "Thanks for your help. Text me when you're available next week and we'll have our first flip chart session."

Standing, she secured her bag over her shoulder before he encircled her wrist.

"Wait," he said, staring up at her with sad eyes and a small pout that was way too adorable for her pounding heart to handle. "What are you doing this weekend? The parks department just finished the new dog run over by the lake. We could take Kitana there. I bet she'd love it."

"I can't," she said, disengaging from his touch. "I have a crap ton of stuff to do this weekend. But I'll see you next week. Just text me."

"Okay. Bye, Abbs."

"Bye!" she said, sounding like a cheerful idiot when all she wanted to do was crawl in a hole. Bounding to the car, she drove home, cursing herself yet again for agreeing to work with Chad. The agreement would certainly help her campaign but would it destroy her in the process? How long would it be before she developed feelings for him? Sighing, Abby realized that was probably inevitable. Pulling into her complex, she parked and rested her forehead on the steering wheel.

"Please don't fall in love with Chad Hanson, Abby," she said, lightly banging her head against the wheel. "He's just being nice and wants to beat Rydell. You're. Not. His. Type." Every word correlated with a bang of her head on the steering wheel.

Deciding she should probably ice the newly-formed red spot on her head, she huffed a frustrated breath and headed inside.

Spending the weekend alone in comfy sweats was much better than hanging at the dog walk with Chad. Of course, it was. He had his own life and set of friends. Even though they'd agreed on a business arrangement, he had no obligation to hang out with her outside of his campaign duties.

She was just fine hanging with Kitana and bingeing The Crown. Yep, that was much better than spending time with Chad. Repeating the lie over and over in her mind, Abby sprawled on the couch and held the ice pack to her head. After a few minutes, she gave up on the mantra and admitted defeat. Closing her eyes, she recalled the image of Chad in those fucking glasses. Sighing with longing, she slid her hand beneath her jeans, pretending it was his hand touching her deepest place. And, then, she didn't do much thinking at all as she took herself over the edge.

C had sat in the folding chair in Scott and Ashlyn's back yard, not even pretending to enjoy the barbeque on the sunny May afternoon.

"Hanson looks terrible," Peter said to Scott as they stood by the grill, knowing full well Chad could hear him. "I might not even make fun of him for requesting his ribs medium rare—which is a sure-fire way to secure a ticket to barf town. But if he wants them that way, who am I to argue?"

"I like them that way, okay?" Chad said, sipping his beer. "Leave me alone."

"Wow, dude, you're grumpier than Scott. What the hell is up with you?"

"Uh, in case you didn't hear, I lost the election a week ago."

"You seemed fine earlier this week," Scott said. "I was surprised at how well you were handling it."

"Yeah, I'm not buying it," Peter said, loading some ribs onto the tray beside the grill. "Although losing sucks, Chad's not broken up about it. He's smart enough to understand these things happen and he'll be just fine."

"Ooohhhh," Scott said, lifting his brows. "It's about the *other* thing."

"You two are annoying as hell," Chad said, rising and looking over Peter's shoulder. "Those are too done."

"Yours are already on the tray, Your Highness. Relax. And let's just admit what you're too stubborn to say. You're pissed that Abby wouldn't hang with you this weekend."

"Of course, I'm pissed," he said, taking a swig of beer. "I like her, okay? I thought this whole campaign manager thing would get her to hang out with me more but she's fighting it. It's frustrating as hell."

"Well, well," Carrie said, appearing behind them and setting a tray of pasta salad on the table. "Looks like lovable player Chad Hanson has finally met someone immune to his charms."

"Not if I have anything to say about it," he muttered. "I'm working on it, Carrie. Give me a break. These things take time."

"When they mean something, they actually do," she said, palming his cheek. "I'm proud of you, Chad. You might have crossed the threshold of trying your hand at an emotionally mature relationship. That's what Abby's going to need, by the way. She's not some random chick on a dating app."

"I know. She's...different. I love hanging out with her. I can't remember ever wanting to spend so much time with a woman without sex involved. I mean, I think about sex with her...a *lot*...but I also just like chilling with her. It's weird...but cool...but still weird."

"Well, Peter's weird, but I love him anyway. Maybe that's a good thing."

"Hey!" Peter called from the grill.

"If you want me to help you woo Abby, I'm happy to," Carrie said, ignoring Peter's glare.

"Uh, yeah, let me stop you right there," Scott said, striding over to place his arm around her shoulders. "This woman is one of the biggest gossips in Ardor Creek, hands down. Don't tell her anything."

"Hey," she said, swatting his shoulder. "If you weren't my boss, I'd tell you to fuck off. I was instrumental in getting you and Ashlyn together. You're welcome, by the way."

"I think I might have had *something* to do with it, but okay."

"Are we talking about Carrie's awesome matchmaking skills?" Ashlyn asked, trailing down the porch stairs. "She was so helpful when I was stalking Scott. I owe it all to her."

"See?" Carrie asked.

Scott playfully scrunched his features at her, causing her to laugh.

Chad took it all in, realizing how much he wished Abby was there. She would've loved the revelry and would've fit right in with her sharp sense of humor. Determined to ensure she attended the next barbeque, he forged ahead with his master plan.

For the next two weeks, as he and Abby met after work to strategize on the flip charts in their respective living rooms, Chad turned up the charm to a level he'd never implemented. Not on the hot ballroom dance instructor he'd met on Tinder three years ago. Not on the yoga teacher he'd found on Bumble who was insanely flexible. Not even on the Instagram influencer who'd had the most amazing pair of fake boobs he'd ever seen.

By some miraculous stroke of fate, Abby outshined them all. In fact, he'd give up every past sexual encounter for one shot with Abby. Well...maybe he'd keep one of the sexy times with the yoga instructor burned into his memory just for old times' sake, but he was willing to sacrifice the rest, for sure.

"Earth to Chad," the object of his musings droned, snapping her fingers in his face. "I think we're done with the volunteer planning." She pointed at the flip chart and Chad nodded from her couch.

"Yep, looks good. Along with my volunteering at the soup kitchen on Saturdays, we've got a good list of several other pop-up volunteer activities we can schedule through the end of October. They'll draw a lot of people and we can campaign while we work."

"Awesome," she said, placing the cap back on the marker. "Another successful planning session in the books." Glancing down, she regarded her clothes. "Okay, I hate to kick you out but it's almost six o'clock and I've got to walk my little lady before changing into sweats and scrounging up some dinner."

Chad stood, bummed at her desire to kick him out on a Friday night. He wanted nothing more than to hang with her well into the night and thought about asking her to dinner. Unfortunately, every time he'd asked her to hang outside their sessions over the past two weeks, she'd declined, and he was starting to get a complex. Stalling, he pointed toward her hallway.

"Can I use your bathroom?"

"Sure."

Stalking toward the half-bath, Chad gave himself a pep talk and told himself not to be a pansy. Rejection sucked but if he kept asking, he felt he could eventually wear her down.

Chapter 13

♥

Abby rubbed her sweaty palms on her jeans, annoyed at the blood pulsing through her body. Chad had stared at her with such longing before heading to the bathroom that she couldn't deny her own eyes. He wanted her.

In fact, Abby had figured out sometime over the past two weeks that Chad was employing a shit-ton of charm to get her into bed. That had to be all it was, right? She was an anomaly because she didn't fall into bed with him the second he gave her that killer smile. A challenge he needed to vanquish so he could go back to dating skinny women who were ten years younger.

After their meeting at the diner, he'd shown up to their first strategy session with flowers, stating they were a gift to honor her win.

"Red roses?" she'd asked, smelling them. "That's...well, carnations would've been fine, or maybe some champagne, but thanks."

"Champagne," he murmured, nodding. "Got it."

She'd shot him a look, wondering what there was to get, and moved on...until she arrived at his apartment for their next session. Abby had entered his living room only to find champagne and chocolate-covered strawberries spread across his coffee table.

"This is fancy for a casual planning session," she'd muttered.

"You said you wanted champagne," was his chipper response as he handed her a glass. "We can formally celebrate."

She clinked her glass with his and only drank half, although she would've liked to drink more since it was a nice brand. But having more would've meant letting her guard down and she was determined not to do that around Chad. If she did, she might do something stupid like beg him to stroke her hair again. Or kiss her. Or rip off her jeans and...

Clearing her throat, Abby clutched the mantel, returning to reality. For some reason, Chad was trying to seduce her. There had been other instances, like how he always managed to brush her hair off her shoulder or stared at her lips like they were his next meal. Over her dead body. Abby had enough drama in her life and just couldn't see herself taking the leap to whatever place Chad wanted to go.

His efforts were equal parts annoying, adorable, and obvious. She could see how other women would fall for them but she was stronger than that, right? Getting involved with Chad could be disastrous on so many levels...or, it could also be...fun? She did enjoy hanging out with him during their planning sessions and found him incredibly knowledgeable about local politics and Rydell Industries. But was she mentally prepared to enter into a sexual relationship with the person who'd led her down the path of so much self-doubt? Crossing that chasm seemed impossible.

"It's a bad idea, Abby," she whispered to herself, turning to stare into the mirror that hung on the wall above her mantel. It sat in the middle of a frame with metal arms that looked like sun rays, and she studied her eyes, noting they were laced with both fear and longing. Clutching the end of the mantel with shaking hands, she shook her head. "You cannot sleep with Chad Hanson."

"You talking to yourself, Abbs?" he asked from the other side of the room. "I want in on the conversation."

Turning, she observed his cute smile and the tuft of hair that hung over his forehead. Feeling her world begin to crumble, she felt the rush of tears. "I need you to leave, Chad."

Straightening, he stood firm as concerned eyes drifted over her. "What's wrong?"

"Nothing," she said, shaking her head. "I just need you to leave. I appreciate your help but it's time for you to go home."

He took a tentative step forward. "What if I told you I don't want to go home?"

Swallowing, she shook her head again. "I can't do this, Chad."

Desire flared in those stunning green eyes.

"Do what, Abby?"

"Please," she cried, hating the tears that clouded her voice. "I just need you to go. Good night." Turning, she hoped he'd get the hint and leave her alone as she was so used to being. God, she just wanted to be alone.

C had studied Abby's back, her shoulders stiff as she clenched the end of the mantel. White knuckles seemed to glow beneath her flushed skin. He could almost feel the emotion as it vibrated from her frame and he hurt for her.

"Abby..."

Whirling, she inhaled a deep breath and gave a succinct nod. "Sorry. I freaked out for a moment there. I think it's because I need to eat. I'm fine, Chad. Honestly. Thanks for spending all this time with me but I'll let you get back to whatever you need to do on a Friday night. Have a good weekend."

He gazed at her, overcome with how beautiful she was as the blue locks of her hair rested atop her shoulders. The tips of the strands flirted with the mounds of her breasts above the neckline of her shirt, and he imagined dragging one of the strands across her nipple. Fuck. He wanted her so damn much.

"Stop looking at me like that."

"Like what?"

A muscle ticked her jaw. "Like you want to have sex with me."

Chad's brows lifted. "That's going to be tough because I *do* want to have sex with you."

"No."

Breathing a laugh, he took a step forward. "No?"

"Absolutely not."

Taking another tentative step, he slowly lifted his hand, attempting to brush the hair off her shoulder. She recoiled and the gesture sent a small crack down his heart.

"Abby—"

"It's not happening."

His eyes darted between hers as arousal pulsed through his body. Lust swam in her brown orbs, as well as trepidation and fear.

"Are you afraid of me?" he whispered, terrified of the answer.

"Of course not." Her chin lifted defiantly. "But if you think I'm going to get naked in front of the person responsible for sowing the majority of self-doubt I've spent years overcoming, you're batshit crazy."

Chad felt the insane urge to cry. It was ridiculous for a forty-one-year-old grown-ass man but he felt it anyway. Self-loathing threatened to choke him as he struggled with the regret of his actions all those years ago.

"I'm so sorry, Abby—"

"I don't want to discuss it."

Taking one more tentative step, he closed the distance between them. The pulse fluttered at her neck and her cheeks were flushed, making her look exquisite. God, he hated what he'd done to her all those years ago. He wished so badly he could change the past. Lifting his hand, he gently cupped her cheek, thrilled when she didn't pull away.

"If I could go back and relive that day, I'd make so many different choices, Abby."

"I'm sure you would. My presence here has reminded people you're not perfect. It's not good for your political image."

"I don't give a shit what anyone else thinks. All I care about is that I hurt you."

She rolled her eyes. "Okay."

Breaths mingled as they studied each other, two wary soldiers in a battle filled with past pain and regret.

"I don't blame you for dismissing my words but it doesn't make them less true. I deeply regret everything that happened that day. Especially now, when you're using it as an excuse to deny you want me just as much as I want you."

Scoffing, she shook her head. "How can you think I'd enjoy having sex with you? I'd be consumed with doubt the entire time, wondering if you found me flabby or gross. I'm not one of your skinny Soul Cycle girlfriends, Chad. I have cellulite and dimples and, well, it's not pretty."

He slowly stroked her cheek. "I want to see every fucking dimple, Abbs. Show me."

"No."

Smiling at her grit, he ran his thumb over her lip, elated when she exhaled a ragged breath.

"Tilt your head back," he commanded softly.

"No."

Placing his fingers under her chin, he gently tilted her face to his.

"Your lips are the stuff of wet dreams, babe." He caressed them with the pad of his thumb as she shuddered. "I want to taste you."

Those gorgeous eyes clouded with tears, shattering his heart into a million pieces.

"Abby," he said, his voice rough with emotion. "Please don't cry, honey. God, you're breaking my heart."

"Why are you doing this?" she asked, her tone equal parts anger and confusion as she swiped an errant tear. "You can have anyone you want. Is it some weird game to you? Get Abby into bed so you can add another notch to your belt?"

"Low blow, sweetheart, but I guess I deserve it." Stepping forward, he aligned their bodies. "Let me be clear: I'm doing this because somewhere along the way, you've become the person I think about all the fucking time. When I wake up. When I'm falling asleep. When I jerk off—"

She grimaced and he chuckled.

"Yep," he said, shrugging. "All the damn time, Abby. I don't give a damn how many dimples and blemishes you have. At this point, you could probably chop off my—"

Her features scrunched. "Ew."

"I was going to say *arm*," he said, laughing. "But if you want to go dark, be my guest."

"Well, it's a natural conclusion to draw," she remarked, rolling her eyes. "Lorena Bobbitt and all."

"Right," he said sardonically, arching a brow. "Well, I was going to say you could chop off my *arm* and I'd forgive you as long as you kiss me."

"I'm not really a fan of blood or I'd probably consider it."

Lowering his head, he gently nudged her nose with his. "I have to taste you, Abby. Just once."

"One kiss and you'll drop it?"

"Yes," he lied, slowly gliding his arms around her waist. In reality, he would need a million more kisses from Abby to sate his thirst for her. But, for now, he'd agree to one if she'd take pity on him and kiss him back.

"Put your arms around my neck."

Brown eyes searched his as heavy breaths rushed through her lips.

"Abby," he said, tightening his hold around her waist. "Slide your arms around my neck."

She complied, damn near causing his knees to buckle as she finally embraced him. Tilting her head back, she licked those full, luscious lips, sending every ounce of blood in his trembling body to his dick. Inching closer, he touched his lips to hers, inhaling her quick intake of breath as he pushed them open.

The sound she made—somewhere between a moan and a whimper—was so damn sexy, he almost blew his load right there in his favorite pair of khakis. Drawing her close, he plunged his tongue inside her mouth, searching. Her tongue met his, sliding and caressing as he growled against her. Lifting his hand, he speared his fingers in her thick, multi-colored hair and tugged, allowing him greater access.

She tasted like rain and spring and everything else he'd ever craved in his life. Drowning in her taste and smell, he pushed his throbbing erection into the juncture of her thighs. Those gorgeous breasts smashed against his chest, causing him to curse the human who'd invented shirts. Whoever he was, he was evil, because nothing should be separating his naked chest from Abby's breasts.

Tiny mewls escaped her throat as she worked her tongue against his. Lost in her, he struggled to breathe as his body threatened to inflame. Her nails speared into his neck, the pinpricks of pain almost sending him over the edge. Expelling a breath, he drew back and nibbled her lip before resting his forehead against hers.

Her lids lifted to reveal eyes swimming with arousal.

"Why did you stop?" she whispered.

"Because I'm about to blow my damn load like Willy Franklin in eighth grade."

A laugh escaped her throat. "Holy shit, I forgot about that. Mrs. Connaughton caught him jerking off in the closet of the music room."

Chuckling, he nodded. "Poor Willy."

"I mean, his name didn't help. Poor guy. He had it worse than me."

Chad brushed his lips against hers, dying to kiss her again but needing to breathe for a moment.

"You're not a terrible kisser," she said, grinning.

"I'm even better in bed." He chucked his brows.

Huffing a breath, she shook her head. "I'm not sleeping with you, Chad."

"Okay."

"I'm serious. I don't think I'll be able to turn off my brain and enjoy it. Sorry, buddy. Cynthia Andrews is divorced now and you always had a thing for her in high school. You should jump on that."

"Cynthia has nothing on you, babe."

"Um, yeah, she's about a size four to my size fourteen. I've got a lot on her."

"I have no idea what those numbers translate to, but if a fourteen means you have an ass like yours, I'm in." Sliding his hand down, he gripped her ass, squeezing before drawing her closer.

"I don't remember saying you could grab my ass."

Feeling his lips form a pout, he slid his hand up to the small of her back. "Sorry."

Her lips curved as mirth sparkled in her eyes.

"What?"

"I hate it, but you're really cute right now. I think I could command you to do anything and you'd do it."

"Anything but murder, probably." Closing one eye, he considered. "On second thought, murder is fine if it means I can touch your ass again. Who's it gonna be? Old man Smitty from the pub? I mean, he's a really nice guy but if he needs to take one for the team, I'm sure he'll understand. I'll tell him it's for the cause of alleviating my severe case of blue balls from needing to touch Abby Miller."

Snickering, she bit her lip. "You're ridiculous."

He grinned, so thankful to be in her arms. Gently stroking her face, he asked, "What will it take?"

"Huh?"

"For you to let me make love to you. What will it take, Abbs? I'll do anything."

Sighing, she lifted a shoulder. "I don't know. I have a lot of hang-ups about being with you that way, Chad. Do you know how many people called me Flabby Abby and said awful things to me? They spray-painted that stupid nickname on my locker and threw stuff at me when I walked down the hall and...well, I don't want to dredge up the past. Suffice it to say, it was really painful. I ran to D.C. as fast as I could and never looked back."

"Until you returned to gain revenge against your greatest enemy."

Laughing, she nodded. "Yep. Part of my plan was to secure some sort of requited justice. It sounds weird when I say it out loud but I went through a lot of therapy and eventually realized I wanted to return to Ardor Creek and rewrite the narrative...and secure a *smidge* of payback against you."

He arched a brow. "What did your therapist say about that?"

"She assigned me a bunch of forgiveness meditations. I told her I downloaded them while I secretly plotted my master plan."

"Damn, that's hot. You know, I'm kind of digging this whole revenge thing you've got going on. Let's have rage sex. We can bang while you scream how much you hate me."

She gave him a droll look. "I'm not going to hate fuck you, Chad."

"Come on. Now I'm really into it. God, you'll look so sexy with your cheeks all flushed as you stare me down. Let's do it."

Annoyance clouded her features and she stepped toward the center of the room, causing him to frown. "Don't pull back. Sorry. We can just regular fuck. It doesn't have to be a hate fuck."

Laughing, she ran a hand through her hair. "God, you're so weird."

"Are you into that? I can be weird if it leads to sex."

"Okay," she said, showing her palms. "Enough. It would take a lot."

His brows drew together.

"For me to be able to sleep with you," she clarified. "I never expected you'd want me or that you'd actually be nice and want to help me win. It's thrown a wrench in my plan to hate you forever."

"And, I'm devilishly handsome," he said, pointing at his face. "Don't forget that part."

"Whatever." She rolled her eyes. "I don't sleep with someone unless I'm dating them. I'm just not into casual sex or one night stands."

"Let's start dating, then. First date: seven o'clock tonight. That will give you time to walk Kitana and I can run home and change. Gotta ditch the tie," he said, running his hand over it. "I'll take you to dinner wherever you want. Lolita's has great Mexican or we could do the fancy American restaurant behind Main Street."

She stared at him as if he were daft.

"What?" he asked, lifting his hands. "Do you not like Mexican?"

"We can't start dating like that," she said, snapping her fingers.

"Why not?"

"Because you're a serial dater with a revolving door of women. I'm not signing up for that."

"Hey, I only date one woman at a time. I believe in getting to know someone. When the relationship runs its course, I move on. That's how dating works, Abby."

"I know how dating works, thanks."

"Then date me," he said, stepping toward her and cupping her cheeks. "Come on. It will be fun."

She studied him as the silence grew.

"Abbs?"

"Hold on. I'm debating whether or not it will be fun."

Chuckling, he arched a brow. "Okay. How long will it take?"

"I don't know."

He stood there, content to let her mull since he was touching her again. Finally, she licked her lips and sucked in a breath.

"Okay. Let's do Mexican."

Elation surged through his frame. "Yeah?"

"Yeah, only because I'm starving and on the verge of 'hangry'. But I'm not one of those 'salad girls' you probably date. Grilled salmon and lettuce for every meal? No, thanks. I'm going to inhale chips and salsa, and most likely a beef burrito, like my life depends on it. It's probably going to turn you off."

"No way," he said, loving her sense of humor. "Let's get guacamole too. And an extra order to go that I can eat off your body later."

"So weird," she said, shaking her head.

"I think you secretly like that I'm weird. You must've dated so many buttoned-up political guys in D.C. I'm just small-town, quirky mayor weird. It's kind of hot. Admit it."

Her grin was adorable. "Maybe a little bit." She held her thumb and index finger an inch apart.

"After Mexican, we can bang, right? We'll officially be dating."

"Depends on how much salsa I eat. Sex is great but salsa is everything."

"Can't argue with that logic. Okay, hon, I'll pick you up in an hour. I'm looking forward to spending time with you—*without* the flip chart." Leaning down, he placed a soft peck on her lips. "See you later."

"See you later," she whispered.

Hating to let her go, he dropped his arms and turned to walk to the foyer. She trailed behind him, holding the door as he exited.

"Maybe wear some silky lingerie under your clothes so I can imagine taking it off later," he said from her front stoop.

"Sexy lingerie and Mexican? No way, buddy. You're getting functional cotton panties that can expand with my burrito."

"You had me at 'panties.'" Blowing her a kiss, he all but skipped to his car. Abby Miller had finally agreed to date him...well, sort of... and he damn sure wasn't going to squander this fortuitous turn of events.

Chapter 14

T hree hours later, Chad and Abby lay sprawled on either end of her couch, legs extended in front of them as they rubbed their stomachs.

"Why did we order that last burrito to split?" she groaned.

"Because we were starving. Remember?"

"Uggh. I'm never eating again. God, my legs are numb. I've never been this full in my life."

"That was one of the best meals ever," Chad said, sliding his hand over to grab hers. "You're fun, Abbs."

"Correction: I was fun until I ate my body weight in burritos and died a painful death. Make sure they write that in my obituary."

"So dark," he said, shaking his head against the back of the couch. "I never knew you were so dark, sweetheart."

"I'm an avid watcher of the True Crime channel. Don't tell the voters. It's creepy."

Chuckling, he shook his head. "Won't say a word."

Kitana trotted into the room and whimpered, indicating she was ready for her last walk of the night.

"Oh, god, girl. I can't move. Why are you torturing your mom? Give me five more minutes."

"I'll walk her," Chad groaned, slowly lifting from the couch. "Man, that was hard. I was really stuck there."

Snickering, she pointed to the door. "The leash is over there. You sure?"

"Yeah," he said, leaning down to give her a quick kiss. "We're still banging, right?"

"Uggh," she said, palming his face and pushing him away. "I can't even fathom that right now." He frowned as Kitana nudged his leg. "But you're so cute and you're going to walk my dog, so check with me when you get back."

"Ten-four." Waggling his brows, he headed outside as Abby nestled into the couch. Two minutes later, she felt sleep tugging at her consciousness.

"Whoa," Chad said, from somewhere above her. "You're sleeping? Come on, Abbs. We had a deal."

"Lay down and snuggle with me first," she mumbled, burrowing into the couch. "Or, do you not snuggle with the Soul Cycle chicks from Bumble?"

"I'll have you know I'm an excellent snuggler," he said, crawling onto the couch and spooning her.

Abby wiggled against him before exclaiming, "Ouch!"

"What?"

"Your belt buckle is huge. What are you, a Texas rancher? Take it off."

Groaning in frustration, his lips vibrated against her neck as he spoke. "I just laid down, Abby. Geez."

"It's digging into my back."

Sighing, he stood and unbuckled his belt before shrugging it off along with his jeans. Abby's eyes grew wide. "The belt, Chad, not your pants!"

Flashing a satisfied grin, he hopped back on the couch. "It's all or nothing, hon." Drawing her back into his front, he aligned their bodies. "And we can't bang if I still have my pants on."

She shimmied her jean-covered ass against his crotch, half-thankful and half-annoyed he'd left on the boxer briefs. "We'll totally bang in a minute," she said, already feeling herself fade. "Just need to digest that last burrito..."

C had's eyes flew open and he searched the dark room, trying like hell to remember where he was. As long as it wasn't a bachelor party and there were no dead hookers, he figured he was okay. Glancing down, he realized Abby was in his arms, and his heart flooded with joy. They must've fallen asleep on her couch after their epic Mexican dinner.

Lightly touching his nose to her neck, he inhaled her scent, closing his eyes at the sweet smell. God, she smelled so fucking good. He had no idea if it was perfume or body spray or whatever women did for that sort of thing, but it was heaven. Placing his lips on her neck, he began to trail kisses over the smooth skin.

"Mmmm..." she moaned, burrowing into his body as his dick stood to attention. Was he wearing pants? Glancing down, he remembered he'd taken them off but left on his boxer briefs. Better than nothing.

Resuming the nibbles on her neck, he slid his arm around and cupped her breast. She pushed into his palm and he felt her nipple pebble underneath her shirt and bra. Fuck, he couldn't wait to have those nipples in his mouth. Trailing his fingers to the tight bud, he lightly pinched and she gasped.

"Chad?" She turned her head and gazed at him with hooded eyes. "I'm really confused right now...don't process things well when I wake up."

Lifting his hand, he stroked her cheek. "We fell asleep on your couch." Reaching for his phone from the side table, he checked the time. "It's one thirty-eight in the morning."

"Oh," she said, biting her lip. "Didn't mean to fall asleep. Sorry."

"Don't ever apologize for falling asleep when your body is smashed against me, Abbs. Got it?" He pushed his erection into her ass.

"Got it."

Brown eyes darted between his, and Chad could see the wheels turning in her mind.

"I don't know what to do here. Do you want to stay? We can go to my room."

"Do you want me to stay?"

"Coward," she said, grinning.

"Fine, I want to stay. But if I do, I'm definitely going to want to have sex, Abby. I don't want to play games with you. We're too old for that shit."

Gnawing her bottom lip, she pondered. "Okay. But I have conditions."

"Let's hear 'em."

"First, we have to brush our teeth, because, Mexican and sleep. Ew."

Laughing, he nodded. "As long as you have an extra toothbrush, I'm in."

"Sure do. Second, we do it with the lights off."

"No way," he said, shaking his head. "Hard no. I want to see you, Abby."

Her eyes clouded with the now-familiar self-doubt and he wanted to kick himself for the part he'd played in it so long ago. "How about this? We'll brush our teeth and go to your room—with the bedside lamp on—and I'll show you mine before you show me yours."

"You'll show me your perfectly sculpted chest before I show you my rolls of belly fat? Um, yeah, no thanks."

"I'm insanely attracted to your body, honey." He stroked her hair as he spoke, hoping she would believe him because it was true. "I literally think about touching you every other second of the day. I want to see every part of you. Please don't hide yourself from me."

She glanced down before reclaiming his gaze. "Let's brush our teeth while I contemplate."

"Done." Standing, he extended his hand to her. She took it and they trailed to her bedroom, where she flipped on the bedside lamp. He followed her into the adjoining master bathroom and admired her ass as she bent over to rummage through the counter under the sink.

"Here," she said, handing him a single-packaged brush. "Courtesy of my last visit with Dr. Jobe. No cavities, thank goodness. The toothpaste is there." She motioned with her head to the cup beside the sink. "You go first and I'm going to check on Kitana. She's probably sleeping on her dog bed in the kitchen."

Nodding, Chad brushed his teeth, loving how forthright she was. Banging while having Mexican sleep breath wasn't terribly sexy. Good call.

She returned, closing the door behind her, and stepped into the bathroom.

"She's asleep and clutching the old bone I gave her weeks ago. She's so cute."

"Will she be mad I'm having sexy times with her mom?" He chucked his brows.

"Who knows? If she starts pawing at the door, we'll have to let her in. She's spoiled, the little brat. It's all my fault."

"It's all yours, hon," he said, stepping from the bathroom so she could take care of business. Afterward, she stepped outside, her green toenails peeking out under the cuffs of her jeans.

"Okay," she said, rubbing her thighs. "How are we going to do this?"

Slowly approaching, he encircled her wrist and drew her beside the bed.

"I'll take off my shirt and then you'll take off yours." Grasping the hem of his shirt, he tugged it off and threw it on the chair in the corner of her room. Her eyes darted over his nipples and the smattering of hair as her teeth toyed with her lip.

"Shit. You're really hot, Chad."

The words sent shivers of elation down his spine. "So are you, hon. Come on. Your turn. Shirt off."

Sighing, she clutched the hem of her shirt and pulled it over her head. Her hair fell back over her shoulders and black bra as she dropped the shirt. "Here you go," she said, slightly shrugging. "Flabby Abby in all her glory."

Compassion swamped him as he closed the distance between them. Sliding his fingers under her chin, he tilted her face to his. "You're so fucking beautiful, Abby," he said, placing a sweet kiss on her lips. "I'm so sorry I hurt you. I wish I could fix it."

"I know," she whispered, running her thumb over his lips. "It helps when you look at me like that. Like I'm pretty and you don't want to look away."

"You are pretty, honey," he said, tugging her toward the bed. Sitting on the edge, he drew her to stand between his legs. "I always thought you were so pretty. Even all those years ago."

"Liar," she teased, sliding her fingers through his hair.

"Nope," he said, gliding his hands behind her back to unclasp her bra. "That's a hundred percent true, Abbs. Believe me or not, but it's just a fact."

He slid the bra down her arms, baring those magnificent breasts. She released his hair to let the garment drop to the floor before sliding her fingers into the thick tresses again.

"You were supposed to take off something else," she said, pouting.

"I already lost my pants in the living room so we're even now."

"I'm not sure that's a logical argument, but okay."

Chuckling, he slid his hands up her sides. His heartbeat accelerated at the way her skin trembled beneath before he cupped her breasts. "Holy shit," he whispered, gently massaging them. "They're so pretty."

"Well, they're too big and require a sports bra the size of Maryland when I work out, but if you like them, I guess that's good."

"Oh, I like them," he said, licking his lips before touching them to her nipple. Rimming the pebbled bud with his mouth, he gazed up at her. "Abby," he whispered.

"*Please...*"

Moved by her plea, he closed his lips around the tight little nub, sucking it as she fisted his hair. Lowering her hand, she speared her nails into his neck, finding a stronghold as he tasted her. Feeling the taut bud tighten against his tongue, his fingers toyed with her other nipple, bringing it to a stiff point before pinching it.

"Oh, *god*," she moaned, head falling back as she pushed against him. "Pinch it harder."

He complied, squeezing her nipple with his fingers as he gently bit the other. She shuddered in his arms and he felt his cock twitch, longing to be deep inside her warmth. Trailing a row of kisses to her other nipple, he drew her inside his mouth as he gazed up at her.

She returned his stare with eyes so full of lust, he sent a silent prayer of thanks to the universe. For a while, he'd been unsure if she would open herself to him. But now, staring into her soul, he realized how amazing she was to bare herself to the one person who'd ripped her apart so long ago.

"You're so beautiful, sweetheart," he whispered against her breast before sucking her nipple back between his lips. He wanted to say more—to say something profound—but his arousal-ridden brain couldn't find the words.

After playing with her breasts for a while, he drew back and reached for the button of her jeans. Unfastening it, he lowered the zipper.

"They're tight," she said, grinning.

"Oh, I know." He nipped at her breast while inching them down. "These jeans are my favorite item of clothing ever invented."

Laughing, she shook her head. "I had no idea you liked curvy women, Chad."

"I don't like any woman but you," he teased, shimmying her jeans down her thighs. She stepped out of one side, then the other, and he tossed them aside. "Well, look at these functional cotton panties. Chad likey." He toyed with the lace at the top.

"They gave the appropriate amount of expansion and I am sufficiently pleased."

Smiling up at her, he hooked his finger under the band. "Can I take them off?"

She gave a shy nod. Overcome with how cute she was, he dipped his fingers beneath the fabric and dragged them off her legs. She stood before him, naked, and he took a moment to gaze at her beauty.

Curves and hollows led to thick thighs that Chad suddenly wanted wrapped around his head for the rest of his life. Yep, he could just live between Abby's thighs forever and he'd die a happy man.

"I swear I work out," she said, lifting a shoulder. "It helps but I'll never be skinny."

"You're perfect, Abbs," he said, sliding his palms over her lower abdomen to her hips and down her thighs. "I've never seen anyone more perfect."

"I'm sure Britney from Tinder would disagree."

"Britney chewed like a horse. She had nothing on you."

Throwing her head back, she gave a hearty laugh. "Of course, you would've dated someone named Britney from Tinder. Wow. I was joking, but okay."

"She also had this weird tooth that stuck out right here," he said, pointing to his incisor. "It was really uncomfortable when she was sucking my—"

"Okay," she said, tugging his hair. "That's enough about Britney."

Grinning, his hands continued their trek over her body. "Honestly, Abbs, I've never even come close to feeling this way about anyone else. I think I should be scared but, for some reason, I'm not."

Sighing, she rested one knee on either side of his hips, straddling him as he cupped her ass. "Keep saying romantic stuff like that and I'll forgive you for dating Britney."

God, he loved her sense of humor. Gripping one luscious butt cheek in his hand, he slid the other around to find her core. Searching, he found her wet and slick, and he gritted his teeth. Staring into her deep brown eyes, he slid his finger into her tight warmth.

Her resulting exhale washed over him, full of desire and longing. Gliding his finger back and forth, he closed his eyes against the onslaught of pleasure at finally touching her most intimate place.

"More," she cried, and he inserted another finger, dragging it back and forth as her slick walls clenched him tight.

"Can I get you off this way?" he growled.

"Yeah," she nodded, her forehead against his. "Go deep and hook your fingers and rub my clit at the same time. I can help if you need—"

Gasping, she broke off when he hooked his fingers against the tiny spot deep inside. "Right there," he said, thrilled he'd found it.

"Mmm-hmm," she said, working her hips against him.

Placing the heel of his hand on the top of her mound, he pushed the folds apart and stimulated the swollen bud while his fingers moved inside her. She pushed against him, undulating her hips in the most erotic lap dance he'd ever seen. Overcome with the need to make her scream, he lifted his lips to hers and drew her into a passionate kiss.

She moaned into his mouth, licking his tongue with ardor as she rode him. Chad was so turned on, he was pretty sure he was going to come in his boxer briefs, but he didn't give a damn as long as she got off. Breaking the kiss, he sucked her bottom lip between his teeth.

"You have no idea," he whispered into her mouth. "I've imagined this for so long."

She whimpered, increasing the pace of her hips as she drew him into another kiss. His tongue warred with hers until she broke the kiss and buried her face in his neck.

"*Oh, god...*" she groaned, biting his neck.

Chad hissed at the prick from her teeth and felt her begin to spasm against his hand. Determined to take her high, he slammed his fingers into her pussy until she shattered. Screaming his name, she held on for dear life as her body quaked, the soft strands of her hair tickling his chest.

"No more," she moaned, and he immediately relaxed his hand, content to feel her pulse against him. Eventually, her muscles relaxed and she melted into a puddle of sated lust in his arms.

She slid her legs across the bed, wrapping them around his waist as her face remained buried in his neck. Content to hold her, he stroked her hair while his other hand cushioned her ass.

"Babe?" he called softly, not wanting to detract from her high. "You okay?"

"Worse than the burrito," she mumbled.

"What?"

"I'm more incapacitated now than I was after I ate the extra burrito. Help."

Overcome with laughter, he buried his face against her skin, realizing making love to Abby Miller was going to be fun. Sexy and meaningful and fun.

"That was amazing, Abbs."

Lifting her head, she assessed him as her features drew together. "What?"

"That was amazing for me but I don't know how it was amazing for you. You didn't come yet."

"Believe me, I was close for a second there," he joked, nipping her lips, "but it feels good to make you feel good, hon."

"Aw, that's sweet. But I'm totally okay with making you come now. What do you want me to do? We can bang or I can play with you for a while. I'm open."

"While I appreciate that, I'm pretty sure I'm going to last about thirty seconds, so we should probably move straight to banging."

"Straight to banging it is, sir," she said with a salute. "Do you have a condom? All mine expired months ago and I keep forgetting to buy more."

"Not even for Larry with the huge mole? I can't believe you guys barebacked. What if you'd gotten pregnant with a little Larry?"

"Wow, you're really killing my lady boner with that image. I'd suggest you stop immediately."

Chuckling, he pecked her lips. "I've got condoms in my wallet, which is in the living room. Be right back." She scampered onto the bed and he all but sprinted to the living room and grabbed his wallet. Stepping back inside her bedroom, he softly closed the door.

She rested on the comforter, hair fanned out over the pillow, rubbing her legs together. Chad took a mental snapshot, pretty sure he'd remember this moment for the rest of his life. Feeling himself harden, he tugged off his underwear and found a condom in his wallet.

"You're really lucky because I shaved my legs this morning," she said, biting her finger like damn sex goddess. "Usually, it's hit or miss."

Rolling on the condom, he placed a knee on the bed and ran his palm over her leg from ankle to thigh. "Smooth."

"Yeah, I've got pretty nice legs, actually. The universe didn't shaft me all the way."

Sliding over her, he wedged his knee between her legs. "The universe didn't shaft you at all, sweetheart. I'm so hot for you." Gripping the base of his cock, he aligned the head with her opening. "Do you want me to rub your clit first?"

"No way," she said, encircling his neck with her arms. "I'm ready—"

He slowly pushed inside as soon as the words left her mouth, causing her to laugh atop the pillow. "Someone's eager."

"You're fucking right I'm eager, honey," he gritted, advancing inch by inch into her tight channel. "Fuck, I'm going to blow so fast. I'm so turned on right now."

Lifting her arms, she pressed her palms flat on the headboard. "Then fuck me hard and make it good."

He circled his hips, dragging his straining cock against her swollen walls. "You sure?"

She nodded, her hair sliding against the pillow, and he rested his weight on one straight arm as he slid his hand behind her knee. Lifting her leg high, he pulled back before surging deep with one full thrust.

She moaned from the pillow, those wet lips open as she screamed his name, and Chad finally saw the vision he'd been imagining for so many months. Abby, open and groaning beneath him as he claimed her. Feeling possessive, he hammered into her body, needing her to know she was *his*.

"You're mine now, Abby," he growled, lowering to his forearm and gripping her hair. "You know that, right?"

Emotion clouded her eyes and he felt himself falling. Pleasure tingled at the base of his spine as he worked his cock into her trembling body.

"Tell me, honey," he whispered, drawing her into a heated kiss before pulling back. "Tell me you feel it too."

She cried his name and he lost all semblance of rational thought. Burying his face in her neck, he surged inside her taut channel, unable to do anything but burrow deeper into her luscious body. Feeling something snap, he grunted against her skin before he exploded, shooting jets of release into the condom as his body racked with tremors. She wrapped her leg around him, drawing him even deeper as he succumbed to the orgasm.

Every muscle in his body turned to jelly as he collapsed, loving how she wiggled underneath him. Her fingernails roved over his scalp in movements so pleasurable, he wanted to feel them forever.

"Holy shit," he breathed, nuzzling her neck.

"Mmm-hmm," was her lazy response.

"God, Abby, fucking you is hands-down my favorite thing in the world. I want to do it several times a day from here on out, okay? Just say yes. Don't think. A succinct 'yes' will suffice."

Chuckling, she continued the soft strokes against his scalp. "Yes."

Breathing a sigh of relief against her skin, he closed his eyes.

"Chad?"

"Hmm?"

"We need to get rid of the condom."

He grunted against her neck. "Can't move."

Huffing, she pushed his shoulder. "Go throw it away so we can cuddle and maybe we can do it again after we sleep."

"Fine, you evil woman." It took all his energy to walk to her bathroom and dispose of the condom but he managed. Returning to bed, he noticed she'd crawled under the covers and was nestled on her side facing the wall.

"Turn off the light too."

"Is there anything else I can get for the lady before I retire?" he grumbled, turning off the light before crawling into bed.

"Don't be an ass," she said, snuggling into him as he spooned her.

"Fair warning, I'm going to touch your boobs while we sleep." Sliding his hand over one of the mounds, he cupped it and drew her closer.

"Fine. Just don't drool on me. Everything else is open game."

"Everything?" he asked, pushing his sated cock into the crack of her butt. "Even butt stuff?"

"Go to sleep, Chad," she droned.

Snickering, he kissed the back of her neck. "Night, honey."

"Night," she mumbled. "And I do."

"Hmm?"

"I...feel it too. Just wanted you to know. Okay, going to sleep now. Night."

Closing his eyes, he breathed in her scent, so thankful she'd spoken the words. Sliding his leg over hers, he drew her into his body and let himself sleep.

Chapter 15

♥

Abby awoke encircled by something heavy and warm and...snoring. Struggling to make sense of the strange sensations, she lifted her lids to find Chad wrapped around her like a python ready to choke its next victim. Internally chuckling at the thought, she turned her head, noticing his face was burrowed into her neck as he snored. His leg was thrown over her thighs and his arm snaked across her stomach, ending with his hand that cupped her breast. Well, he *had* warned her he was going to touch her boobs so she couldn't really fault him there.

Assessing the situation, Abby tried to recall ever being held so reverently. There was something so sweet and possessive about his embrace, and her heart lurched. He hadn't been kidding about being an epic snuggler. Chad was holding her as if he never wanted to let go and it was...adorable. Damn it, it was fucking adorable.

Signing, she studied the ceiling, wondering how long it would take her to fall head over heels in love with him, especially if he held her like this after they made love. Accepting reality, she realized she was doomed. There was no way in hell she wasn't going to fall, especially now that they were sleeping together. Deciding she'd need to process that realization after coffee, she glanced at him again, wondering if he was a hard sleeper. Would he wake up if she tried to extricate herself?

Since there was only one way to find out, she began slowly moving underneath him, sliding along the sheets as he continued to snore. When she was free, he mumbled something unintelligible and shifted, burying his face in the pillow. Seconds later, he began snoring again and she snickered. After throwing on some sweats, she headed to the kitchen and brewed the coffee before walking Kitana. Afterward, she poured a cup and headed back to the bedroom, sipping it while assessing her sleeping lover.

It was still early on Saturday, so perhaps he was just a late sleeper who enjoyed sleeping in on the weekends. She, on the other hand, had a Saturday ritual that she was intent on keeping, especially now that she was intimate with Chad. Setting the mug on top of her dresser, she rummaged inside and located the yoga pants and sports bra.

Removing her sweats, she shimmied on the yoga pants before struggling with the sports bra. Getting her breasts into the thing was always a massive feat and she turned to find a smiling Chad gazing at her, hands resting under his head on the pillow.

"Uh, good morning, creepy lurker," she said, still struggling with the damn garment. "How long have you been watching me?"

"Since the yoga pants," he said, the low tone of his sleep-filled voice sending shivers down her spine. "Watching you get into those was hot. I think watching you get out of them will be even hotter."

Rolling her eyes, she managed to finally get the sports bra situated. "Well, that's going to happen after my workout, if it happens at all."

"Working out at seven-fifty a.m. on a Saturday. Impressive, Miller."

"It's a habit I formed years ago," she said, shrugging a tank top over the sports bra. "I get up and work out five days a week and one of them is always Saturday. I grumble about it the whole time but I always feel great afterward."

"You have a gym here in the complex?"

"Yep. It's pretty nice. They have weights, machines, and my favorite of all, the elliptical."

He grinned. "Your sarcasm is tangible."

"Yeah, I hate it," she said, shrugging. "But it's a necessary evil if I want to maintain this fountain of beauty," she joked, gesturing to her body.

"I think your body is gorgeous, Abbs," he said softly.

"Thanks," she said, rubbing her arm since she felt awkward. "Well, anyway, it will take me about forty-five minutes and then we can, uh, I don't know, get breakfast somewhere if you want?"

He studied her as he contemplated. "Can I work out with you? I can use the gym as your guest, right?"

"You can, but I'm not sure if that's a good idea. I'm not one of those cute gym girls with the ponytail and go-getter attitude. I hate every minute of it and drop multiple curse words as I struggle not to beat the shit out of the machine. Not a good look if you want to maintain any sort of attraction to me."

Sitting up, he scratched his head and yawned, and Abby felt her knees turn to jelly. Freshly-awoken Chad was probably the sexiest thing that existed on the planet. How did he just wake up like that? Annoyed, she crossed her arms.

"Well, while you pose for World's Hottest Peeping Tom over there, I need to get to it."

Shrugging off the covers, he stood and approached, seemingly unconcerned he was naked as a jaybird. Trying like hell not to stare at his junk, she maintained eye contact with him.

"I can run home and change and be back in fifteen minutes." Lifting his hand, he ran the backs of his fingers over her cheek. "Wait for me, Abbs. I need to work out anyway. Let's do it together."

She wrinkled her nose. "If you're okay with the fact that last night might be the first and last time we bang, then, fine. Because I'm telling you, it's not pretty."

"You're pretty," he whispered, brushing a soft kiss on her lips. The sweet gesture damn near buckled her knees. "Give me fifteen minutes."

"Okay," she said, backing away before she did something stupid like swoon into his naked body. "Get on with it then. I'll finish my coffee while I wait."

"Thanks." Locating his clothes, he donned them and gave her one more kiss before heading out.

Padding into the kitchen, she sat at the tiny table and drank her coffee. Kitana stared at her, a bone between her paws, and Abby scowled.

"Don't look at me like that," she said while Kitana panted, tongue hanging slightly from her mouth. "It's really hard to tell him 'no', okay? He's so damn cute. It's annoying."

Kitana sighed and began chewing the bone, obviously done with the conversation.

A few minutes later, Chad appeared, looking fresh and chipper in his workout attire. Meanwhile, Abby felt every bite of last night's Mexican feast firmly implanted on her thighs. Did her dimples show through the fabric? Damn, she hadn't even considered that.

"Ready?" Chad asked in the foyer.

"Yeah." After grabbing her iPad and earbuds, she led him around the corner to the fitness center and used the fob to unlock the door. Once inside, he assessed the room and lifted his brows.

"This is nice," he said, glancing around. "Way nicer than my apartment's fitness center. I might have to work out with you more often. They have a great selection of equipment and weights."

"Let's see how this session goes," she muttered, eyeing the elliptical. "I usually pop in my earbuds and watch something on my iPad while I'm working out. I'm not someone who enjoys conversation while I'm sweating profusely."

Chuckling, he nodded. "Okay, I'll leave you alone. But I might glance at you here and there just to see how you're doing."

"And, by that, I think you mean you'll watch my boobs jiggle while I'm doing the incline."

Covering his heart, he sighed. "Abbs, you already know me so well." Leaning down, he brushed her lips with his. "Have fun, babe." Pivoting, he headed toward the weights, and she allowed herself to stare at his ass in the gym shorts because, well, she was only human.

Facing the elliptical, she completed some stretches before climbing on. Setting up her earbuds and iPad, she chose a course and got down to business. Every once in a while, she'd glance at Chad as he lifted barbells by the mirror. He usually caught her looking and would respond with a wink or kiss in the reflection. After her obligatory thirty minutes, she hopped off and chugged water from one of the tiny cups attached to the dispenser.

Chad sauntered over, glistening and flushed, while she was soaked and huffing. Annoyed, she arched a brow.

"Having a good workout?"

"Yep," he said, taking a cup and dispensing water before throwing it back. "Feels really good. I usually run or use the gym at my place. It's a nice way to start the day."

Nodding, she gulped the water before tossing the cup in the wastebasket. "Well, I'm done. Do you need more time?"

"I'd like to do a few more reps on some of the machines if that's cool?"

"Sure, I'm going to head home and make fresh coffee and I'll leave the door unlocked. Kitana will bark when you come in but just pet her and she'll calm down."

"Okay, see you in a few. Thanks."

She trailed back home and put on a new pot of coffee before opening the fridge and assessing. She had eggs and could make an omelet but wasn't sure if Chad would rather go out. Deciding to wait, she pulled open the drawer and opened the pill pack as Kitana barked by the front door.

"The beast let me live," Chad joked, walking into the kitchen. "She's a teddy bear under all that fur."

"Tell me about it," Abby said, placing the pill on her tongue before taking a sip of water to help wash it down. "She's a great dog. She's a little aggressive around men but, otherwise, she's really sweet."

"You popping pills on me, Abbs?" he teased, leaning his hip on the counter.

"Birth control," she said, shrugging. "It helps with my acne and raging PMS."

"Sexy." He arched a brow. "That means we could scrap the condoms, right?"

Abby's eyes darted between his. "That's a big step, Chad. I'd want us both to get tested and I wouldn't feel comfortable with you being with anyone else."

His lips curved. "I'm okay with that."

Facing him fully, she crossed her arms. "You're telling me that after one date and one night in bed together, you're ready to be exclusive?"

Tilting his head, he lifted a shoulder. "Yep. I think that's what I just said."

"Exclusive means you can't date anyone else."

"Thanks, Merriam Webster. I'm aware of what exclusive means."

Huffing a breath, she ran a hand through her hair. "Like, you can't message anyone from Tinder or Bumble on the side."

"Fine. I'll delete the apps. I haven't used them in a while anyway."

"Right," she said, rolling her eyes.

"I haven't, Abbs." He tucked a strand of hair behind her ear. "Ever since I saw you at the pub in January, I haven't really been interested. I was fixated on the campaign and, well, I was kind of fixated on you."

She swallowed, which was difficult since her heart was fully lodged in her throat. Narrowing her eyes, she studied him.

"What?" he asked, looking perplexed.

"I'm just trying to figure out why you're into me. I mean, I'm pretty rad in some areas but I took away something you loved. I'm wondering why you don't hate me for it."

Grinning, he slid his palm over her arm and clutched her hand, lacing their fingers. "I could never hate you, hon. I'm bummed about the primary, for sure, but it brought you back into my life so there were some positives too."

"It's hard for me to think when you say sweet stuff like that."

"Then, don't think," he said, drawing her closer as their bodies brushed. "Just say 'yes'. Let's do this, Abbs. Summer is starting and it's my favorite time of the year. The gang has a cookout almost every weekend, and we go to the lake and on hikes up by the reservoir. I want you there with me for that stuff. I like hanging out with you."

"I do like hiking," she said, eyes narrowing, "and I kind of like you..."

Laughing, he leaned down, staring into her eyes. "Then, let's do it. Let's be exclusive and see where it takes us."

She gnawed her lip as she contemplated. "You're sure?"

"I'm sure."

"Okay," she whispered, telling herself to be cool although, deep inside, she wanted to do a hundred cartwheels around the kitchen.

Never in a million years would she have imagined Chad would ask her to be exclusive. Squeezing his hand, she gazed into his eyes, floored by the sentiment that stared back at her.

"You're in?"

"I'm in," she said, yelping when he drew her into his body and cemented his lips to hers. She melted into him, kissing him passionately as her hands roved over his back. Holy shit! She was now officially dating Chad Hanson. It was a full-circle moment for the shy, awkward girl she'd been so long ago. Drawing back, she caressed the hair at his temple as he panted above her.

"Abbs?"

"Hmm?"

"I think we totally need to bone to cement this new phase of our relationship."

Throwing her head back, she laughed. "Okay, but I'm super gross."

"So, let's shower together."

"Uh, yeah. I need to work my way up to that level of self-confidence." Chuckling at his frown, she ran a finger over his jaw, loving the prickly stubble. "But how about you shower while I cook us some omelets, then we'll eat, then I'll shower, and then we'll bone?"

"Sounds good," he said, nipping her finger. "But we're going to work on this confidence thing because I need to see you wet in the shower. But," he said, lifting a finger when she opened her mouth to argue, "I'll accept separate showers for now." Brushing a kiss on her lips, he pulled back and gestured with his head down the hall. "I'll be out in a few minutes. Thanks for cooking."

"Sure. Do you need some clothes? I not sure I have anything that would fit you."

"I have some extra workout gear in the car I can wear."

"The hot water in the shower takes a minute so just let it run and you'll be good."

"Gotcha," he said, lifting a hand as he trailed down the hall.

She whipped up the omelets while he showered and they ate breakfast in the kitchen while they chatted. After showering, she stepped into her room wrapped in a towel and found a shirtless Chad sitting on her bed.

"Wow. No build-up before getting down to business, I guess."

"Oh, there's going to be buildup, hon," he said with a wicked grin. "It's just going to happen while my lips are touching your skin." Motioning with his hand, he urged her closer. "Come on, Abbs. Ditch the towel. Let's make this relationship official."

Inhaling deeply, she grabbed the top of the towel and tugged before tossing it to the floor. The desire that flared in his gorgeous green eyes was all she needed to see. Diving in with her whole heart, she all but rushed the bed and fell into his arms.

Later that day, Chad sat on a bench at the dog park, arm around Abby's shoulders as they watched Kitana play with the other dogs. She was having a grand ol' time and so was Chad. Finally, after all his careful planning, he'd snagged Abby. Feeling pleased with himself, he glanced over to find her grinning.

"What?"

"You're gloating," she said, nuzzling into his side. "Is it because you got me into bed? I swore I wasn't going to sleep with you. I was so sure I wasn't your type."

"You're totally my type," he said, waggling his brows. "And, yes, I'm definitely gloating at the fact you found me irresistible."

She rolled her eyes. "Whatever."

Chuckling, he swiped a tuft of hair from her cheek blown there by the warm breeze. "Tell me about D.C. How did you end up working for Senator Dawkins?"

"I kind of fell in love with politics when I was in college at Georgetown. Politics infiltrates every facet of life in D.C. and several of my classmates volunteered for various campaigns. I decided to volunteer for Senator Dawkins when he was running his first campaign to fill Representative Steiner's seat in the House of Representatives."

"That's cool. I'm guessing you enjoyed it."

"Yep," she said, nodding. "I really did and I made some friends, which wasn't easy for me, but the other volunteers were nice and a lot of them were quirky like me."

"Are you quirky?" he asked, squinting.

"You know I am." She swatted his chest. "I like being that way now, but when I was younger it was hard, especially because I was shy too. Anyway, I made some good friends and Senator Dawkins was impressed with me. When I graduated college, he asked me to come on board as one of his junior advisors."

"Nice. He was a major power player in congress until he retired."

"Sure was," she said with a firm nod. "During his two terms as senator, he accomplished so many things. I was honored to serve as one of his advisors and eventually moved up to senior advisor. It was nice that he was from Scranton. I felt like I was contributing in some way to Ardor Creek—and the rest of Pennsylvania—even though I'd left it behind."

"What made you decide to come back? Besides wanting to crush me, obviously."

Sighing, she gazed at Kitana in the distance as her lips formed a soft smile. "I loved all aspects of working for the senator but my favorite meetings were always with local officials. You know, county representatives, town council members, and mayors. The mayors were always the best. They cared so much about their towns and knew them intimately."

"Small-town mayors are pretty awesome." He huffed on his fingernails and rubbed them on his shirt.

"Okay, let's keep the ego in check," she said, scrunching her features and giving him a playful glare. "Anyway, I realized how much I wanted to stay in politics after Senator Dawkins retired but I didn't relish the cutthroat world of D.C. politics. I wanted something smaller and more enjoyable. After thinking long and hard about all the mayors I'd met with, I decided it would be cool to try and run somewhere."

"And you could also get some killer revenge."

"Yes," she said, rubbing her palms on her thighs. "I won't lie and say the thought didn't excite me. I'd grown into someone stronger and more confident, although I can always still grow in that area.

Somewhere along the way, I got the idea I could run for mayor in Ardor Creek and accomplish two goals: get some payback against you and become a small-town mayor like all the ones I'd met with over the years. Plus, I thought it was ridiculous that Ardor Creek had never elected a female mayor and wanted to change that."

"And here you are. Mayor-elect Abby Miller." He squeezed her shoulder. "You should be really proud of yourself, Abbs."

"Well, I'm not mayor-elect yet," she said, shrugging. "I still have to beat Rydell."

"We're going to beat him, hon. I'm fully dedicated to the cause."

"So, what will you do?" she asked, kicking the ground with her toe. "Now that I've ousted you?"

"Ouch."

"Come on, you must have other aspirations besides working at the store. You're a great mayor, Chad, but there's so much more you can do."

Sighing, he shook his head. "I don't know. I think I'm putting it off because I don't want to admit I lost somewhere deep inside."

She cupped his jaw, turning his head so he was forced to gaze into those deep brown eyes, swimming with empathy. "I'm sorry I beat you, Chad. Not for me—because I think I'm going to kick ass if I win in November—but for you, because I think you really love being mayor. It hurts that I took away something you love. I never expected to feel torn up about it. But," she held up a finger, "I do think this could be a blessing in disguise for you. If you search deep within, I think you'll find that you'd become a bit complacent and weren't challenging yourself. You're an exceptional politician and I think you should contemplate running for a higher level office."

His eyebrows drew together. "Like county clerk or something?"

Laughing, she shook her head. "That's not nearly high enough. State Senator Lawrence's seat is opening up next year. I think you should run for his spot."

"For state senator?" He rubbed his chin, contemplating. "I've never thought about it."

"The seat is in Ardor Creek's district so you could remain here. I'd help you with the campaign. I'm well-versed in state and federal politics and would be happy to help."

Chad smiled at the offer. He knew Abby fetched a pretty hefty consulting rate with political clients and was humbled by her offer to help. "How much will it cost me? I'm going to be out of a job in January."

"I'll do it for free as long as you keep plying me with Mexican. I mean, a girl has to eat."

"I'd be a fool to pass up that deal." Pursing his lips, he let the idea simmer as he held her. "It's an interesting idea, Abbs. I need to think about it but I appreciate your faith in me. It means a lot." He gazed down at her, noting how cute her button nose and flushed cheeks were in the afternoon sun. Feeling like the luckiest guy in the world, he kissed the tip of her nose. "And I like the idea of running for something else but staying in Ardor Creek. I still love it here even though the people are over me."

"Ardor Creek loves you, Chad. I'm not even going to feel sorry for you on that one. You're the poster child for this town and always will be with that handsome face and charming personality."

"Keep going," he said, circling his hand. "I need more."

"Okay, I think we're done here." Standing, she placed two fingers between her lips and elicited a shrill whistle. Kitana's head snapped to attention and she ran toward them, into Abby's outstretched arms.

"That's a good girl," she said, rubbing Kitana's back in furious motions. "Were you having fun with the other pups?"

Kitana barked and Chad stood, stretching as she talked to the dog. "The whistle thing is sexy, Abbs. Makes me wonder what else you can do with your mouth."

Straightening, she shot him a glare. "Do you think about sex every *other* minute of the day or is it just on a constant loop in your head all the time?"

"When I'm near you, I think about sex *every* single minute, babe, especially when you're in those jeans." Tugging her wrist, he drew her closer. "We talked about those jeans and exactly what state they put me in."

Rising to her toes, she brushed her lips against his. "Want to take them off and show me?" The words vibrated against his lips as his body slammed into overdrive.

"Geez, Abbs, are you trying to make me blow it in the dog park? Fuck, you're so hot right now. And yes, I definitely want to take off the jeans. Let's go." Extending his hand, he shook it impatiently.

Those full lips curved into a wicked smile she took his hand. "Why, Mr. Mayor, I thought you'd never ask."

Clutching his woman's hand as she clutched Kitana's leash, he led both ladies from the park so he could put his dirty mind to good use.

Chapter 16

Abby's first official week with Chad flew by and before she knew it, the weekend was right around the corner. Chad was adorable as they lay in bed Thursday night after eating the sushi he'd brought over for dinner. He was staring at her with that goofy grin as his head rested on his hand. They'd made love and were now in a sex-sushi coma, which Abby found quite heavenly.

"That had better be the last time we have to use a condom, Abbs," he said, trailing a strand of her hair over her nipple. "I'm ready for full bang mode."

Laughing, she nuzzled into the mattress, relishing the soft strokes against her sensitive skin. "I should get the results back tomorrow morning. Yours came back fast."

"I told Dr. Matthews to expedite them."

"Of course, you did."

Chuckling, he continued the lazy strokes until his expression turned serious.

"What?"

"Scott texted me today that they're having everyone over on Saturday. I'm planning on heading over after I'm done at the soup kitchen. You're going to come, right?"

She wrinkled her nose. "I have to check with my other suitors but, yes, I should be available."

He looked relieved, causing her eyebrows to draw together. "Did you think I wouldn't want to come?"

"I just don't want you to think I don't take your campaign seriously. I do and I understand you're going to be spending a lot of weekends campaigning—and I'll be campaigning for you too—but I want you all to myself for a few weekends at least."

"I'm going to go into full campaign mode after July 4th. Figured I'd give myself a month or so to take a break from the grind."

"That's perfect. We can chill and settle into this thing for a while before we have to go full force. I'm still going to manage your campaign, Abbs. We've already come up with tons of awesome ideas and I have so many more buzzing in my head. We're going to cream Rydell."

"Hell, yes, we are and you didn't think I was letting you off the hook, did you? I'm definitely still taking advantage of your free campaign manager skills. You're my secret weapon."

His eyes roved over her breasts as he stroked them with her hair, and she ran her fingers over his cheek. "Chad?"

Green eyes lifted to hers as he smiled. "I'm just honored that you believe in me, hon. I'm kind of a self-taught politician. I don't have a master's degree or all the experience you have. It makes me feel legitimate or something."

"You've been mayor for eight years," she said, shaking her head on the pillow. "That's the best kind of experience one can have."

"I guess," he said, kissing the valley between her breasts. "I've been thinking a lot about what you said. You know, the state senator thing? Half of me thinks I might actually be able to do it and the other half thinks I'd be laughed out of the election."

"By whom? Being mayor is a perfect stepping stone to that position. Especially a two-term mayor."

"And then what?" he asked with a sparkle in his eyes. "US senator? President? Would you vote for me for president?"

Laughing, she bit her lip. "Oh, Chad, you dear, sweet man. Don't you know that I'll be running for president? You can be my first man."

"I'd be honored to be your first man," he said reverently, "and Kitana can be first dog."

She must've heard her name because Kitana's snout appeared through the crack in the door before she pushed it open. Trotting over, she hopped on the bed and crawled in between them.

"Well, that cuddle session is officially over," Abby said, stroking her fur. "Like I told you, she gets a bit jealous."

"I get it, girl," he said, petting Kitana. "I don't want anyone else touching your mom either."

Abby's heart melted at the words—and at the fact that Chad was besotted with her dog. "She really likes you."

"I like her too." He kissed her nose before wiping his lips with the back of his arm. "Even if she gives sloppy kisses like her mom."

"Hey," she said, swatting him. "I'm not a sloppy kisser."

"Okay."

"You're going to pay for that."

"Ohhh, yes, make me pay," he said, shimmying past the dog to nuzzle into her side. "I think I'll like being punished by you."

Kitana began barking furiously and Abby groaned. "Okay, we have to walk her. Well, I have to. You can come with me if you want to walk off the sushi."

"I'll come," he said, sliding off the bed. "And then the three of us can huddle in here and watch the new true crime episodes you DVR'd."

Rising, she cupped his face. "Are you trying to say the perfect thing? Because that was pretty much it."

"I've got you figured out, Abbs," he said, grinning as he pulled on his sweatpants. "I'm leaving my shirt off, by the way. Let's blow Martha's mind."

Abby snickered. "Oh, god, yes! She might faint when she sees us all sexed up. This is the stuff of her gossip-filled dreams."

"Well, let's not keep her waiting."

Abby slid her hand into his, ready to give Martha a show as they walked Kitana under the star-filled sky.

On Saturday, Abby was nervous as Chad drove them to Ashlyn's. Although his crew had always been nice to her in high school, they'd been in the popular crowd while Abby had been a pariah. She'd had fun at Carrie's sip and see, and hoped she felt as relaxed during the cookout as she had that day.

"You okay, hon?" Chad asked, squeezing her hand as he held it atop her thigh.

"Yeah. I'm nervous. That probably sounds weird but this is dredging up all my memories of high school. I've finally got an in with the cool kids. Hope I don't blow it."

"I'm pretty sure you're the cool one now that you've creamed me, but we'll see."

His teasing was sweet and comforted her as they puttered through town.

A few minutes later, they turned onto Ashlyn's gravel driveway. Once parked, Abby opened the back door and grabbed Kitana's leash when she jumped out.

"You ready to meet everyone, girl?"

Kitana barked.

"Remember, be nice, okay? And no jumping."

She followed Chad around the house to the back yard, where a bunch of folding chairs were set up on a patio surrounded by a grill and long table covered with a checkered plastic tablecloth.

"Abby!" Ashlyn called, jogging over and hugging her with Carrie close behind.

"Hey, guys," she said, hugging them both. "Thanks so much for having me."

"We're so glad you're here, sweetie," Carrie said.

"Well, aren't you sweet?" Ashlyn asked Kitana, rubbing her fur. "Oh, Abby, I love her."

"Thanks, Ashlyn. I'm hoping she doesn't jump all over everyone. I'll keep her leashed until the excitement wears down."

"Hi, Chad," Chad said, mock annoyance in his tone as he glanced around the back yard. "Great to see you. How are you?"

"Oh, stop," Carrie said, swatting him. "Obviously, we're happy to see you but this is Abby's first cookout." Embracing him, she placed a peck on his cheek. "There, are you happy now?"

"Sure am. Give me another one here so we can make Peter jealous," he said, pointing to his other cheek.

"She's already banging the mailman from what I hear, so I abandoned jealousy months ago," Peter called from beside the grill. "Go ahead, man. I'm dead inside."

"So dramatic," Carrie said, rolling her eyes. "The boys are racing Scott around the woods somewhere. They had too much energy and he offered to run some of it off. I can't wait for their summer soccer leagues to start in July. For now, we're their entertainment and it's exhausting."

"But I have something really cool for them when they come back," Ashlyn said, pulling a key from her back pocket. "Last year they found a box buried in the yard that I believe was left there by Sally Pickens. After an exhaustive search of the attic, I found this key and it opens the box!"

"Sally Pickens from the ghost story?" Abby asked. "I remember that story from years ago. She passed away in the attic from a broken heart."

"In *that* attic," Ashlyn said, excitement in her dark green eyes as she pointed toward the house. "I tested the key to make sure it worked and then closed the box right away. I want the boys to open it."

"Wow, that's super cool. I didn't realize your house was Sally Pickens' house."

"Yep," she said with a nod. "My grandmother lived here until she passed away a few years ago and left the house to me. That's how I met Scott. I basically stalked him until he agreed to renovate my house. We all have to do inventive things to push people a bit, right, Chad?" She arched her brows.

"Right," he said, grinning.

"Okay, what am I missing?" Abby asked.

"Let's just say Chad was really interested in being your campaign manager," Carrie said, threading her arm through Abby's. "I won't out him but I'll say it was a really cool plan. Now, let's get you a drink."

"I think you just outed me anyway, Carrie," Chad called as they strolled away from him toward the table covered with various wine bottles and an ice-filled bucket of bottled beers. "Don't give away my secrets. I just won her over and don't want to blow it."

Carrie winked. "He's so cute when he talks about you, Abby. It's so nice to see. Do you want beer or wine or something else?"

"Wine's fine," Abby said and Carrie poured some into a red solo cup. "And he is really cute. He asked me to be exclusive after the first date. I was floored."

"Oh, I know," she said, pouring a cup for herself. "He's beside himself over you. It's awesome. Being mayor has been Chad's only love for years. I think that might change with you and I'm over the moon." Lifting her cup, she toasted, "May you finally be the one who domesticates Chad Hanson."

Laughing, Abby touched her cup to Carrie's. "I'm not sure about that but I appreciate the sentiment. Cheers."

They settled in as Abby said hello to Peter, Mark, and Teresa before Scott and the boys bounded around the corner. They halted, all three out of breath, and rested their hands on their knees as they recovered.

"I'm too old for this," Scott said, panting. "I used to be such a good runner. What happened?"

"I don't remember you being that fast," Ashlyn muttered.

"Quiet, woman. I run circles around you."

"In your dreams, buddy."

Carrie handed them all bottled waters which they gulped before straightening. Assessing her, the oldest boy asked, "Are you the new female mayor? Mom said you're going to be really good."

"Well, I hope I'll be the first female mayor. I have one more election to go. Your mom was really helpful when I was campaigning."

"Don't remind me," Chad muttered.

"Hey, I canvassed for you too," Carrie said.

"I might forgive you since it's Abby. Otherwise, I was planning to get revenge by making your yearbook glamor shot my Facebook profile picture."

She gasped. "You wouldn't."

"Totally would," he said, lifting his beer. "But I'll let it go this time."

She shot him a playful glare before running her hand through her son's hair. "This is Sebastian and this is Charlie." She placed her arm around his shoulders.

"Hi, guys," Abby said. "This is Kitana."

"She's pretty," Sebastian said. "Can I pet her?"

"Sure, but approach slowly, okay? It takes her a few minutes to warm up to strangers but she's really nice once she feels comfortable with you."

Nodding, Sebastian approached, hand outstretched and Kitana sniffed it before licking it.

Laughing, Sebastian scratched her under the chin. "Hey, Kitana. Good girl. What's Kitana mean?"

"Kitana is a really important princess in the Mortal Kombat world. It's a video game I used to play all the time when I was younger."

"I love video games," Sebastian said. "I just got three new games for my Nintendo Switch because I got good grades last year."

"We bribe them," Carrie whispered loudly. "It's terrible but I love the result."

Chuckling, Abby held up her hands. "No judgement here. I'd love to play video games with you sometime, Sebastian."

"I play too," Charlie said.

"Well, then I'll play with both of you. Sounds like fun."

Ashlyn chose that moment to reveal the key to the boys, who responded with wide eyes and gasps of excitement. Lifting the withered wooden box from the table, she placed it in Sebastian's hands while handing Charlie the key.

"Why don't you turn the key while Sebastian holds the box, Charlie?"

Charlie stuck the key inside and turned, his face a mask of curiosity. The latch clicked and the top of the box sprung open. Reaching inside, Sebastian pulled out a stack of what appeared to be letters, tied together with a string.

"Okay, let's be really careful," Carrie said, taking the letters from Sebastian and walking toward the table. Untying the string, she separated them and lifted one from the pile.

"Can I read it, Mom?" Sebastian asked, reaching for it.

"I want to read one too," Charlie pouted.

"You both can read one," she said, handing each of them one of the folded pieces of paper.

"I'll go first," Sebastian said.

Charlie nodded and Carrie gave a "whew" before wiping her brow. Abby snickered at her obvious relief at Charlie's concession.

"That was very diplomatic, Charlie," Abby said. "You'll make a great politician one day."

Charlie beamed as Sebastian unfolded his letter and began to read.

"My darling Patrick,

You left me to fight a valiant war, and for that, I do not begrudge you. But there are so many words I would've said if I'd known the ones we spoke that day were our last. I ache for you when the world is cold as vehemently as I ache for you on the scorching summer days. How can one survive a season without you? It's been twelve seasons now. Three long years. How many more must I bear before we are reunited in a world where I bask in the glow of your love? Until that day, I will wait for you, my darling, in the house we shared when we were happy together.

Love, your Sally."

"Dramatic much?" Peter muttered to Scott.

"Hey!" Carrie said, shooting him a glare. "That was beautiful. And don't act like you're not just as romantic, Peter Stratford. You showed me all the sweet things you wrote about me in your journal. You're not fooling anyone."

He blew her a kiss as Charlie unfolded his letter and began to read. It relayed similar sentiments and Abby slipped her hand into Chad's, squeezing as she smiled into his eyes. He winked and she felt her heart flutter. Yep, she was a goner. Sighing, she gave in to the emotion and decided there was no point in denying she was bound to fall in love with him. She had other things to worry about and he seemed pretty enamored with her too, which was reassuring.

After the letters were read and examined by the group, Chad declared that some of them should be given to the local historical society for examination and possible donation to the small museum on Main Street. Abby thought it a lovely idea that showcased Chad's reverence and appreciation for Ardor Creek.

Eventually, Abby felt comfortable enough to let Kitana off the leash and the boys played with her in the yard. Kitana relished every minute and Abby realized she'd be exhausted when they got home. That was good because a sleeping Kitana meant she could have sexy times with Chad, which she was really looking forward to since they'd exchanged test results. He hadn't stayed over last night due to a mayoral dinner function he'd attended on Main Street, so she was pretty much ready to jump his bones after the cookout.

She had a fantastic time, especially when Grant and Emily awoke from their naps and she could hold the little cuties. The tight-knit group was more like family than friends, and Abby felt honored to be included.

About an hour after sunset, Chad took the last sip of his beer and tossed the bottle in the recycling bin. Smiling at Abby, he rubbed her upper arm.

"Ready to go, babe?"

"Yeah," she said, whistling to Kitana. She trotted over and Abby attached the leash. After a round of hugs, they trailed to the car. "You okay to drive?"

"Yep," he said, sliding behind the wheel. "I nursed that last one for two hours. Didn't want anything obstructing our first condom-free bang fest."

"Wow, that's a lot to live up to," she teased. "Hope I'm up to the challenge."

"Oh, I have no doubt, sweetheart," he said, waggling his brows as he drove.

When they arrived at her apartment, she walked Kitana one more time before she settled in with a bone on her dog bed. Entering her bedroom, she closed the door, noticing Chad brushing his teeth in the bathroom.

"Guess it was a good idea for you to bring the overnight bag," she said, sliding off her sandals. "I might let you stay over."

"Is that so?" he asked, striding from the bathroom and brushing a kiss on her lips before removing his shirt. Encircling her wrist, he drew her close.

"Wait," she said, holding up a finger. "I need to brush my teeth and wash my face and do the whole regimen. I've been wearing makeup to bed when you stay over but that's not my normal routine. Women over forty have this whole thing we do," she said, circling her hand over her face. "I want to look pretty for you but I need to cleanse and moisturize."

Laughing, he nodded. "Moisturize away. I'm sure you'll still look gorgeous, Abbs."

Closing one eye, she assessed him. "How old were the women you dated before me? Late-thirties?"

His eyes grew wide. "Uh, yeah, some of them."

"Wait. Early-thirties?"

"Some of them."

"Twenties?"

Rubbing the back of his neck, he seemed to struggle for the right answer. "I mean, does age really matter in today's dating world?"

Crossing her arms, her mouth fell open. "Chad, am I the oldest woman you've ever dated?"

He frowned. "No."

"Oh, my god. You're a terrible liar. I am!" She poked his chest.

"Ouch. Geez, Abbs, I don't care about that stuff, okay? It's more about the attraction for me."

"When's your birthday?"

"August 7th."

"Thank god. Mine's September 29th. At least you're older than me. I'm not sure I could've handled it if you were younger."

"You don't look a day over twenty-five," he said, tugging her close and pecking her lips.

"Okay, I'm going to brush my teeth while I try not to develop a complex." Heading to the bathroom, she muttered to herself in the reflection as she completed her regimen. "*What do you talk about with a twenty-five-year-old when you're forty? Do you tell them about the war? Walking uphill in the snow both ways barefoot? It's absurd.*"

"I can hear you!" Chad called from the bedroom.

"That was the point," was her cheeky reply.

His chuckle filtered through the room and she grinned at her reflection. Stepping back into the bedroom, she found Chad lounging underneath the covers.

"I had fun today," she said, removing her tank top before sliding off her jeans. "Thanks so much for inviting me."

"Just the first of many, hon." His eyes sizzled with arousal as he watched her undress. "Keep going."

Grinning, she unhooked her bra and slid it off before shimmying her underwear down her legs. Naked, she sauntered toward the bed and planted one knee beside his hip before straddling him.

"Look at you," he whispered, sliding his hands over her abdomen before cupping her breasts. "I want to taste you, Abbs."

"Where?"

Sliding his thumbs back and forth over her rapidly pebbling nipples, he gave her a sinister grin. "I want you to sit on my face."

She recoiled. "No way. Do you have a death wish?"

"If it's taking my last breath between those sexy thighs, then, yes, I think I do." He slid his hands down, reverently caressing her thighs as his breaths grew heavy.

"I'm afraid I'll crush you."

"No way, babe. It's a huge turn-on for me. Please?"

"Chad, I'm too heavy—"

Flipping them over, she squealed at the rapid movement before he slithered over her body. "Why do you say stuff like that, Abbs?" he asked, caressing her cheek. "Your body is perfect to me and when you say things like that, it reminds me of our shitty past. I want to let that stuff go."

Exhaling a deep breath, she shook her head on the pillow. "It's just hard for me. Being overweight is something I've struggled with my whole life. I was finally able to lose most of it but I don't want to disappoint you."

"Abby," he whispered, running his thumb over her lips. "I'm awed by you, hon. The way you charged into town and won everybody over. It's amazing. You're so fierce and I'm obsessed with every inch of your body because it's part of you."

"Oh, man," she said, tracing her finger over his jaw. "That's really good. Kind of cheesy but really good."

Laughing, he drew her into a kiss before drawing back. "I like to try things in bed. Maybe I'm weird—"

"You are weird. But I like that about you."

"Anyway," he said, rolling his eyes. "If I ask you to try something, I want you to be open and I need you to know I'm grateful you let me touch you. Anywhere. It's kind of a fucking miracle."

Chuckling, she nodded. "Okay. I'm open."

"Good." He waggled his brows before flipping them over again. Resting her palms on his chest as she straddled him, she bit her lip.

"Should I just slide over you?"

His lips formed a sexy smile as he nodded. Gripping her hips, he urged her toward his face. Abby clutched the headboard and slid over him, resting her knees on either side of his head.

"Like this?"

"*Fuck*," he whispered, squeezing the sides of her ass as he nuzzled against her folds. "Yes, babe, like that. Come closer."

She lowered onto him, telling herself to relax and enjoy the sensation. Chad emitted a pleasure-filled moan as he moved beneath her, running his tongue between her folds. Closing her eyes, she clutched the headboard and began to move her hips.

His fingers tightened on her ass, moving her over his mouth as he sucked and nibbled her most intimate place. There was something so sexy about having all the power—knowing she controlled every aspect of the moment as he strove to give her pleasure.

His tongue speared inside her core and she cried his name, unable to control the movement of her body. She rode him, hips undulating as he growled against her skin, the vibrations sending delicious shivers to every cell in her body.

Sliding up her folds with his tongue, he drew her clit between his lips, sucking the engorged nub as she writhed against him. It created a different sensation—one so pleasurable she threw her head back, releasing every inhibition so she could focus on *feeling*. Chad moaned, the sound one of pure contentment as he loved her. His movements relayed his joy at her ability to open herself to him, and it unlocked something deep in her heart.

"*Chad...*"

He groaned against her pussy as he drew her closer, his hands now holding her ass in a death grip that was so possessive, she felt *claimed*. His ministrations against her trembling body were so intimate...so raw...and she felt the orgasm looming on the horizon.

"Oh...*god*...I'm going to come..."

His resulting lust-filled grunt shot straight through her frame and her spine snapped, causing her to clench the headboard as the climax took over. Holding on for dear life, she began to spasm against his tongue, feeling her wetness gush into his waiting mouth. Giving in to the toe-curling sensation, she arched her back and let the orgasm rack her body with shudders.

Eventually, she came down from the high, expelling a ragged breath as she released the death grip on the headboard. Glancing down, she met Chad's eyes, noticing they were swimming with satisfaction and lust.

"Oh, boy," she said, slowly sliding down his body to sprawl over him. "Someone's *really* proud of himself."

Chuckling, he ran his fingers through the hair at her temple as she caressed his face. "As long as you felt good, I'm damn proud of myself."

"I'm all over you," she whispered, dragging her finger over the wetness that covered his mouth and chin. "Fuck, that's sexy."

"Come here," he said, pulling her into a deep kiss as he positioned her over his body. Surrounding the base of his cock, he guided it to her core and aligned himself with her opening. Breaking the kiss, he stared into her eyes as he began to push inside.

"*Chad...*"

"Yeah, honey," he said, sliding his cock against her swollen inner walls. "There you are. So sweet and wet..." He gripped her hips, moving her against him as he rocked into her body.

Abby stared into his eyes, understanding this was so much more than sex...for her, at least. Undulating against his strong frame, the moment was profound because she'd never experienced such raw intimacy with anyone else.

"Don't get scared, babe," he said, sliding his fingers into the hair at her nape. "I know it's intense."

Understanding he'd seen the fear in her eyes, and loving how well he could read her, she lowered her lips to his as they moved together. A few moments later, he growled into her mouth and flipped them over, lifting her leg as he began to fuck her hard.

"Is this okay?"

"Yes," she cried, nodding from the pillow.

"*Fuck*," he grunted, his hips working into her body as he pistoned back and forth. "So close, hon...*oh, god*..."

With one last deep groan, he threw his head back and began pulsing jets of release into her desire-ravaged body. Abby could feel every jerk of his cock inside her, making her feel so connected to him. Clenching her inner walls, she strove to pull him deeper inside, hoping to give him even more pleasure.

"Oh, god, you're squeezing me," he said, the words ragged as he breathed a laugh. "I might never stop coming."

She slid her arms around his shoulders, drawing him close as the shudders eventually died down. He burrowed into her neck and surrounded her, holding her so tight she struggled to breathe. Tapping his arm, she mumbled, "Too tight."

"Sorry," he said, immediately relaxing his hold but still sprawled over every inch of her body. "I'm a stage five clinger after sex. You've probably figured that out."

"It's so cute," she said, trailing her fingernails over his back. "I never imagined player extraordinaire Chad Hanson would be a cuddler."

"I love it," he said, snuggling into her. "Especially with you."

"Okay, stop saying sweet things like that. It's not fair."

Chuckling, he kissed her neck. "All part of my master plan, babe."

Stroking his skin, she stared at the ceiling, wondering what Chad's future plans were. Did he want to get married? Did he want kids? She figured he'd want to stay in Ardor Creek because he loved it but maybe he had dreams of living somewhere else one day. They were serious questions that led to serious discussions she was suddenly terrified of having.

"Stop thinking, Abbs," he mumbled against her neck.

"I'm not thinking."

"Yes, you are. I can hear the gears shifting in your brain. Turn it off and cuddle with me."

Sighing, she relaxed against him and closed her eyes, drifting toward the darkness as she wondered where the future would take them. Would she end up with Chad Hanson after everything they'd been through? Eighteen-year-old Abby would've found it unbelievable. Now, she found it...possible. Sliding into sleep, she marveled at the unpredictability of life and how inexorably things could change with the passing of time.

Chapter 17

♥

C had would always remember that summer as the one where he fell slowly and reverently in love with Abby Miller. May turned to warmer days in June and they spent most nights together as Chad's tenure as mayor wound down and he prepared to help Abby take his place. Sometimes, she would look at him, those brown eyes filled with concern and a slight bit of hesitation, and ask if they were moving too fast. Chad would always reassure her, realizing the connection they'd formed was rare, and he wanted to foster it.

"Thank god you have me, Abbs," he teased one day as they sat at the dog park. "You worry about everything."

"I just don't want you to get tired of me," she said, throwing the yellow ball toward the fence so Kitana could race after it. "We're spending a lot of time together."

"Who else would I spend time with?" he asked, brushing her hair off her shoulder. "I'm happiest when I'm with you. I don't see the problem."

Kitana returned with the ball and Abby gave him a sly glance. "What do you think, girl?" she asked, petting her under the chin. "Sometimes I think he says this stuff just to see if I'll believe it."

"Maybe I just say it to get you into bed," he joked, chuckling at her scowl. "Either way, it works pretty well. You're mad for me, Abbs."

"Wow. I knew you had an ego but this is next level."

"Come on, you love it. Doesn't she, girl?" he asked, bending down to pet Kitana.

Abby sighed and Chad felt his lips curve. Yep, he was pretty sure she was head over heels for him, which made him ecstatic. After so many years, he was finally ready to settle down if things felt right. He'd never been against marriage since his parents had a great marriage filled with lots of love and laughter before his mom passed. Rather, he'd just never felt the urge.

He'd had a few relationships that lasted several months—Britney with the wayward tooth being one of them. Although he'd cared for her, he hadn't *craved* her like Abby. Chad's desire to be near her was on some sort of obsessive level he'd never experienced. As he'd told her the first night they made love, it probably should've terrified him, but it didn't. *At all.* Which was so fucking weird...but, also, pretty damn great when he took the time to ponder it. It meant they *fit*—quite perfectly, in his opinion, and he was smart enough not to squander it.

They spent most nights at her place since it was Kitana's home too, and Chad loved learning Abby's little quirks as they grew closer. First, she was a stickler for the bedtime teeth brushing and face routine. Sometimes, he would try and seduce her into bed before she went "full ritual" but it was tough. He guessed there could be worse things than waiting ten extra minutes to bang someone with minty fresh breath and glowing skin. Plus, the habit was rubbing off on him and he was pretty sure he'd never have a cavity again.

She also loved eggs—like, omelet for breakfast, egg salad sandwich for lunch, and quiche for dinner—loved eggs. Chad found it hilarious and chided her for it but she usually just rolled her eyes and made him something egg-related as well. So, basically, eggs became Chad's new favorite food, whether he liked it or not.

She hated jogging, although she loved hiking, and they took Kitana on hikes several times a week over by Reservoir Park. It housed multiple trails perfect for working up a sweat—and maybe a few hidden spots where he could steal kisses from Abby before Kitana got jealous and nudged him away.

And, maybe best of all, was her obvious love for Kitana. Abby was an awesome dog mom and showed her tons of affection. Chad knew she'd be that way with her own kids one day and he slowly grew into the idea of them having kids together. It was a colossal leap and he understood the relationship needed time to breathe before they tackled the subject. Content to let it simmer, he threw himself into the multitude of work and play that comprised the busy summer.

Abby was now a fixture at their weekly cookouts and fit in perfectly with the group. When the July 4th barbeque rolled around at Carrie and Peter's home, Ashlyn gathered everyone around for a special announcement.

"I'm very sorry to tell you that Carrie's wine buddy will be temporarily taking a break," Ashlyn said, lifting her red solo cup, "because your very good friend and my favorite grumpy contractor has managed to knock me up again!"

The group cheered and Carrie said, "That just means more wine for me since this baby maker is closed." She pointed at her stomach while everyone laughed.

Several rounds of hugs followed and Chad patted Scott on the shoulder as he beamed. "Wow, man, congrats. I'm so happy for you guys."

"Thanks, Chad," Scott said, elation consuming his expression. "After everything with Ella and Tina, it's such a damn miracle. I'm so thankful for Ashlyn."

"She's amazing. You're one lucky son of a bitch."

"Says the man dating our next mayor. You've seemed to find someone pretty awesome too."

"Yeah, I'm super into her, man," Chad said, sipping his beer. "I think this might be it."

"Holy shit," Scott said, shaking his head. "I'd almost given up hope."

"Don't be a dick. I just needed a little more time than you guys. Some of us age like fine wine."

"Or, like a really terrible fungus," Peter said, appearing behind Chad and throwing his arm over his shoulders. "You're like a really bad toe fungus, Hanson."

"Where do you come up with this stuff?" Chad asked, eyebrows drawing together. "It's like your brain thinks something stupid and you just word barf it out."

"Word barf," Peter said, rubbing his chin. "I like that one. Totally stealing it. Thanks, bud." He trailed toward the table and held up a finger when Carrie approached. "Gotta write this down, honey. Chad's giving me gold over here." He made a note in his phone.

"Do I even want to ask?" Carrie arched a brow, looking at Chad.

"Nope," he said, shaking his head.

"I didn't think so." Sighing, she resumed gushing over the news with the rest of the ladies.

That night as he was driving home, Abby reached over and grabbed his hand.

"Okay, I don't want to make this weird or into some big discussion. I'm not sure we're ready for that yet. I just want to get a basic idea so don't freak out. A clear, simple answer will do."

"Okaaaaaay," Chad said.

"Do you want to have kids? I'm only asking because we're both at an age where we need to do it relatively soon so we're not on walkers at our kids' high school soccer games."

"I'm not sure that would be so bad. You'd look pretty hot on a walker, leaning over so your ass stuck out in those amazing jeans—"

"Chad," she interrupted, her tone annoyed.

"What? It's true. Don't hate the messenger."

Sighing, she rolled her eyes and looked out the window. "Forget it. It's too early to bring it up anyway."

Squeezing her hand, he tugged it when she wouldn't look at him. Finally, she turned her head and he grinned. "I want to have kids, Abbs. Probably two max because, like you said, we're old as fuck."

"Speak for yourself," she huffed, shimmying into the seat. Sparing him a glance, she said, "And I want to have kids too, in case you were wondering. Two is perfect. Okay, that's all."

"Is that all?" he asked, loving how annoyed she was. Abby was so damn cute when she was annoyed. "Anything else I can answer for the lady?"

"Nope."

"Want to know my favorite color?"

"Nope."

"It's blue. Probably why I was so obsessed with your hair."

"That's great."

He could barely control his snicker as her cheeks inflamed with irritation.

"Want to know my philosophy on life? It's a doozy. You see, it all started with the Big Bang—"

"God, you're so annoying. I'm sorry I asked."

Laughing, he reached over and poked her arm. "Come on, Abbs."

"Ow!"

"Man, you're so riled up. It reminds me of the pub that day. You were this close to sitting on Smitty's lap." He held his thumb and index finger an inch apart.

"If only I'd taken that path," she sighed. "I would've dodged a bullet."

"Oh, you've done it now, babe." Pulling into the parking spot in front of her apartment, he jogged around and tugged her from the car before grabbing Kitana's leash as she hopped from the back.

"Chad!"

Bending down, he picked Abby up and threw her over his shoulder. Tugging Kitana behind them, he trailed to the front door.

"What are you doing?" she squealed, lightly pounding his back with her fists. "Put me down."

"No way," he said, inserting the key she'd given him into the lock of her apartment door. It creaked open and Kitana ran inside. "Sex with exasperated Abby is my favorite. We're getting down to that right now." Looking to his left, he waved. "Oh, hi, Martha. How's it going?"

"Fine, Mr. Mayor," she called from her stoop. "Are you two okay?"

"Just fine," he said, giving a salute. "Abby was mean to me so I'm carrying her inside so she can apologize. She'll probably have to get on her knees—"

"Everything is fine, Martha," Abby interrupted, sounding like she wanted to strangle him. "Chad ran out of roofies so I'm still half-conscious and he needed to carry me. Have a good night!"

They giggled with glee as he carried her inside and down the hallway, tossing her on the bed. "Roofies, Miller? Come on. I haven't used roofies in years."

Tossing her head back on the comforter, she laughed, the sound so melodious that Chad felt his heart click. One more piece that fit into place every time he fell a bit more in love with her. Lowering his lips to her neck, he trailed kisses over the pounding vein and over her jaw, coming to rest on her lips.

"Poor Martha," he said against her lips. Abby shivered beneath him and his body grew tense with desire. "We really need to stop torturing her."

"I think it's a fair price to pay for being so nosy," Abby said, sliding her arms around his neck before wrapping her legs around his waist. He drew her into a blazing kiss, determined to show her with his lips and tongue how much he adored her. And then, several minutes later, the little minx just so happened to get on her knees, although an apology wasn't exactly what she gave him...

Chapter 18

♥

Sterling Rydell's first commercial aired two days after July 4th, yanking Chad and Abby from the playful summer days straight into the campaign. It set the tone for a spiteful race, which Chad had never experienced in Ardor Creek. But Charles Rydell was determined to ensure his son's win so Sterling could approve his shady proposals, and the campaign would be bankrolled by his endless wealth.

Abby saw the ad first as she was watching the evening news in the living room. She had a thing for David Muir but Chad figured that was okay since he lived two hundred miles away. If he ever came to Ardor Creek, Chad would have a nice discussion with ol' David explaining that Abby was off-limits. For now, he'd let it go.

Stepping into the living room with a fresh beer, he noticed Abby's shocked expression as she sat on the couch holding the remote. She seemed frozen and her mouth hung slightly open as Kitana panted beside her.

"Abbs?" he asked, slowly approaching. "What's wrong?"

"That son of a bitch," she said, her expression filled with disbelief.

"Who?"

"Watch this." Clicking the remote, she rewound the feed sixty seconds. A dog food commercial came on and his eyebrows drew together. "Uh, are we changing Kitana's food?"

"Shhh," she said, waving her hand. "It will come on after this."

The dog food commercial ended and another one began. Sterling Rydell's smiling face appeared in front of an American flag.

"If there's one thing Ardor Creek understands, it's the need for change," the narrator said, his tone low and compelling. "That was proven when the residents chose Abby Miller in the May primary. But now there's a new challenger, one who will create an influx of prosperity and bring fresh ideas to Ardor Creek."

"I'm Sterling Rydell and I care deeply about Ardor Creek," he said, sounding more like a robot to Chad than a person. "It's time we revitalize this town and make it into the thriving paradise we want to see."

"Paradise?" Chad said, rubbing his neck. "What a cheeseball."

"Wait, here's the kicker," she said, pointing at the TV.

"Don't fall for Abby Miller's flabby policies," the narrator continued. "Vote for Sterling Rydell in November. Sterling Rydell: the choice today for a better tomorrow."

She paused the TV and lifted her gaze to him. "That asshole knows."

Chad swallowed. "He used the word 'flabby' to describe your policies." Dread coursed through him as he began to realize the implications.

"It's a fucking signal," she said, standing and rubbing her palms on her thighs. Pacing around the living room, anger rose in her tone with every word. "We called them 'word drops' when I worked for Senator Dawkins. Words your opponent would place in media spots to indicate they had dirt on you."

"I'm trying to follow you, Abbs," he said, lowering to the chair in the corner as she paced.

"They know about the stupid nickname. 'Flabby policies,'" she said, making quotation marks with her fingers. "They're signaling to me that they're going to drag out the old nickname the more I fight them."

Standing, Chad set his beer on the table and approached her. Rubbing her upper arms, he struggled to understand. "So, this is only the first instance? You're saying they're eventually going to go full force and bring out the Flabby Abby name in their campaign?"

"Yes," she said, eyes wide as she huffed a breath. "It's actually brilliant. Remind everyone in town of my pariah status when I grew up here. It will bring the Butches and Heathers out of hiding and they can give interviews about how inept and unpopular I was. Then, flood local media with the message that Sterling is strong and has a fresh vision much different from the loser they'll portray me to be."

"Shit, that's dirty."

Nodding, she rubbed her forehead. "I'm used to dirty. We saw it all the time in D.C. I just didn't think I'd see it in Ardor Creek."

"Just another example of Rydell's dishonorable tactics. He probably hopes bringing up old wounds will throw you off your game."

"Exactly," she said, arching a brow. "But he's got another thing coming if he thinks this will shake me. It just makes me want to decimate him even more."

"Fuck, babe, I know this is important and needs attention but I just have to pause and tell you how fierce and gorgeous you are right now. Is this how you were in D.C.? Because I'm here for it."

Breathing a laugh, she ran a hand over her hair. "I was pretty badass."

"No doubt." Leaning down, he brushed a kiss over her lips. Drawing back, he studied her.

"What?"

"Should we address the elephant in the room that this is ultimately my fault? I don't want you to resent me, hon. If you need to punch me or something, you can."

She squinted. "I'll hold that offer for a later date but this isn't your fault."

"I'm the one responsible for that stupid nickname. One terrible mistake that will haunt me forever."

"You know what?" Cupping his cheek, the corner of her lips curved. "Fuck 'em. That was a long time ago and I'm such a different person now. Plus, the guy who destroyed me back then is kind of into me now and that's a really good narrative. If you're willing to go on the record."

"On the record that I'm crazy about you?" he asked, sliding his arm around her waist and pulling her close. "Definitely. I'll shout it from the top of the damn firehouse."

Laughing, she nodded. "I'm not sure we'll need to go that far but our story is kind of cute. Current mayor falls for next mayor despite their difficult past. I can work with that."

"And she falls for him too," he said as his lips formed a pout. "Don't forget that part."

"Eh, maybe. We'll see how it goes."

"You wound me, Mayor Miller," he said, covering his heart. "Why does the lady break my heart so?"

Grinning, she rose to her toes and pecked his lips. "I don't know why you fall into that weird old-school prose but it's pretty damn cute."

"Obviously," he teased, rolling his eyes.

"Chad?"

"Yes?"

"Go get the flip chart. My mind is humming with a million ideas. We've got work to do."

Laughing, he gave her a salute. "Yes, ma'am." Trailing to the den, he located the flip chart and markers, ready to help his woman.

Abby threw herself into the campaign, ready to officially claim her title as the first female mayor of Ardor Creek. She and Chad had come up with a bunch of ideas in their pre-dating planning sessions which she implemented right away.

First, she set up a ton of new volunteering opportunities, both for kids and adults, finding them a great way to give back and help the community while also allowing her access to the residents. She organized road clean up events along the local highway between Ardor Creek and Battle Falls, thrilled when over a hundred residents showed up to the first two events. They were so successful that she organized a lake clean up event in late July where Ashlyn offered to supply free food from Grandma Jean's Gourmet to the volunteers.

Multiple people attended the event and they removed tons of trash from the lake and surrounding woods and walking paths.

After the trash had been loaded into the garbage trucks to be hauled away, thanks to Chad's careful planning with the waste management department, Abby sat with her friends as she devoured two of Ashlyn's delicious pulled pork tacos.

"God, I was starving," she said, taking a huge bite as she sat atop the blanket on the soft grass. "Thanks so much for doing this, Ashlyn. I feel bad you gave everything away for free."

"Consider it a donation to my favorite mayor's campaign."

"Ouch," Chad said, grimacing from his spot beside Abby.

"Favorite *new* mayor," Ashlyn corrected. "You'll always be my favorite current and former mayor, Chad."

"I'm not sure that makes me feel better, but okay." He rubbed his chin.

"What if I whipped up some garlic fries for you? I know they're your favorite."

"I'll never turn down garlic fries," he said, beaming.

"Coming right up." Scott stood and helped her up before sitting back down on the checkered blanket spread next to them.

"You're so attentive to her, Scott," Abby said in between bites. "It's so cute."

"She's carrying precious cargo so I'm a bit overprotective. She says I'm a hoverer but I don't care. We're taking care of our girls, right, buddy?" he asked, ruffling Grant's hair as he sat on the blanket, playing with a toy truck.

"I was so excited when Ashlyn told me you were having a girl," Carrie said as she held Emily in her lap beside him. "She and Emily are going to be best buds. Right, sweetie?" Emily gurgled as drool ran down her chin.

"I'm happy it's a girl too." Glancing down, Scott ran his hand over the grass. "Of course, it brings back so many memories of Ella."

Abby's eyes welled as she observed his sad expression, unable to even imagine losing a child. The thought was heartbreaking.

"But I think the best way to honor her memory is to love these two little buggers as much as humanly possible. Right, bud?"

Grant gazed up at Scott and uttered an unintelligible jumble of noises that were so cute, Abby felt her biological clock kick into high gear. Chad tickled her arm and she swatted him away. His green eyes twinkled as if he knew her thoughts and she glowered at him before resuming eating her taco.

"Anyway," Scott continued. "I've been talking to Teresa again too. It's nice because I have full access to her now. She won't let me pay her, which is annoying, but I'll be getting her some fantastic bottles of wine as an extra wedding gift to even things out."

"I'm so excited about the wedding," Carrie said. "Too bad Teresa and Mark couldn't be here today but they're deep into last-minute wedding prep. Speaking of, Chad's a really good dancer, Abby. Can't wait to see you guys tear it up on the dance floor at the reception."

"I'm not a great dancer," she said, wiping her hands after finishing the last taco. "Maybe he can just dance with you guys so I don't do something stupid like fall on my face and accidentally flash my lady parts."

"No way," Chad said, shaking his head. "You're cutting it up with me, Abbs. That's non-negotiable."

She shrugged. "If you want your toes smashed from me stepping on them all night, be my guest."

Peter chose that moment to appear, still wearing the orange vest they'd worn as they cleaned the lake. "Okay, let's be honest. I'm super-hot in this thing, right?" He pointed to the vest.

"Oh, brother," Carrie muttered, rolling her eyes.

"Come on, Care Bear, you know you want me all alone in nothing but this vest. I could see you swooning over me when I was over there talking to Donna and Dan. Do we need to go to the SUV so you can release your ravenous desire for me?" He pointed to the parking lot.

"Do you guys hear something?" Carrie said, looking around. "Sounds like some sort of annoying bird cawing in my ear—"

Peter lowered beside her and placed a sloppy kiss on her neck. "Okay, we can wait until we get home. Not sure you'll make it though. You seem really into me right now."

"Hold your daughter, please," she said, pulling Emily back before he took her. "Take the vest off first, Peter. And use the antibacterial gel before you hold her."

Wrinkling his nose, he followed her direction and took Emily, cooing to her as Carrie stood. "I'm going to go round up the boys."

"Kitana's having such a great time playing with them," Abby said, shielding her eyes with her hand as she observed them in the distance. "I think we'll both have tired kids after they're done."

"That was the plan," Carrie said with a cheeky grin before she trailed away.

Abby saw two people approaching in her wake and her heart fell to her knees.

"Hey, Flabby Abby. How you doing? Heard you were going to be cleaning up the lake today. Looks like the whole gang's here."

"Hi, Butch," she said, sensing Chad tense beside her.

"Can you not call her that, man?" Chad said. "I think we're all a little old to be using nicknames."

"You're the one who started the whole thing," Butch said, lifting his hands. "If you don't like it, that's your fault, man. Sterling Rydell has no problem using it either. I think he calls her Flabby Abby in almost every commercial now."

"Yes, I'm aware," Abby said, encircling Chad's forearm when he tried to stand up. She was pretty sure he wanted to punch the bastard and that wouldn't be a great story to follow her volunteer efforts. "It shows Sterling's ineptitude that the best weapon he has against me is some stupid name from high school. Doesn't bother me in the least."

"And why should it?" Cynthia Andrews asked beside Butch, her arm laced through his. "You're not nearly as heavy as you were in school, Abby."

It was a veiled insult and Abby's nostrils flared as she strove to remain calm.

"In fact," Cynthia continued, "you're the latest in the long line of ladies who've dated our esteemed mayor. I was sure you were going to ask me out after my divorce, Chad, since we all know about the little crush you had on me in high school, but Abby must've caught your eye first."

"Which worked out well for me," Butch said, grinning as Cynthia extended her hand, showing off a sparkling engagement ring. "We got engaged last night."

"Congrats, guys," Peter said. "Are you going to get married before or after Cynthia's next nose job?"

"Excuse me?" Cynthia gasped.

"Watch your mouth, Stratford, or I'll shut it for you. You all were always a bunch of snobs who thought you were better than everyone else."

"Except for Abby," Cynthia said. "No one would even speak to her in high school."

"Okay, I think we're done here," Scott said, standing and gesturing toward the lake. "It's a nice day so let's not ruin it, guys. Ardor Creek is a small town and there's no need for hostility. High school was a million years ago. I think it's time we all moved on."

"Of course," Cynthia said, peering around him to wave at the group. "Sorry that got so nasty, guys. No hard feelings. And I'd like to wish Abby the best of luck in the race."

"Thanks, Cynthia," she said, watching Chad flex his fist out of the corner of her eye. He looked very much like a man who wanted to charge Butch Connors and beat the shit out of him.

"Butch and I have decided to vote for Sterling because we love the idea of modern new developments, especially since we want to buy a place now that we're engaged. But it's nice to see a close race and I'm sure you'll do just fine. Ta ta!"

They strolled away, Chad gazing after them with murder in his eyes.

"Relax," she said, squeezing his arm. "They're idiots. And Peter wasn't kidding about the nose job. I think her nose is half the size it was in school. I have no problem with plastic surgery but she has a lot of balls to call out my weight."

"What a bunch of assholes," Chad said, turning to look at her. His eyes swam with sorrow and she breathed a laugh.

"Chad, it's fine. I've lived through way worse than that. Screw 'em."

"You're so much more beautiful than she'll ever be," Chad said, palming her cheek. "You know that, right, Abbs?"

"Thank you," she whispered, overcome with how he looked at her sometimes. Like she was the only woman in the world and he was so lucky to be with her. It made her heart skip a beat as he caressed her cheek with his thumb.

"Hanson's a goner, dude," Peter mumbled to Scott.

"Totally," Scott murmured. "Should we have a funeral for his dating app profiles? Chad, thirty-eight, who gives excellent massages, and Chad, thirty-seven, who loves watching rom-coms both need a proper farewell."

Chad glared at them. "Will you two shut the hell up?"

"Massages and rom-coms?" Abby asked, expressing mock mortification. "I haven't gotten either of those things. Maybe I need to go on Bumble and meet Rom-Com Chad."

"You know what? Screw all of you guys. I'm going to get my fries from Ashlyn." Standing, he scowled at them before walking away.

"Wait," Abby called, snickering. "I love massages. Do you do hot stone ones too?"

He shot her the bird, not bothering to turn around as he approached Ashlyn's food truck.

"Oh, man, he's pissed. You might have to calm him down, Abby."

"I'll take care of it. Don't worry, guys. Thanks for having my back, Peter."

"Sure thing," he said with a nod. "You're in the crew now, Abby. We protect our own here in this lovely but sometimes dramatic little town."

"I wasn't sure how easy it would be to acclimate when I moved back but I love it here."

"Glad to hear it since we're going to ensure you're our next mayor," Scott said.

"Well, it looks like I lost two votes," she said, gazing at Butch and Cynthia as they walked toward the lake. "Rydell's messaging is great. I'm doing my best to educate the residents on how disastrous his developments will be if he skirts the regulations."

"He only hires contractors who install sub-par building materials," Scott said, shaking his head. "They cost less but are vulnerable to damage and some don't meet the proper fire retardant standards. That huge fire they had in Dunmore last year was in one of Rydell's developments. The fire spread so quickly that the residents had to abandon it before they could grab their pets and most of them perished."

"That's terrible," Abby said, knowing she'd fall apart if something like that happened to Kitana. "I won't let him bring his shady practices to Ardor Creek. It's just not happening."

Carrie returned with the boys and Kitana and gave them a confused look. "Why is Chad eating fries by himself and pouting on the bench over there?"

Abby looked at Peter and Scott before they all broke down snickering.

"It's a long story, honey. Let's just say Butch made an appearance with Cynthia and they're engaged."

"I'm not sure why that would make Chad pout, but okay. Ready to go, guys?" She ran her hand over Charlie's hair. The boys nodded and everyone began to pack up for the day. Abby approached Chad as he sat on the bench finishing the fries.

"You're pouting worse than Carrie's boys," she teased, sitting beside him.

"I just needed some fresh air. Butch really pissed me off...and then Peter and Scott really pissed me off."

Laughing, she ran her fingers through the hair at his temple. "Don't be a big baby. I'm glad they outed you. I want one of these famous massages from forty-one-year-old Chad from the pub."

Arching a brow, he pondered. "I'm not sure you're ready for one of my massages, babe. It's probably going to make you fall even more madly in love with me and make you beg me to marry you or something."

"Me?" she asked, batting her eyelashes. "I only want you for your flip chart skills." She made an X over her heart.

"Liar," he said, giving her a sexy grin.

"Prove it."

Grabbing her hand, he tugged her back to the blankets so they could gather everything and head home. After walking Kitana, Chad showed her his massage skills, which she confirmed were rather epic and declared were off-limits to anyone but her for the foreseeable future.

Chapter 19

♥

The Friday before Mark and Teresa's wedding, Abby sat in her home office finishing up her last consultation. Chad would be home from town hall by four and she was looking forward to the weekend. Not only because of the wedding but also because Sunday was Chad's birthday. She'd cooked up some little surprises and was excited to celebrate with him.

Her cell phone buzzed a few minutes after the Zoom ended and she smiled at the caller ID.

"Senator Dawkins," she said, surprised at the call. "I just had visions of you calling me in the dead of night when there was a crisis. How are you?"

His chuckle traveled over the phone. "I'm just fine, Abby. Retirement is treating me well. I do miss the beltway excitement but Betty is happy to have me all to herself. Well, most of the time, I think."

"Betty is the most patient political spouse I know. You owe her big time."

"I sure do. Convincing her to marry me was the best campaign I ever won."

"Aw," Abby said, reminded of how sweet he was with his wife and family. Senator Dawkins was a shrewd politician, while still remaining respectful, but he was always a puppy dog when it came to Betty. "That sent a shiver down my romantic heart."

"You sound good, Abby. I'm glad to hear it. I'm calling because I've been keeping an eye on your race. Rydell is playing dirty."

Sighing, she traced her finger over the desk. "Yep, he's drudged up my old high school nickname and is pouring tons of money into campaign ads. I just can't compete with him there since I get donations from smaller organizations and individual citizens but I'm running a killer ground campaign."

"I would expect nothing less. You were my best political operative by far. Don't tell John London I said that. He was a worthy second but you refused to accept failure."

She basked in the praise from someone she greatly admired. "Thanks so much for saying that. I loved working for you and do miss it, although I'm really enjoying local politics. And I haven't spoken to John in a while now. The last time we texted he was working for Senator McLean's reelection campaign."

"Unfortunately, McLean lost his primary so John is out of a job. Or, he was until I spoke to him yesterday."

Abby's brows lifted. "Oh? Who hired him?"

Senator Dawkins cleared his throat. "I did."

"But you're retired. Or did you decide to run one more time?"

"Lord, no. Betty would have my hide. But I'm highly invested in another race and I hired John to work on that one."

Abby's heart began to pound. "Whose race?"

"Why, yours, dear. I'm thrilled with what you're doing in Ardor Creek and feel that Pennsylvania needs more female mayors in suburban and rural areas. I hired John to help you win."

Abby worked her jaw, unsure of what to say. "Wow, that's...well, I'm a bit shocked, Senator."

"How about you call me Robert now that I'm retired, Abby? And please don't turn down the offer because it's something I really want to do. I can't publicly campaign because it would pull me out of retirement and my health hasn't been so great."

"Oh, I'm sorry to hear that. Is there anything I can do?"

"Betty's got me eating oatmeal and wheatgrass so that might kill me before the cholesterol does. But, no, I'll be fine. The only thing I want is for you to agree to let John help you with the campaign."

Abby contemplated the offer. "I mean, of course, I'd love to have his help but he's way too qualified to work on a small-town mayoral campaign."

"When I spoke to him he seemed over the moon about it, Abby. I know you two were close."

"We were. I spent more time with him than half my ex-boyfriends."

"That might be why they became exes, dear."

Abby grimaced. "Touché."

"Think of this as my campaign donation. I'll be paying John the same salary he was earning on McLean's campaign and covering his living expenses. He already sent me a lovely bed and breakfast he found in Ardor Creek where he can stay until after the election in November."

Abby was shocked at the good fortune but smart enough to accept the amazing offer. "Well, okay, then. If he's fine with staying here and working on my campaign, I'm all for it. Cassie will love it too. I'm assuming she's coming along?"

"I don't want to get into John's personal business but he and Cassie have been separated for about a year, Abby."

"Oh, no," she said, recalling John's wife. She'd always been rather cold to Abby but John had spoken about her with such reverence that she'd assumed they were happy. "I'm so sorry to hear that."

"I'm sure he'll tell you when you see him. Expect a call from him on Monday. Now, get out there and win this campaign, Mayor Miller. We're all counting on you."

"I'm so honored you would do this for me, Senator Dawkins. I have no idea how to repay you. Thank you so much."

"Just win, Abby. That's how you can repay me. And call me Robert from now on, okay?"

"Okay, Robert," she said, feeling weird because she held him in such high regard. "Thank you."

"Call me anytime you need me, Abby. Take care."

The phone clicked and she leaped from the chair, jogging in place as she chanted. "This. Is. So. Fucking. Awesome!" She squealed and heard a chuckle from the door. Pivoting, she saw Chad with a shit-eating grin, arms crossed as he leaned against the doorframe.

"I thought you said you couldn't dance, Abbs. Those moves are killer."

"Oh, hush," she said, running toward him jumping into his arms. He caught her and she wrapped her legs around his waist before cementing her lips to his in a blazing kiss.

"Wow," he breathed after she'd all but sucked his face off. "Who are you, where is Abby, and can we bang before she gets home?"

Throwing her head back, she laughed. "I think that's some sort of veiled dig about how uptight I am but I don't even care right now. Chad! I have amazing news."

"Tell me, hon," he said, brushing her hair off her forehead.

"You can put me down first."

"No way," he said, clutching her butt cheek. "I've got you right where I want you. Tell me."

She updated him on the news and his resulting grin was adorable. "That's amazing, hon. I know you were bummed about the recent poll that showed you and Rydell neck and neck. This will definitely help."

"Totally. I'm so amped up. We need to celebrate."

"I'm ready," he said, chucking his brows.

She lifted a finger. "Sex is good but we can do that later. I have something else in mind."

His eyes narrowed. "Oh, I know exactly what it is."

Smiling into each other's eyes, they exclaimed in unison, "Mexican!"

Laughing, they agreed she deserved a celebratory feast and after walking Kitana, they headed to Lolita's to destroy a hefty meal of chips, salsa, and burritos.

Mark and Teresa's wedding was held on a sunny afternoon beside a sparkling lake that sat on a large estate about twenty miles north of Ardor Creek. They chose to keep the wedding small, with Mark's sister, Justine, serving as maid of honor and Teresa's brother, Lionel, serving as best man. Justine's daughter, Avery, was the flower girl and Abby thought her adorable as she trailed down the aisle dispersing flowers as she approached Mark and Teresa.

They stood under a white altar that Scott had fashioned for them as one of their gifts, and Chad was the officiant.

"Well, I'm beginning to see that something is in the water in Ardor Creek," Chad said, opening the ceremony. "All my friends are getting married and taking advantage of my mayoral status to get free officiating services."

The crowd laughed before he continued.

"Although my term as mayor will be ending soon, I have an in with the next mayor so if anyone else needs an officiant, just let me know. I'll only take a small finder's fee."

"We all know who's getting married next!" Ashlyn called from her seat beside Abby.

"Shhh!" Scott scolded, glaring at her.

"What? It's true. Okay, I'll be quiet now."

"Okay, now that we've heard from the peanut gallery," Chad said, "I think it's time we got on with this lovely little ceremony."

Teresa and Mark spoke so reverently as they exchanged vows and it moved something inside Abby. At one point, she soaked her tissue all the way through and Ashlyn handed her a fresh one. Quietly thanking her, Abby sighed wistfully as Chad wrapped up the ceremony.

"By the power vested in me as mayor of our favorite little town, I now pronounce you husband and wife."

Their kiss was so sweet, so full of promise and hope, as Avery jumped up and down beside them. Her excitement was palpable and Mark picked her up, situating her on his hip before he grabbed Teresa's hand and held it high in the air. Everyone cheered as they walked down the aisle, Justine and Lionel behind them, and headed into the reception hall.

The guests stood to follow them inside and Abby sauntered toward Chad, loving his cheeky grin.

"Are you freaking out because I'm walking down the aisle toward you?" she teased, sliding her arms around his waist as they stood by the first row of seats.

"Nope," he said, brushing a kiss on her lips. "It's good practice."

"For when I marry Chris Hemsworth? You're damn straight it is."

"Well, before you leave me for Chris, I'd love a drink." Sliding his arm around her waist, he led her inside and they ordered drinks from the open bar before sitting down at their table. The band leader introduced Teresa and Mark and they strolled hand in hand to the table at the front of the room. Music played as servers came around to confirm everyone's order and Abby struck up a conversation with Teresa's parents, who had traveled from Spain to attend the wedding. She found them lovely and was deep in conversation with them an hour later when Chad appeared at her side, hand extended.

"Okay, Abbs. I warmed up the dance floor for you but the band's going to play a few slow ones. I know you can do it. Come on."

"I'm a terrible dancer," she said to Teresa's mother as she stood. "Please have 911 queued on your phone in case I break his toes." She laughed and Abby followed her handsome partner onto the wooden dance floor.

Sliding an arm around his neck, she slipped her hand in his as he placed his other arm around her waist. Drawing her close, he kissed her temple. "You look so pretty in your dress, babe."

"Thanks. You look like a million bucks in that suit."

Resting his forehead against hers, he stared at her, lust and emotion simmering in those gorgeous green eyes. "I wish we could bust this joint and head to the room but I guess we have to stay until it's over."

Laughing, she nodded. "Yes, I think that's how these things work. Let's have some fun for a few hours and then we'll christen the room. It's nice that the estate accommodates overnight guests. That means we can let loose and not worry about driving."

"You're going to let loose?" he teased.

"Yes." She wrinkled her nose. "I'm already kind of tipsy."

"I'm finally going to get to bang Drunk Abby? Never thought I'd see the day."

Snickering, she shrugged. "As long as I don't get too drunk. Carrie's on a mission with the wine. Stay tuned."

Hours later, as the reception wound down and after the band played their last tune, Abby sat at her seat observing Chad talk to Peter, Scott, and Mark as they stood by the bar. They had the comradery of old friends and their elation for Mark was palpable. She noticed their buddy Gary walk over and join the conversation, remembering how nice he'd been in school. He'd been another shy student like her but had always been kind during the brief encounters they'd had.

Chad looked her way and grinned, indicating he knew she was wasted. Yep, Abby had consumed *way* too much wine and now all she wanted to do was lay in the comfy hotel bed and pass out. Of course, she wanted to rock Chad's world with amazing sexcapades but was suddenly unsure she had the energy.

"Oh, no," he said above her, and Abby's eyelids flew open. She hadn't even realized she'd closed them. "Someone's about to pass out. Come on, hon, let's get you to bed."

He bent down, sliding his arm around her waist and lifting her to her feet. Leaning into his side, she let him lead her from the reception area and down the hallway to their room.

"I'm so sorry," she said, shaking her head as he slid the plastic key in the door. "You were dancing and I was drinking and...man, I think I drank too much."

"It happens to all of us," he said, leading her into the room where she promptly fell on the bed, dress, shoes and all. "Okay, Cinderella, let's get you out of those clothes and maybe brush your teeth before you crash on me."

He tugged her hand and she groaned before finally giving in and letting him pull her to her feet. She dragged off her dress and shoes, and Chad appeared by her side with a tank top from her bag.

She shrugged it on and ambled to the bathroom, wondering why she wasn't embarrassed to be wearing only a tank top and panties in front of him. Probably because it was Chad, and he was pretty much the greatest person in the world. Ever. Giggling at her silly drunk thoughts, she somehow managed to brush her teeth and wash her face before wandering to bed. Crawling under the crisp sheets, she snuggled into the pillow and burrowed under the covers.

Chad eventually slithered in beside her, warm and naked, and drew her against him. Placing her cheek on his chest, she sighed.

"I fucked up the wedding sex. I'm so sorry. We were totally supposed to be banging right now. I don't usually get this tipsy."

A deep chuckle reverberated through his chest as he stroked her hair. "It's okay. You're so damn cute right now, babe. It's nice to see you relax."

"I'm so relaxed," she said, rubbing her nose against the prickly hairs on his chest. "And I realized something when you were forcing me to brush my teeth."

"*Forcing* is a bit much, but okay."

Snickering, she slid her leg over his thighs, loving how the hairs tickled her skin. "I think you're my best friend. Besides, Kitana, obviously. But you're a close second. I don't even feel the need to wear pants around you anymore."

"Well, that's my favorite sentence you've ever said to me."

"Of course, you'd love that I don't need to wear pants," she mumbled as she drifted toward sleep.

Breathing a laugh, he pressed his lips to her temple and whispered, "That was a good sentence too but I meant the other one. I think you're my best friend too, Abbs."

Sighing, she snuggled into him, so tired she couldn't open her eyes. "You're not mad, right? I'll make it up to you tomorrow. So much banging in your future..."

His reverent chuckle was the last thing she heard before she succumbed to the darkness.

Chapter 20

♥

C had awoke to the smell of...strawberries. Yes, he must've somehow fallen asleep in a field of strawberries because the aroma was *everywhere*. Hell, he could even taste them on his tongue. Opening his mouth, he felt the tip of the fruit, so sweet as he sucked it deep. Working his lips, he struggled to make sense of his surroundings.

Abby's breathy moan invaded his consciousness and he lifted his lids to find her sprawled above, cheeks flushed and lips wet as she pressed her breast into his mouth.

"Happy birthday," she whispered, the rasp in her voice sending sparks of arousal to every cell in his frame. "I figured the best present I could give you was waking up with my boobs in your face. You seem kind of obsessed with them."

His brain was so fogged with desire, he couldn't even laugh. Making love to her was all he could comprehend as he trailed his tongue over her nipple before sucking it between his lips. She moaned his name as his arms surrounded her, wishing he could meld into her somehow.

Popping her nipple from his mouth, he murmured, "Why do you taste like strawberries?"

"I figured you liked them since you served them with the champagne after the primary." Lifting a tiny white tube, she shook it and chucked her eyebrows. "Strawberry edible birthday lube. I put it on my breasts and now I'm going to put it on you." Reaching down, she encircled his throbbing cock and lightly tugged.

"Babe, we can just fuck," he said, covering her hand to stop the ministrations. "I'm hard as a fucking rock."

Her lips formed a pout. "Don't you want me to suck you? It's the present I was most excited to give you today."

Breathing a laugh, he ran his fingers over her cheek. "Okay, but you have a lot of faith in me. I might not last long. Waking up with your tit in my mouth is enough to make me blow my load."

"Well, I'll suck you off, and then we can cuddle, and then I'll do it again."

"That's literally the best offer I've ever had. Go ahead."

She smiled, looking pleased with herself, causing him to chuckle. Tossing off the covers, she dispensed some of the lube on her palm and rubbed her hands together, spreading the liquid. Kneeling beside his thigh, she grasped the base of his cock with her hand and cupped his balls with the other. Her lips formed a shy smile as she gazed at him, moving her hand back and forth over his shaft as she gently massaged his balls.

Chad closed his eyes, determined to think about sports stats...or paint chipping...or his grandmother's favorite old sweater that smelled like mothballs—anything that would keep him from blowing his load while the woman of his dreams was caressing him like a goddamn sex goddess.

"Does it feel good?" she asked, quickening the pace of her hand along his length.

"So fucking good," he said, running his fingers over her thigh.

Grinning, she repositioned and lowered her face to his cock, placing soft kisses along the length as she jerked him with her hand.

"It's your birthday so you can have full reign. If you want to grip my hair and move my head, I'm okay with that."

Expelling a breath, Chad thrust his fingers into her hair, gazing at her as she lifted the tip of his cock to her lips. Smiling into his eyes, she opened her mouth and slid over him, causing Chad to groan as he watched her devour him.

"Abbs," he whispered, clenching her hair as she sucked him. "God, this is so fucking hot."

She purred against his length, her head bobbing back and forth as she continued to caress his balls. She worked him like a champ, sliding her mouth over his slick cock as she hollowed her cheeks. The suction was so intense, he knew he wouldn't last long.

"I'm going to come, babe," he rasped. "It's just too fucking good. Pull back if you need to."

She increased her efforts, sucking and tugging until he thought he might go mad. Little hums of desire emanated from her throat, the sounds vibrating against his engorged cock, sending his body into overdrive. Unable to hold back, he shouted her name and began to come.

She sucked him dry, drawing each jet of his release into her mouth, taking everything he gave her. Chad's body quaked and shuddered as she mewled around his length. Struggling to catch his breath, he released his grip on her hair, letting his hands fall limp on the mattress.

"My god, woman," he said, releasing a sigh. "Go easy on me. I'm an old man now."

Laughing, she popped his cock from her mouth and wiped her bottom lip. "Happy birthday."

Huffing a breath, he shook his head. "I don't want to move but I have to go to the bathroom. Can you go for me?"

"Um, I'm not sure science has figured that out yet." Resting her cheek on his thigh, she grinned.

Groaning, he sat up and kissed her forehead when she rolled away. "Be right back. That was epic, babe."

After taking care of business, he crawled between the sheets and pulled her close, aligning their bodies. Her breasts smashed into his chest and she slid her leg over his thigh, drawing him closer.

"Strawberry lube," he said, kissing the tip of her nose. "Aren't you just a basket of surprises over here?"

She wrinkled her nose. "Maybe it's weird but you're kind of weird in bed so I didn't think you'd mind."

He rubbed his chest against her breasts, slick from the lube. "I love it. I can think of a bunch of other things we can do with lube."

"I'm sure you can." She playfully rolled her eyes. "Anyway, that's just the first of many surprises today. I love birthdays and I'm going to make yours special. And, I can make up for totally passing out last night. That was an epic party foul."

"It's fine, hon. You were saying some pretty sweet stuff. I was pretty sure you were going to drop the L-word."

Biting her lip, she shook her head. "You're saying it first."

His eyebrows lifted. "Is that so?"

"Yep. I'll just wait until you say it and then I promise I'll say it back. Whenever you're ready."

"You're saying it first, Miller. There's no way you can hold out longer than me. You're crazy about me."

Her features contorted in playful exasperation. "How can you be so cocky yet so likeable at the same time? It blows my mind."

"It takes practice," he teased, urging her to lie on her back. Trailing kisses down her neck, he blazed a path to her nipple. "Now be a good girlfriend and let me taste these strawberry nipples."

Moaning her acquiescence, she threaded her fingers through his hair and drew him close. Chad loved her with his lips, and then with his body, knowing the words weren't far off, no matter who spoke them first.

Abby spent the rest of the day making Chad feel special. After another epic blow job session in the hotel room, they headed home and picked up Kitana from her neighbor. Not Martha, since she was more of a cat person, but a lovely woman named Julie who ran the local pet rescue. She fostered quite a few dogs in constant rotation and loved watching Kitana.

Abby agreed to go jogging with Chad, although she hated it with a passion. But it was something he enjoyed and he suggested she bring Kitana along, so it wasn't terrible. Afterward, they showered and cuddled on the couch where she finally agreed to watch Terminator and Terminator 2 with him. He was obsessed with the movies and seemed appalled she hadn't ever seen them. Once they were finished, she turned and gaped at him.

"Oh, my god. Chad. That was so good. Linda Hamilton is so badass."

"I tried to tell you, babe," he said, shrugging. "Terminator 2 is even better than the first one but I had to make you watch them both."

"Are the rest of the movies as good?"

He scrunched his features. "They're okay. There's one with Claire Danes where she's pretty hot."

Swatting him, she stood and grimaced. "I don't care about that. I just want to know if it's worth watching."

"We can give it a go one day. And if it sucks, we can just make out."

"Deal."

Pointing to the kitchen, she said, "Well, I'm ready to cook you dinner. Enjoy this moment because it's not happening again until next year. I hate cooking."

"Why do you hate cooking so much?"

"Because it takes forever. I'm hungry the first ten minutes I start cooking and just want to eat."

"That's fair."

Leaning down, she kissed him. "Want another beer?"

"I'm so digging Attentive Abby. Yes, I'd love one."

"Don't get used to it, buddy."

After grabbing him another beer, she got to work preparing two sirloins she'd picked up at the store. That, along with mac and cheese, and mashed potatoes, was about as much as she could handle.

They ate at her small kitchen table, Abby scolding him when he fed Kitana a piece of his steak from the table.

"Chad! I don't want her to become a beggar. Don't do that!"

"She looked at me with those big brown eyes, Abbs. Come on. I have no willpower when either of you look at me like that."

She decided to let it go since he was being sweet but shot him a look of warning every time he even glanced Kitana's way. After dinner, she served the cupcakes she'd made, placing a candle in one of them so Chad could make a wish.

"I was going to buy forty-two candles but I couldn't afford it. It's just too many."

"Ha. Ha." He rolled his eyes. "You'll be forty-two soon, babe."

"Don't remind me."

Eventually, they headed to bed and she snuggled into him as Kitana nuzzled into her backside. He stroked her hair as they watched a true crime documentary and she felt so content.

"Thank you for everything today, Abbs," he said, kissing her forehead as he stroked her hair. "You made my birthday so special."

"You're welcome. Do you want to bang again? I can probably rustle up the energy."

Laughing, he shook his head. "Thanks for the appealing offer but I'm happy to hold you, hon. You gave me two blow jobs today. I'll quit while I'm ahead."

Snickering, she ran her hand over the prickly hairs on his chest before yawning. "I always knew you were smart under those dashing good looks..." she mumbled into his chest. Five minutes later, she was dead to the world.

Chapter 21

♥

The next morning, Abby hopped out of bed, ready to start the new phase of her campaign. Her phone rang promptly at nine a.m. and she kissed Chad as he was walking out the door before answering.

"Hi, John," she said, unable to control her grin. "I just want you to know you've got a very happy candidate over here. I'm so excited you agreed to do this."

"Hey, Abby," his deep voice said. "I'm thrilled too. It allows me to help you and come out of unemployment. Win-win."

"Definitely. So, there's a diner on Main Street where we could meet. Want to meet there at ten?"

"Sounds good. I've already brainstormed several ideas I want to go over with you."

"Perfect. See you there."

She dressed in black dress pants, a silky red blouse, and sandals, and put her hair in a bun liked she'd often done in D.C. Senator Dawkins had always encouraged originality and had never minded the quirky appearances of some of his staff members. Some had nose rings, tattoos, mohawks, and several other non-mainstream styles. The senator was clear that he encouraged individuality but when the occasion called for it, he expected a certain level of professionalism. Abby had worn her hair back most days so the streaks wouldn't detract from her purpose, although she was thankful her boss encouraged his staff's uniqueness.

Entering the diner, she noticed John sitting at one of the booths. He looked the same as ever: straight nose, slick, coiffed dark hair, and striking blue eyes. He stood when she approached and she remembered his height. He'd played college basketball and was six-foot-six to her five-foot-eight inches tall.

"John," she said, giving him a strong hug. "It's so nice to see you. How do you like the bed and breakfast? Are they treating you okay? George and Lina are amazing but I can put in a special request if you need me to," she said, referencing the owners.

"It's perfect, Abby," he said, squeezing her before releasing. They slid into the booth and he flashed a brilliant smile. "George and Lina are great and they're ardent Abby Miller supporters."

"Yep," she said, nodding. "They love my idea of encouraging wineries to build on the outskirts of Ardor Creek. I think they see lots of dollar signs if I get that resolution passed."

"No doubt. Have you eaten?" He picked up the menu. "I ate an English muffin from the continental breakfast at my place."

"I ate an omelet at home so I'll just get coffee." The server came by and they ordered before getting down to business. Pulling out a notebook, John began flipping through.

"You've made a good start here, Abby, but I see several places where we can improve. The latest polls only have you up by a few percentage points."

"I know," she said, sighing. "The Scranton Times-Tribune and the county paper do polls every week or so. The last one had me at fifty-two percent and Sterling at forty-eight."

Nodding, he ran his finger over his notes. "We can definitely increase that spread. I don't want to mess with your ground game because you're killing it. The volunteer activities have had great returns."

Arching a brow, she said, "Someone's done their research."

"I want to earn every penny the senator is paying me."

"I couldn't believe it when he called me on Friday," she said, resting her chin on her hand. "I feel incredibly lucky he would do this for me, and that you would drop everything to help me."

His expression fell a bit. "Well, things haven't been so great after McLean's loss. That one hurt. I'm not used to running losing campaigns."

"His extramarital affair and subsequent text chains released to the media didn't help," she muttered.

"Yeah, he kind of sunk himself. And, while we're discussing misfortunes, I might as well address my separation. Senator Dawkins told me he let it slip."

Reaching over, she covered his hand. "He did and I'm so sorry, John. I always liked Cassie." It was a slight lie but why kick a man when he was down? "If you want to talk, I'm happy to listen. Sometimes you just need to vent in these situations."

"Thanks," he said, turning his hand and squeezing hers. "I won't mince words: it fucking sucks. Marriage is hard, especially when you have a job as stressful as mine, and we ended up growing apart. It's been tough but I'm happy to have this opportunity to focus on something new." His gaze was sincere and filled with...yearning?

Swallowing thickly, Abby smiled before drawing away. She certainly didn't want to give him the impression she was interested in anything other than the campaign. She and John had never had a hint of anything sexual between them, most likely due to the fact that he'd been married and off-limits.

"Of course. I'm thrilled you want to help me and have the time to dedicate to my tiny campaign." She held her thumb and forefinger an inch apart. "Okay, hit me with these great ideas. I'm ready."

"First, we need to find some people who've been hurt by Rydell Industries who can go on the record. Residents who lived in his developments, and business owners who were negatively affected by his shady practices."

"It's a good idea and I've thought about it but I don't have a ton of money for commercials. I'd rather spend the donations I get on local community activities, but I can certainly spare a percentage to feature people hurt by Rydell in a few commercials."

"I think you should take it further than that," he said, leaning forward. "Let's bring them to Ardor Creek. Pay for their lodging and have them stay for a while. Entrench them in the activities you plan so they can tell their stories in a natural setting. We can also set up some town halls where they answer questions about how Rydell Industries has affected their lives."

Abby straightened, considering. "I mean, it's a great idea but I'm not sure I have the funds for that. Nor, do I have the time to track these people down and convince them."

"Well, what do you think I'm here for, Abby?" he asked, pointing to himself. "Put me to good use. And Senator Dawkins is willing to foot the bill for anyone who agrees to spend some time in Ardor Creek."

"That's too much, John—"

"He was insistent, Abby, and told me not to let you talk me down. He was very clear that I had to be firm since you were always a tougher negotiator than me. It would hurt my feelings if it wasn't true."

Laughing, she shook her head. "You were always so fierce. We made a good team."

"We did." His eyes sparkled as he gazed at her. "And the senator is rich as shit, Abby. He's written several bestselling books and wants to leave a legacy behind. I think he sees you as part of that legacy. You earned this."

Blowing a breath through puffed cheeks, she pondered before nodding. "Okay, let's do it."

"Great. I'll spend this week tracking down people who can take the time to speak about their experience. I have some other ideas too about creating a nickname for Rydell since he's latched on to this Flabby Abby thing for some reason."

She rolled her eyes. "It was my nickname in high school and something I'm never going to escape. People here remember it and it reminds them of my pariah status. I'm well-adjusted enough to admit it's a good tactic. I think Sterling is hoping it will throw me off my game."

"Well, it's kind of ridiculous because you don't embody anything about that nickname. You're stunning and badass, so I'm not sure he hit the mark."

"Thank you," she whispered, the little girl inside still so stunned when people said things like that to her. Her inner voice would always be her worst critic and she had to constantly remind herself that she was a strong woman who'd created a rich, meaningful life out of that childhood pain.

His lips curved before glancing down at the notebook. "How about this? Sterling 'Ride His Father's Coattails?'"

Wrinkling her nose, she said, "I promised myself I wasn't going to do the nickname thing back to him. It seems so childish."

"It is, but I hate to break it to you, Abby: half of the voters are childish. We live in a world where people need a succinct message. He's railing you with the Flabby Abby nickname. You need to fight back."

"Sterling Ride His Father's Coattails," she said slowly before snickering. "It might just be dumb enough to work."

"Are you denigrating my brilliant idea?"

Laughing, she shook her head. "No, I like it. Okay, we can try one commercial with it and judge the reaction we get. I'm down. This is good stuff. What else you got?"

They spent the next two hours discussing different ideas and Abby felt a jolt of invigoration. Having someone as experienced as John on her side was a huge advantage. They packed up and stepped outside, Abby lifting her face to the warm August sky.

"It's such a nice day," she said, inhaling a deep breath. "I have one consultation this afternoon and then I'm going to take Kitana to the lake."

"How's she doing?" John asked. "I loved seeing her when I would drop off food to you after those long campaign days."

"You always had a radar for when I skipped dinner and would drop off food after our fourteen-hour days."

He shrugged. "It was easy since we only lived two blocks from you. I had to take care of my work wife."

"Yeah, I'm not sure Cassie loved that nickname but you were definitely my work husband. You even got makeup-free sweat-pant-clad Abby when we met on Saturdays sometimes. That's a rare sighting."

Grinning, he rubbed her upper arm. "You always looked fine to me."

Abby stiffened, realizing this was the time to tell him she was in a relationship because it was obvious he was into her. So weird. She'd just never imagined John in a sexual nature.

"John—"

"Um, hi," Chad said, approaching them on the sidewalk, surprise and a slight bit of anger in his tone. "Is there some reason you're touching my girlfriend, man?"

Abby pulled back and faced him. "Chad, this is John London. The man who's graciously agreed to help me win the campaign." Her tone was firm as she shot him a look that said, *Be nice.* "John, this is Chad—"

"Her boyfriend," Chad said, extending his hand and shaking it as he sized John up. "Just in case there was any confusion."

"Chad!" she hissed.

"Nice to meet you, Chad," John said, shaking his hand. "I read about you in the campaign articles and wondered if the stories about you and Abby dating were true, especially since she beat you in the primary. Takes a confident man to date someone who defeated him."

"Well, she deserved it," Chad said, narrowing his eyes before releasing John's hand. "And I'm on board with the message that Ardor Creek is ready for a change and ready for its first female mayor." Placing his arm around Abby's shoulders, he drew her into his side.

"I'm right there with you, man. Abby, I'm going to head back to the bed and breakfast and get to work. Call me if you want someone to join you at the lake later. I'd love to see Kitana." Giving a wave, he turned and walked to his car.

Facing Chad, she wiggled out of his hold. "Is there some reason why you're acting insanely jealous? That was super weird, Chad."

His eyes grew wide. "Excuse me if I'm pissed. Imagine my surprise when I'm walking down the street to meet Scott for lunch and I see some tall dude who looks like Henry Cavill touching my woman. He was legit *gazing* at you, Abbs. Geez."

"I've known him forever. We were really good friends in D.C."

"Did you guys ever...?"

"He was married!"

"So? I know a lot of married guys who cheat on their wives."

"Not John," she said, shaking her head. "He's a good guy, Chad."

"Well, I'm not blind. That guy wants you, Abby. It's obvious by the way he was staring at you."

Cupping his cheeks, she bit her lip to contain her smile. "This jealousy thing is so cute. I can't believe you're overreacting like this."

"He's never allowed to touch you again," he said, his lips forming a slight pout. "I'll chop off his arm. His perfectly sculpted arm. Don't make me do it, Abbs."

Laughing, she shook her head. "You're ridiculous." Rising to her toes, she kissed him. "I'm heading to the lake around three. If you're free, you can come with me."

"I have meetings for the rest of the day or I would. But he's not allowed to come with you," he said, jerking his head toward where John's car had been parked.

"Oh, you dear, sweet man. You think you have a say in what I do with my time. It's so adorable."

"I mean it, Abbs," he said, sliding his arm around her waist and drawing her close. "And how does he know Kitana anyway? I thought you said she hated men."

"We used to work at my apartment in D.C. sometimes. She didn't like him at first but she eventually warmed up to him."

"Well, I hope she shows some loyalty. I want the be the only man she likes from here on out."

Chuckling, she caressed his cheek. "Wow. You're really worked up. Okay, I have to go. I'm going to debate whether your intense jealousy is cute or annoying. I think it's both but we'll see." Giving him one last peck, she began trailing to her car.

"I mean it, Abbs! Solo walks only."

"Goodbye, Chad!" she droned, waving as she walked away.

"Remember who introduced you to Terminator and Lolita's. He's got nothing on me."

She just waved again before sitting behind the wheel and heading home, laughing the entire way at his adorable, if slightly annoying, reaction.

C had spent the week bogged down by meetings, which was a bit frustrating since it gave him less time to spend with Abby. The weekly farmers' market and summer street fair were now in full effect and ensuring those ran smoothly was one of Chad's main functions as mayor. He was also putting a lot of time into planning the Halloween parade, fall festival, Thanksgiving, and Christmas parades since those would be the last of his tenure.

Each day spent at town hall running the town he loved was one day closer to the last, which filled him with a latent melancholy. Thankfully, he had Abby, who seemed to sense his sadness and constantly reminded him that there were bigger and brighter opportunities on the horizon. Campaigning for her was invigorating and he was determined to ensure her win. There was no one he'd rather pass the mantle to.

The appearance of John London was a curveball Chad hadn't expected. He'd been mulling the idea of looking for a ring and proposing to Abby sometime around the holidays. By then, he figured they would've settled into the relationship enough to feel comfortable taking the next step. As she'd mentioned a few times, they weren't getting any younger. Oh, and there was one last very important factor: Chad loved her with all his heart.

He hadn't said the words aloud yet, especially since their silly discussion about wanting the other to say it first. But he was in—all the way—and finally understood the sentiments voiced by Scott, Peter, and Mark when they spoke about their wives. Abby was everything he'd ever wanted but never found, and he couldn't wait to marry her and build a family.

Of course, John London seemed to want the same. Chad had barely known the guy a week and had only observed him in a few interactions with Abby, but he was quite transparent about his affection for her. If Chad saw him rub her arm one more time, he was pretty sure he was going to break the guy's perfect nose.

He remarked on it as they were driving to his dad's house to have dinner with him and Mrs. Connaughton. Chad had finally set up the dinner and was excited to spend some quality time with his dad.

"John was staring at your ass during the walk around the lake today," Chad said from behind the wheel as he drove.

"He was not," she said, shaking her head. "You're paranoid."

"He's got a lot of balls to invite himself on our Friday afternoon walk, Abbs. That's you, me, and Kitana time."

"He found four people with very touching stories who can spend some time here and want to go on the record. He wanted to update me and I thought you'd like to hear the update as well."

"I think he'd like to do more than *update* you," he muttered.

"Okay, the jealousy thing was cute but it's shifting toward annoying. I have zero romantic or sexual feelings toward John. How can I when I'm dating loveable Ardor Creek mayor Chad Hanson?"

He turned his head and gave a slight pout. "Keep going."

Laughing, she arched a brow. "I think you know exactly how cute you are. Now, let's get to the good stuff. Do you think your dad and Mrs. C. are banging? I mean, ew, but also, go Donald and Mrs. C!"

"I have no idea but we're going to do some reconnaissance tonight. Honestly, I kind of hope they are. Dad's been in that big house all by himself since Mom died and I want him to find some happiness."

"That's so sweet. Okay, I'm on it. Hanson and Miller, Ardor Creek's finest investigators, will crack the case."

"You watch too much True Crime TV, babe," he said, pulling into his dad's driveway. "I worry about you."

She shot him a playful glare before they exited the car and trailed up the front steps. Donald pulled the door open and Chad inhaled the aroma emanating from the kitchen. "Hey, Dad," he said, hugging him. "It smells great."

"Claire insisted on cooking although I told her a hundred times we could order in or I could try to make something. She says she misses cooking for people. Hi, Abby."

"Hi, Mr. Hanson," she said, embracing him.

"I told you to call me Donald, young lady."

"Yes, sir," she said, smiling. "Thank you so much for having us over."

"I'm glad you two could take some time from your busy sched-
ules to visit your old man. Come on in. We'll have a drink in the
living room while Claire finishes cooking."

Donald ushered them into the living room and disappeared to
the kitchen where he grabbed beers for himself and Chad, and a
glass of wine for Abby. Once they were settled, Claire stuck her
head around the corner and waved.

"Hi, Mrs. C.," Chad said, beaming. "I'm so glad we're finally doing
this."

"Me too. Donald and I have actually had a few dinners together
now. Once when he was nice enough to come over and screw
in those fancy lightbulbs for me and once when we ran into each
other on Main Street. But this is the first time I'm having dinner
here and I'm so thrilled to see you both."

"Screwing in lightbulbs, Dad?" Chad said, arching a brow.
"You're really going the extra mile for customer service—"

"That's lovely to hear, Mrs. C.," Abby said, swatting Chad since
Donald's cheeks were reddening and he appeared uncomfortable.
"Who knew all these years later we'd be having dinner with our
favorite music teacher?"

"Who knew, indeed," Claire said, grinning. "Okay, I'll be done in
a few minutes. Donald, do you want to set the table?"

"Sure," he said, rising from the couch while Chad and Abby
offered to help. He told them to stay put and exited the room.

Abby whipped around and whispered excitedly, "They're totally
banging!"

"I know," Chad said, eyes wide as he digested the fact his dad was
into someone besides his mom. It was...a bit strange but if there
was anyone who could make him happy, it was Mrs. C. "I'm happy
for them."

"Don't embarrass your dad," she scolded, holding up a finger.
"He's obviously uncomfortable. Let's not make it awkward for him."

"I'll try but it's so fun to see him sweat."

Her eyes narrowed. "I'm suddenly realizing you have this slightly
evil streak..." Trailing off, she rubbed her chin.

"It's all in good fun, babe. Come on, let's help him. I'm starving."

They helped Donald finish setting the table before Claire served an amazing dinner of chicken pot pie, Caesar salad, green beans, and cornbread. Afterward, Chad was stuffed and sat back in his chair, rubbing his stomach. "I think I'm gestating a food baby here. That was awesome, Mrs. C. Thank you."

"You're welcome," she said with a nod. "And speaking of babies, when am I going to get some grandbabies from you two? And, yes, I think of all my former students' babies as my own grandbabies. My kids live so far away that I mostly see my real grandbabies over video chat."

"I don't know," Chad said, glancing at Abby. "This one's running a mean campaign," he pointed to her with his thumb, "so I figure after she wins, we should probably discuss it."

Abby's cheeks inflamed, making her look so cute, and he leaned over and kissed her temple. "We'll have to see if she's willing to go the distance with me. I'm not sure if you've noticed but she's much smarter and better looking than I am. I'm putting up a good fight though."

"He's okay," she teased, rolling her eyes. "I might consider having that discussion with him *after* the election," she said, shooting him a look, "because that's my main focus right now."

"I totally understand, dear," Claire said. "We're all so proud of you. I can't wait to see you sworn in as the first female mayor. I'll be in the front row at your inauguration."

"Thanks, Mrs. C. That means so much."

"Well, I say we have a nightcap in the living room before you kids head home," Donald said. "I've got to get up early in the morning and reattach the gutter that fell off during that last terrible storm."

"Donald, you shouldn't be climbing the ladder," Claire said, concern lacing her features. "I don't want you to fall."

"I'll come help you, Dad," Chad said. "What time?"

"Probably around eight if that's not too early. Claire invited me to go to the winery up by Laceyville and we want to get on the road by ten or so."

"Eight is perfect. Abby loves to work out with me on Saturdays but I'll skip tomorrow. Will you be okay without me, hon?" he teased.

"I think I'll survive," she muttered.

Once they were home, Chad lay sandwiched between Abby and Kitana as they were drifting to sleep.

"Do you think Mrs. C. stayed over at your dad's? She was still there when we left."

"Not sure. I'm happy for them but I don't really want to imagine my dad banging anyone, especially Mrs. C."

Snickering, she nodded. "Totally get that. I had fun tonight. Thanks for inviting me."

"Thanks for coming, hon."

The next morning, he left Abby to her solo workout and headed to his dad's, noticing Mrs. C.'s car still parked in the driveway. After parking beside it, he checked the time, noting it was eight a.m. sharp. Trailing up the front porch stairs, the door was yanked open and he was met with a surprised Claire Connaughton.

"Oh, dear," she said, patting her uncombed white hair. "I was supposed to be gone when you arrived but we, um, got held up..."

"Hi, son," Donald said, appearing behind her and looking cha-grined. "Claire, uh, stopped over to pick up her pans from last night."

"Oh, Donald," she said, swatting his chest. "He's smart enough to know I stayed over. Let's not lie to the boy." Facing Chad, she held her head high. "I loved Mr. C. with my whole heart, Chad, just as I know your father loved Karen. But they're not here and we only have a few years left to enjoy our time on this planet. After careful consideration, I've decided I'd like to spend the majority of the time I have left with your father."

Chad held up his hands, unable to control his grin. "I'm here for it, Mrs. C. I'm thrilled to see you two together."

"You are?" Donald asked.

"Yes, Dad," he said, patting his shoulder. "I want you to be happy. This is hella cool. I think Mom would approve."

"I think she would too," Claire said. "I feel like Karen and Mr. C. are up there in heaven pushing us together somehow."

"As long as you're okay with it, son," he said, rubbing his neck.

"One hundred percent," he said with a nod. "Now, let's get those gutters reattached so you two can visit the winery. Sounds like a fun day. I'm attending a volunteer event with Abby after the soup kitchen so I'm ready to knock it out."

"Oh, yes, Lana Reinhardt will be running the soup kitchen today. I'm slowly transitioning more responsibility to her so I can spend more time with my, well, I guess 'boyfriend' is the right word? Although we're probably too old for that." She smiled at Donald.

"Works for me," he said, kissing her forehead. "You'll be back at ten?"

"On the dot." Trailing down the stairs, she waved goodbye and walked to her car.

"Son, if you want to talk about this, I'm happy to discuss it."

Cupping his shoulder, he shook his head. "It's cool, Dad. Don't make it weird. Come on, let's get to work."

Striding to the back yard, they got down to business under the warm morning sun, Chad grinning the entire time at the fact that they were both under the spell of two amazing women.

Chapter 22

♥

T he blistering days of August rolled into comfortable September days that were consumed by the campaign. With only two months left until the election, Abby knew she had to dedicate everything to the final stretch to secure her victory.

John was extremely helpful and the surrogates he'd recruited to help her campaign were invaluable. There was Joan Carter, a woman whose daughter had moved into one of Rydell's properties built on a severely contaminated site in Western Pennsylvania. Her daughter had developed severe health issues and now lived with Joan because she couldn't work. They were convinced the lack of proper remediation contributed to her health issues and Joan was willing to go on the record while her husband stayed at home with their daughter. There had been some concern that Rydell would retaliate with a libel lawsuit, which Abby had discussed with Mark Lancaster.

"Rydell can always file a suit," Mark said, "but I doubt he'll do it for one squeaky wheel. People like Joan and her daughter are flies to be swatted to people like Rydell. But, if she's worried, I would offer to represent her for free if he does retaliate."

"I can't ask you to do that, Mark," Abby said, floored by the offer. "My campaign would pay you and, if I didn't have enough funds there, I would pay you myself."

"Consider it a donation, Abby. I'm invested in your win and I'm also so happy to see you with Chad. He's crazy about you and you're part of our crew now. Let me do this for you. Like I said, it's improbable they'll sue her anyway. I have a feeling that once the campaign is over, Charles Rydell will move on to another town where he has better odds of building something without strict regulations."

Abby had reluctantly agreed, humbled by his offer and friendship.

The next witness they found was a woman from Rydell's property in Dunmore that had burned to the ground before anyone could save their pets. Judy Farrell had lost two cats, a dog, and her pet parakeet in the fire, along with all her belongings, and she was pissed as hell about it. She was a spitfire and made a compelling case.

The last witnesses were a retired couple whose son had worked on several of Rydell's sites as a heavy machine operator before he'd passed away from cancer. The couple firmly believed their son died as a result of not getting proper protective equipment in the contaminated environments and Abby was moved by their story.

Armed with her surrogates, she and John secured them rooms at the bed and breakfast while Senator Dawkins footed the bill. They all attended Abby's events, telling their stories to everyone who would listen. The news of Rydell's nefarious practices and disastrous effects began to spread and Abby felt a shift in the campaign. If they maintained the momentum, she felt confident she would win in November.

Meanwhile, she noticed a slight shift in Chad's mood. She could tell he was sad to leave office and his snarky comments about how much time she was spending with John were starting to drive her a bit crazy. As much as she insisted she wasn't interested in John, he seemed more surly as the weeks wore on.

The tension came to a head one mid-September night when she and John were in the Ardor Creek library filming her last commercial in the very room where she'd kicked off her campaign. The four witnesses were all speaking on camera about their experiences and they were running way over on time. Checking her phone, she realized she wouldn't be done until at least ten p.m. She was supposed to meet Chad at Lolita's at seven and dialed him, dreading the conversation since she had to cancel.

"Hey, babe. You already at Lolita's? I was just about to leave my apartment."

"We're running behind," she said, rubbing her forehead. "I don't think we'll be done until nine or ten at least."

Silence stretched over the phone and she could sense his frustration. "I've barely seen you all week, Abbs, and you call me at six-thirty to cancel? That's really shitty."

"I'm sorry," she said, inwardly admitting he was right. "I lost track of time and thought maybe we could speed things up, but it's not going to happen."

"So, what? You're going to finish up and have dinner with *John* afterward?"

"I don't appreciate the tone, thank you very much, and, yes, we'll probably grab something or order delivery. We're at the library surrounded by a camera crew and my campaign surrogates. I'm not sure what you think is going to happen."

"I think this guy wants to get into your pants and you're spending way too much time with him."

"This election is important to me and I have two months left to win it. I'm sorry if that doesn't work for you but I'd appreciate a tad more support."

"There are things that are important to me too, Abbs. You fucking ripped the thing I love most away from me, and I wasn't even pissed because it brought you into my life. But I'm struggling here and I'm pretty torn up about having to leave office in January. I just wish you cared more but I guess all you care about is winning."

Guilt surged as she struggled to balance her need to support him with her drive to win. "Of course, I care. But I also know you're going to go on to even bigger and better things, Chad. I'm going to help you achieve them but I need to win my own race first."

"Fine," he said, sighing. "Do you want me to go over and walk Kitana?"

Her heart melted at his sweet offer. "That would rock. Man, now I feel even worse."

"Good. I solely made that offer so you'd feel terrible," he teased.

Laughing, she bit her lip. "Well, it worked. Please don't be mad at me. Stay at my place after you walk her. I promise I'll save some energy so we can bang when I get home."

"Okay, I only slightly hate you now."

Abby giggled. "Thank you. I'll see you later."

Returning to the task at hand, they continued shooting the testimonials and interviews as Abby's stomach grumbled. John approached her when they were on a shooting break and cupped her upper arms.

"Are you hungry? We should order food."

As if on cue, Chad entered the room, carrying bags of food that read *Lolita's* on the outside. His eyes latched onto hers and she realized he was *pissed*. Glancing up at John, she noticed he was still holding her arms.

"Did you bring us Mexican?" she asked, drawing away from John and walking toward him. "Wow, that's above and beyond. Thank you."

He just gave a curt nod and headed toward the long table on the far side of the room, depositing the bags before drawing her outside into the hallway.

"Thank you so much," she said, attempting to slide her arms around his neck before he pulled away.

"Why in the *fuck* is that guy always touching you? I'm not okay with that, Abby."

"Please don't fight with me here," she pleaded, stepping closer. "This was such a nice gesture and we're making progress inside. You can stay if you want."

"Do I need to stay? Has that guy tried anything with you? I'm going to murder him if I see his hands on you again."

"Whoa," she said, showing him her palms. "That's an absurd overreaction, Chad. He's my campaign manager—"

"*I'm* your campaign manager."

"Well, unofficially, yes, I guess you still are. You've been so helpful setting up events and campaigning for me. But John is an expert and our relationship is strictly professional."

"I get it. He's got the fancy poli-sci degrees and I'm just a small-town hick who happened to become mayor because I'm so gosh darn likeable. Would you rather be with someone like him who's all polished and stale? The guy's got the personality of a rock."

"Well, I'd appreciate it if you didn't insult him since he's gone above and beyond to help me."

"And I haven't?"

"Of course, you have," she said, frustrated. "Both of you have been extremely helpful. And the Mexican is a nice touch." Tentatively sliding her hands over his chest, she formed a pout. "If you stop arguing with me, I'll let you touch my boobs as soon as I get home."

He squinted. "I'm listening."

Grinning, she arched a brow. "And we can bring out the lube again. I'll let you use it anywhere you want."

His eyes grew wide as saucers. "Anywhere?"

Lifting to her toes, she whispered against his lips. "Anywhere."

"Babe, you really know how to negotiate," he said, sliding his arm around her waist and drawing her in for a kiss.

When she pulled back, she wiped the gloss from his lips. "Please don't be mad. I miss you too, Chad. I hate that we haven't gotten to spend a lot of time together lately. After the campaign, this will all die down."

Expelling a breath, he rested his forehead against hers. "I'm sorry, hon. I just miss you and it's really starting to hit me that my term is almost over. I dwell on it more when you're not around."

"I know, and I'm going to make an effort to be there for you more."

"Sorry if I'm being annoying. I probably seem like a needy boyfriend to you. It just took me so long to find you, Abby, and now that you're here, I want to be with you. Like, all the time. I'm probably going to smother you until you run away and hide out on a deserted island or something."

Sighing, she shook her head. "I think that's the sweetest thing anyone's ever said to me." Brushing a kiss on his lips, she threaded her fingers through the hair at the nape of his neck. "I'm so close to dropping the L-word right now. You have no idea."

Grinning, he arched his brows. "I'll say it back after you say it first."

"*You're* saying it first," she declared before drawing back. "Okay, I've got to get back in there. You sure you don't want to stay?"

"Yeah. Kitana and I are going to watch the hot Claire Danes Terminator movie. You're really missing out."

"I hope I can survive," she said, rolling her eyes. "I'll see you later. And thank you for the food. I'm starving. You're amazing."

"Bye, hon. Good luck with the commercial."

Abby reentered the room, thankful a crisis had been averted. Grabbing a plate, she piled it high with food, ready to recharge so she could finish her task and get home to the man she adored.

Chapter 23

Abby's forty-second birthday arrived along with an epic barf session that had her hugging the toilet most of the day. It certainly wasn't how she'd planned to spend her birthday since she'd wanted to spend some quality time with Chad but, sadly, her stomach had other plans.

"I wonder if it was the sushi," he said, stroking her hair as she leaned on the toilet. "I didn't eat that weird-looking crab roll so that might have been the kicker."

"It looked so good on Yelp," she said, shaking her head. "Doesn't matter now since I'm never eating again."

"What can I do for you, hon? I'm sorry you're so sick."

"Just pour me a ginger ale and cuddle with me on the couch. I was planning on banging you multiple times today but I think that ship has sailed."

"I don't care as long as I get to hold you, honey."

The words melted her heart and she ended up having one of the best birthdays ever—in between bouts with the toilet. Snuggling with Chad and Kitana had become her ideal version of pleasure and it ended up being a lovely day despite her nausea.

As October rolled around, Abby continued to battle with nausea and Chad urged her to go to the doctor. The campaign was in full effect but she finally managed to get an appointment with Dr. Matthews, the general practitioner in town the second week of October.

"So, what can I help you with, Abby?" he asked from his stool as she sat on the paper-covered exam table. "We need you healthy so you can win this campaign. All of us are rooting for you."

"Thanks so much for your support, Dr. Matthews. I think I ate some bad sushi a few weeks ago and my stomach hasn't really recovered. I've never puked this much in my life and I have no idea what's going on."

He studied her before looking down at her chart. "It says here you're on ortho try-cyclen for birth control."

"Yep," she said, nodding as she swung her dangling legs.

"Well," he said, lifting his brows. "Have you experienced any fatigue, breast pain, gum sensitivity, or spotting since you began vomiting? And how long ago was your last period?"

Abby straightened, suddenly realizing what he was hinting at. "No way, Dr. Matthews. I cannot be pregnant."

"You're currently sexually active, right?"

She gnawed her lip. "Yes."

"And when was your last period?"

She tried to think back on when she'd last gotten her period. Things had been crazy with the campaign and she never tracked it because she was on birth control and, therefore, her periods had always been very regular.

"I remember it being light a few weeks ago," she said, shaking her head. "Lighter than usual but I just attributed that to stress."

"Have you missed any pills along the way?"

"Here and there," she said, shrugging. "I just always double up if I miss one like the directions on the package indicate."

"Abby," he said, giving her a warm smile. "I've been doing this a long time and have learned that when something seems obvious, it's usually true. I'm going to have you take a pregnancy test and then come back in here and we'll chat."

"Okay," she said as anxiety began to course through her veins. "There's no way I'm pregnant, Dr. Matthews."

Standing, he nodded. "We'll know in a few minutes, dear. I'll send Monica in to administer the test. See you in a bit." He exited the room and Abby noticed her heart was pounding like a damn jackhammer. She couldn't be pregnant, right?

Monica led her to the bathroom where she urinated in a cup before returning to the exam room. Sitting back on the table, she waited for Dr. Matthews.

He entered and looked at the chart before smiling up at her. "Well, Abby, it seems the most obvious explanation was true. You're pregnant. Congratulations."

Abby worked her jaw, trying like hell to digest the information. A thousand thoughts flew through her brain as she tried to process them all. Would Chad be upset? How had this happened? Was it her fault since she'd messed up her pill regimen? Of course, it was her fault. Was Chad ready for kids? They weren't even married yet. Hell, they hadn't even said the L-word yet because of the stupid game they'd decided to play about the other one saying it first. Lifting her thumb to her mouth, she began to chew the nail, which was a habit she'd vanquished years ago. Apparently, it was back and she was freaking the hell out.

"Abby?" Dr. Matthews said, wheeling closer on his stool. "I know this is a lot to process, dear. If you want to discuss it with me now or at a later time, I'm happy to sit down and talk with you."

"I'm just..." Running her hand through her hair, she expelled a breath. "I'm shocked, Dr. Matthews. That's all. I didn't think I would get pregnant on the pill."

"It happens more often than you think, especially if someone is sexually active and doesn't take the pill at precisely the same time each day."

"Shit," she muttered before grimacing. "Sorry. Didn't mean to curse. I'm just blown away."

"I completely understand. This is a lot to digest. For now, I'd suggest you take Benadryl and Vitamin B6 to help the nausea. Both are safe for the baby and should help with the vomiting. If they don't, come back to me and I'll prescribe something stronger."

"Okay," she said, nodding. "Thank you, Dr. Matthews. I just need some time to digest this."

"Of course. Once you speak to your partner I'd suggest scheduling a visit with Dr. Scheff. She's the OB/GYN I refer my patients to."

"Yes, that's who I go to. And I think we all know who my partner is, Dr. Matthews. It is Ardor Creek, after all."

Chuckling, he stood and winked. "It sure is. Don't hesitate to take me up on my offer to chat, Abby. You can just take your chart to Cheryl at the front desk and she'll close out the visit." Wishing her good luck, he exited the room.

Abby trailed up front and paid her co-pay before heading outside into the brisk October day. Closing her eyes, she inhaled the crisp air, wondering what in the hell to do. Wanting to speak to someone, she walked two blocks until she arrived at Grillo Design and Construction. Stepping inside, she was met with a beaming Carrie.

"Hi, Abby. So nice to see you. What are you doing here at eleven o'clock on a Thursday?"

Abby opened her mouth to answer but, instead, began to violently sob.

"Oh, sweetie," Carrie said, rushing over and urging her into one of the chairs. "What's wrong?"

Abby struggled to catch her breath as tears streamed down her face. "I'm sorry. I just...I need to talk to someone."

"Okay, we'll talk, then. Come on. Peter's at the golf course today and Scott's on a site visit. Let's go to Peter's office." She led her down the hallway and Abby sat on the leather couch in the small office.

"This wasn't part of the plan," Abby said, taking the tissue Carrie offered. "We were supposed to say the L-word first, then get married, and then have a baby."

"Oh...wow..." Carrie said, sitting beside her and sliding an arm over her shoulders. "So, you're pregnant. That's definitely a doozy, honey. Now I see why we're swimming in waterworks over here." Rubbing her arm, she spoke in a soothing voice. "Just calm down, sweetie. This is a good thing, right? I know Chad was planning on asking you to marry him after the election. Maybe this will just move things up a bit."

"He was?" Abby asked, hope swelling in her chest.

"Oh, dear," she said, grimacing. "Well, I've just confirmed my status as Ardor Creek's worst secret keeper, although this shouldn't be news to you, Abby. You two are obviously meant for each other."

"We are," she said, nodding as she sniffled. "It's just that things have been strained with the campaign and his ridiculous jealousy of John."

"John is pretty hot, honey."

Abby breathed a laugh. "I don't see him that way at all."

"I know but we all have eyes. Ashlyn and I *might* have had an entire discussion on his butt while we were doing the last lake cleanup. Don't tell Peter or Scott. They'll just tease us for it."

"I won't say a word." She grinned as she made an X over her heart. Blowing out a breath, she wiped her cheeks. "Okay, I'm good. I think I just needed to freak out for a sec."

"Are you going to tell Chad now?"

"I...uh..." Rubbing her forehead, she contemplated. "I have the Rotary dinner tonight and Chad has the Kiwanis dinner tomorrow where he's honoring Nick's diner with the business of the year award. I think I'll tell him on Saturday. We were planning on relaxing since this week's been so crazy. I don't want to tell him in between campaign events. I want to take my time and break it to him when we're at home so we can talk without being interrupted. Do you think it's okay if I wait until Saturday?"

"I think that's fine, sweetie."

"Okay." Fiddling with her tissue, she sighed. "I hope he's not mad."

"Trust me, he's not going to be mad, Abby. He loves you and I'm sure he's going to be thrilled."

"I hope so. I've always wanted kids, Carrie, and I love him so much. I've never said it out loud but it's true. It has been for a while now."

"He loves you too. There's no doubt in my mind."

Feeling much better than when she'd arrived, Abby spent a few more minutes with Carrie before heading home to wash her face, regain her composure and take a nap since she hadn't been sleeping well ever since she'd starting barfing all the time. After her nap, she showered and gazed at her reflection, deciding she looked refreshed even if she didn't feel it.

Donning one of her favorite dresses, she applied makeup and prepared for the Rotary dinner. Chad would be by her side, and John would be there as well, and she hoped there wasn't tension. Lord knew, she couldn't handle anything dramatic since she'd had enough drama for one day. Loading her purse, she texted Chad she was on the way and headed outside to catch her rideshare.

I t turned out that Peter and Scott weren't at the golf course or on a site visit when Abby had her breakdown inside GDC. Instead, they were with Chad in the jewelry store on South Main Street that had recently been rebuilt from the fire earlier that year.

"Okay, you two are the proclaimed marriage experts, so you need to tell me what the hell I'm doing," Chad said as they stood over the jewelry cases. "I like that one but it's kind of gawky. Abby doesn't seem like someone who's into flashy jewelry."

"Definitely not," Scott said, looking over the inventory. "That one's nice. It's simple yet elegant."

"How about I put together a selection of some in that style, Mr. Mayor?" the store owner, Kenneth, asked.

"That would be great, Ken. I want this to be perfect."

"Wow, man," Peter said, crossing his arms as he leaned on the display case with his hip. "You're taking the plunge. I'm impressed you raided Abby's phone to get her parents' number so you could call and ask for her hand in marriage. Very nineteenth century."

"I think that's still a common practice, Peter," Chad said, giving him a droll look, "and I want to do this right. Things have been a bit off with us ever since John came to town. I don't think I've ever hated anyone as much as that dude."

"Not even Lester when he tried to steal my pet turtle in middle school?" Scott asked.

"Eh, he was a close second. But this guy doesn't even try to hide his longing for her. It's pathetic."

"Well, it spurred you to buy the ring and propose faster so maybe it was a blessing in disguise," Peter said.

"Maybe. I just want to make it official. I'm over dating, and Abby and I are old enough to know what we want. I just don't see a reason to wait anymore, although I still need to figure out the perfect time to propose. Sometimes we have these awesome random moments and I think, shit, this would be the perfect time to pop the question. I might just keep the ring in my pocket over the next few days and see if we stumble into one of those moments."

"You're going to carry an expensive ring around in your Old Navy khakis?" Peter asked, grimacing. "Not the best idea you've ever had, man."

"Leave me alone," Chad said, facing the counter as Kenneth returned with the rings. "Okay, guys, give me your honest opinions. This has to be perfect."

They spent almost an hour contemplating before Chad selected a platinum ring with a diamond in the middle and two sapphires on each side. They reminded him of the streaks in her hair and he thought she would love it. After making the purchase, Chad walked to the parking lot behind the store with Peter and Scott.

"Thanks so much for helping me, guys," he said. "I'm so excited to give it to her."

"How did you afford that anyway, man? Don't you make, like, forty thousand dollars a year as mayor?"

"Not that it's any of your business but Dad invested in a ton of stocks years ago and he did really well. He created a trust for me which I inherited when I turned twenty-five. It's not Bill Gates money but it supplements my mayoral income. And if I decide to run for state senate and win, I'll earn eighty thousand a year."

"Doubling your income," Peter said, patting his shoulder. "I like it. You'd make a great state senator, Chad. I think you should run."

"I'm definitely leaning toward it. With Abby's help, I think I can win."

"Who knew back in high school that you, Abby, and Mark would all turn out to be kick-ass politicians? It's pretty admirable, as long as you stay clean and don't turn into someone like Rydell."

"Never," Chad said, grinning. "Okay, I've got to get back to town hall for a budget meeting with Edna for the new croquet court she wants to install by the lake."

"Who in Ardor Creek plays croquet?" Peter asked.

"No idea but she wants it anyway. Welcome to small-town politics. See you guys tomorrow at the Kiwanis dinner. Can't wait to honor Nick. Thanks again." Waving, Chad walked back to town hall, his hand in his pocket clutching the ring the entire way. Come hell or high water, he was giving it to Abby sooner rather than later. Grinning, he realized that probably meant he'd be the first one to say the L-word. As long as she agreed to marry him, that was just fine with Chad.

C had finished his day and headed home to put on a suit for the Rotary dinner. Abby had gotten ready at her house and she'd texted him she was on her way in a rideshare. Calling his own lift, he met the driver outside and mulled things over during the ride. They'd both agreed to take rideshares so they could enjoy some champagne and relax a bit.

When he arrived, Chad saw John in the corner of the banquet hall, talking to Abby as she smiled up at him. Feeling his nostrils flare, he grabbed a flute of champagne from one of the servers holding a tray and headed over.

"Hey, babe," he said, leaning down to kiss her cheek. "Do you want this? I can grab another one." He offered her his glass.

"Oh, no," she said, shaking her head. "My stomach is still acting weird. I'm going to hold off for a bit."

"Did Dr. Matthews say everything was okay?"

"Yep," she said, smiling a bit too brightly, causing a tingle of alarm to shoot down his spine.

"Abbs? Are you sure?"

"We're being rude," she said, gesturing to John. "John was just telling me that he'll be sad to leave Ardor Creek in three weeks when the campaign ends."

"I bet he will be," Chad muttered, taking a sip.

"I know you're not my biggest fan, Chad, and I'm sorry we didn't connect like Abby and I do."

Chad clenched his teeth, wanting to punch the guy right in his square jaw. "Yes, well there's nothing like a great business connection, is there?"

"Okay," Abby said, stepping between them. "Dr. and Mrs. Pearson are here and they're our featured donors for this lovely little dinner. They donated a ton to my campaign at the request of Senator Dawkins and Dr. Pearson is a long-time Rotary member. Let's go say hello, Chad."

Sliding her arm through his, she led him away while John began speaking to one of the female Rotary members who'd approached the bar area.

"That guy is just baiting me now, Abbs. It's not even remotely funny."

"I know," she said, sighing. "I think he's decided it's not worth the effort to be nice to you anymore since you basically hated him on sight. It's a shame because I really wish you two would've become friends. You're both awesome guys."

"With friends like those, better watch your back and be ready for the fatal strike."

"I'm not sure that's *quite* how the saying goes, but I get your sentiment."

The dinner dragged and Chad caught John staring at Abby multiple times throughout the night which didn't help his disposition. After dessert and coffee were served and people started to filter out, Chad began counting the minutes until he could head home with Abby and rip off his uncomfortable suit.

"Well, I think the dinner was a success," John said, approaching Chad and Abby as they stood by the door saying goodbye to guests as they exited. "We're still on for breakfast at the diner tomorrow, right, Abby?"

"Yep. I'll see you there at nine a.m. sharp."

"Sounds good. I'm excited to see tomorrow's polls. I anticipate a hefty margin for you. I think we're in the home stretch."

"I hope so. No offense, but I'm done with campaigning. I just want to win and get to work. And spend time with my man." She grinned up at Chad.

"Well, I guess that's my cue. Night, Abby. Night, Chad."

"Good night," she said as he strode through the door.

"Good riddance," Chad muttered.

Turning, she swatted his chest. "You're incorrigible. He was being nice."

"He's too good looking to be nice. Guys who look like that don't need to be nice at all."

"Need I remind you that *you* look like that? You're hands down the hottest guy I've ever dated, Chad, and you're really nice. Well, most of the time," she finished, lifting her brows.

"Hilarious. Can we blow this joint? I'm melting in this suit."

"Sure. Let me just say goodbye to the stragglers and we'll head home."

Once the goodbyes had been said, they ordered a rideshare home. Abby's eyes drooped as they sat in the backseat and he pulled her close, urging her to rest her head on his shoulder.

"You didn't drink tonight, babe. Is it your stomach?"

"Mmm-hmm," she said, her tone drowsy. "We're going to chill on Saturday, right? I want to spend all day in sweats with you."

"Or naked," he said, kissing her hair. "Either one is acceptable."

Her soft chuckle surrounded them and when they arrived home, Chad noticed her exhaustion as she shrugged off her light coat.

"I'll walk Kitana, hon," he said, running a hand over her hair. "You look beat."

"Are you sure? Because I'm definitely ready to crash."

"I'm sure."

After the walk, Chad prepped for bed and crawled in beside her, pulling her close as she nestled against him. Closing his eyes, he ran over tomorrow's schedule in his head. Abby was meeting John for breakfast but her day was open afterward until the Kiwanis dinner. He had a light day too so maybe they could squeeze in a hike after she met with John. Proposing to her at the top of their favorite hiking trail, with Kitana at their side, would be pretty epic. Mulling the idea, he let it simmer as he drifted to sleep.

Chapter 24

♥

The next morning, Chad whistled as he walked down Main Street under the bright October sun. Figuring Abby was almost done with her meeting, he decided he would meet her at the diner and try to convince her to play hooky with him and head to the hiking trail. But he had one stop to make first.

Striding through the door of GDC, he smiled at Carrie as she spoke into the headset.

"Yes, sir, Mr. Grayson. Of course, we will. Okay, I'll have him call you when he arrives in a few minutes. Thank you." Hanging up the phone, she groaned. "Chris Grayson keeps calling about the patio Scott installed. He says the stones are crooked. I swear, people will always find something to complain about." Straightening in her chair, she grinned. "So, to what do I owe the honor of being graced with our esteemed mayor's presence?"

Striding forward, he pulled the ring box from his pocket. "I know Peter tells you everything so I wanted to show you the ring." Opening the box, he handed it to her with the ring nestled inside. "What do you think? Did I do okay?"

"Oh, Chad," she said, taking the box and holding her hand to her chest. "It's so beautiful. She's going to love it. When are you thinking of proposing?"

"Well," he said, taking the box and closing it before sliding it back in his pocket, "I'm smart enough to know I shouldn't tell you anything unless I want it spread all over Ardor Creek."

She gave him an incredulous look. "Me?" she asked, mouth falling open. "I'm a vault, Chad. A very secure vault."

"We'll need to google the definition of 'vault' together one day," he teased, "but I guess it's okay to tell you I'm thinking of proposing this afternoon. I want to convince her to go hiking on our favorite trail and pop the question while we're there. What do you think?"

"I think it's perfect. Peter told me you called her parents to ask their permission too. It's just so cute, Chad. I'm so happy for you."

"Thanks, Carrie. I was going to wait until after the election but, I don't know." He kicked the carpet with the toe of his shoe. "I just felt the urge to seal the deal. I think it's time."

"It certainly is," she said, green eyes sparkling.

"Okay, what do you know and why don't I know it too?" He narrowed his eyes. "Your eyes always glow like that when you have random juicy gossip."

"How dare you?" she gasped before flashing a grin. "I know nothing and abhor gossip."

"Right." Rolling his eyes, he stepped back when the phone rang. "I'll let you get that. Stay tuned for what I hope is an epic story." Crossing his fingers and holding them high, she waved before he stepped back outside.

Walking to the diner, he resumed whistling until he noticed Abby standing outside the diner, staring up at John London as he held her face in his hands. He leaned down and placed a reverent kiss on her forehead, causing Chad to leap into action. Rushing toward them, he gripped John's fancy, dry-cleaned dress shirt and yanked him away from Abby. Then, he punched the fucker right in his straight, perfect nose.

Abby spent the first thirty minutes of her meeting at the diner with John fighting waves of nausea. If this was what being pregnant entailed, she was ready to consider being a cool aunt for the rest of her life. The nausea thing was for the birds. Of course, the internal joke immediately made her feel guilty since she already in love with the little bugger growing inside her nausea-ridden body. Lost in the musings, she jumped when John waved a hand in her face.

"Abby? You with me?"

"Yeah, sorry," she said, shaking her head. "The polls are better than I expected. The Scranton paper has me up by eighteen points and the county paper has me up by twenty. I think our little power team has made a big difference. I owe you and Senator Dawkins big time."

"Happy to do it. Staying in Ardor Creek has been fun. It's made me reconsider small towns. I always loved the big city but there's something about this place."

"Tell me about your plans after you're done here. I'd love to hear what you have in mind for the future."

He named several candidates he could work for, although he planned to take a break after Abby's campaign for a few weeks. He spoke of Cassie and his desire to hopefully find someone else to settle down with one day.

"I'm so sorry it didn't work out for you guys," she said, sliding her hand over his. "Divorce is really hard."

"It is." Repositioning their hands, he laced their fingers together. "Honestly, our marriage was even harder because there was always someone else I couldn't stop thinking about."

Tensing, Abby pulled her hand away. "John—"

"It's true, Abby. I promised myself I'd work up the courage to say this to you before the campaign was over and you sent me away. I developed feelings for you when we were working together in D.C. I never said anything because I'm not a cheater but, well, Cassie noticed and it eventually tore us apart." Expelling a breath, he ran his hand over his face. "Well, it's finally out in the open. I'm sorry if this makes you uncomfortable. I just needed you to know."

Shocked, Abby opened her mouth, searching for the right words. "I...I don't know what to say, John. I had no idea."

"I know," he said, shaking his head as he laced his fingers atop the table. "When you moved away, I thought it was best you never knew. With you gone, I thought maybe Cassie and I could work things out. But we never recovered and I felt terrible. She eventually had enough and filed for separation."

"I'm so sorry. I wish you two had been able to work things out."

"When I learned about your campaign here, I called Senator Dawkins and offered to help. He was already keeping an eye on your race and we came up with the idea of me moving here for a while to help you."

"Did he know?"

"That I had feelings for you?" He shook his head. "No, although he might have guessed, but it never came up. We both genuinely wanted to help you. But I'd also read about you and Chad, and figured I had a small window to get close to you and tell you about my feelings. I didn't realize you two were already so serious. It put a damper on my plans to win you over, for sure."

"Wow," Abby said, raking a hand through her hair. "I'm floored, John. I never even guessed you were interested."

"I know. That's one of the things I love about you, Abby. You're so humble and never seem to contemplate the fact that half the guys you meet fall head over heels for you."

Shrugging, she grinned. "It's a really hard concept for someone who was called Flabby Abby during a very challenging time in her life."

"Fair enough," he said, smiling. "But I think that experience just made you stronger. You're remarkable, Abby, and I'm so lucky to be your friend. I wish we could be more but I realize now we'll never get that chance."

"Nope. For better or for worse, I'm desperately in love with Chad. Well, he's pretty great, so I guess it's for the better."

"He's a really nice guy. I'm sorry we didn't click. He knew right away how I felt about you. The guy's got some serious radar."

Laughing, she bit her lip. "I told him he was crazy. Oops. I'm never going to live this down."

Sighing, he glanced at his hands before lifting his gaze to hers. "So, where do we go from here?"

Filled with compassion, her lips formed a soft smile. "I'm very sad to say this but I think I have to fire you. You've done a great job and most certainly helped me secure the lead I'm experiencing now, but my relationship with Chad is a million times more important to me than this campaign. I think it's best if we cut ties and you go back to D.C., John."

Nodding, he rested his chin on his hand. "I think that's for the best too."

"Hopefully, after some time, we'll forget this semi-awkward conversation and go back to being friends. I value your friendship and don't want to lose you."

"You won't. Let me go lick my wounds for a while and I'll reach out once I'm ready."

"That sounds perfect."

They asked for the bill and finished up before walking outside. Turning, Abby stared into his eyes, wondering if she'd ever see him again. If she stayed in Ardor Creek and he remained in D.C., the chances were slim.

"Thank you so much for everything, John. I'll never forget how much you helped me. I'm so thankful for you."

"You're welcome." Cupping her face, he leaned down and placed a reverent kiss on her forehead.

Abby saw a flash out of the corner of her eye. Gasping, she lurched back as Chad grabbed John by the shirt and punched him right in the nose.

Chapter 25

♥

"Chad!" Abby screamed, disbelief coursing through her that he'd actually punched John in the middle of Main Street. "What the hell are you doing?" Reaching into her purse, she pulled out a packet of tissues and handed them to John. He removed a few and held them to his bleeding nose.

"I told you I was going to punch this asshole next time he touched you, Abby. I don't care if I go to jail. This guy is *not* allowed to kiss you. You son of a bitch," he said, pointing his finger at John. "I don't know who you think you are—"

"You're right," John said, holding up a hand as he held the tissues to his nose. "I'm sorry, man. That was too far."

Chad's expression fell as he processed the apology.

"Abby, I think I've done enough damage here," John said, breathing a laugh. "I'm going to go ice my nose before it swells to the size of Canada. Nice jab, by the way."

"Thanks," Chad muttered.

"Bye, Abby. Crush that bastard. I'm counting on you." With one final nod, he turned and walked to his car before driving away.

Glaring up at Chad, she shook her head. "You were just dying to punch him."

"What was I supposed to do?" Chad said, lifting his arms. "He was kissing you in the middle of Main Street."

Glancing around, she noticed people had started to congregate on the sidewalk and in the doorways of the surrounding business-es. "Yes, and now we've drawn a nice little crowd. I hope you were trying to make a scene because you've managed to accomplish that feat brilliantly."

"Why was he kissing you? I don't understand why you let him touch you when you know it bothers me."

"Because I fired him and we were saying goodbye."

"You fired him? Why?"

"Because he told me he had feelings for me and I told him I wasn't comfortable with that. We decided it was best to end our working relationship."

His throat bobbed as he swallowed. "Because of me."

"Yes," she said with a nod. "I told him you were more important to me than the campaign or anything else. Once his admission was out in the open, I felt it best we terminate our connection."

"Shit," he said, running his hand through his hair. "Now I feel bad. Will it hurt your campaign?"

Smiling, she shook her head. "I'm pretty far ahead in the polls. Barring some outrageous incident—like my boyfriend punching a guy in the middle of the street—I should be fine."

His lips fluttered as he blew out a breath. "I hope I didn't blow it. I'm sorry, Abbs. I'm a mess lately. With the campaign, and my term ending, and John here...I've just been off. *We've* been off. I hate it because you're everything to me and I don't want any tension between us."

Chewing on her lip, she contemplated him. "I'm going to ask you a question and I'd like an honest, non-joking answer."

"Okay," he said as his eyebrows drew together.

"Do you love me, Chad?"

His eyes widened as he smiled. "Hey, that's not fair. You're trying to get me to say the L-word first—"

"I said a 'non-joking' answer," she said, lifting a finger.

"That's completely unfair—"

"I'm pregnant," she interrupted, lifting her shoulders as his mouth fell slightly open. "How's that for unfair?"

Gaping at her, he worked his jaw, appearing to speak but nothing came out.

"Wow, you're speechless. Okay, I'm not sure what to do with that."

Slowly closing the distance between them, he palmed her cheeks as he stared down at her, puffs of air escaping his lungs in short bursts. "You're pregnant?"

"Yes," she said, feeling her eyes well with tears. "I was going to tell you tomorrow but it sheds some extra light on why I sent John away."

Inhaling several deep breaths, his eyes darted between hers as she grew more uncomfortable.

"Okay, this is weird. Can you please say something?"

His lips curved into that sexy-as-hell smile as he caressed her cheeks with his thumbs. "I only have one question, Abbs," he said, his voice gravelly.

"Okay." She swallowed thickly, wondering if he was going to ask her how she'd fucked up her birth control schedule so badly.

"Are you sure it's mine and not Larry's with the mole? Because I know you guys barebacked—"

Collapsing into laughter, she fell into his arms as he hugged her close. Sliding her arms around his waist, she buried her face against his chest, burrowing into him as the tears began to fall.

"Don't cry, babe," he murmured in her ear, rubbing her back as he held her. "This is amazing. I can't believe you're pregnant. Now I get why you've been barfing so much. It makes perfect sense."

"I fucked up my birth control somehow," she said, sniffling. "I'm so sorry."

"Abbs," he said, drawing back and palming her cheek. "Don't ever say you're sorry about being pregnant with our child. Do you hear me?"

"Yes," she whispered, running her hand under her nose. "I was hoping you'd be happy."

"I'm fucking ecstatic," he said, joy evident in his expression. "When did you find out? Yesterday at your appointment with Dr. Matthews?"

She nodded. "I was going to tell you on Saturday so we could have a whole long discussion and figure things out."

"What's to figure out? I love you and you love me, right? What more do we need?"

Biting her lip, she watched the realization cross his expression.

"Shit, I totally said it first."

"You totally did," she said, giggling.

"Well?"

Cupping his jaw, she ran her thumb over his lips. "Chad Hanson, I'm so deeply in love with you. You're such a warm, caring person who also happens to be extremely hot, and I'm so thankful for you."

"Abbs," he whispered, resting his forehead against hers. "I love you so much, honey."

"Do it now!" a voice called behind Chad. Abby craned her neck to see Carrie standing outside GDC with a smiling Scott Grillo behind her. "It's perfect!"

"Why is Carrie yelling at you?"

Drawing back, he blew out a breath. "Because she knows what I'm about to do. I was going to do it later today when we went hiking but, hell, I think the outgoing and incoming mayors of this amazing little town should share this moment with the residents."

Abby's heart slammed in her chest as she struggled to breathe. "Do what?"

Reaching into his pocket, he pulled out a velvet box. Abby lifted her fingers to her lips as he slowly lowered to one knee. Opening the box, he smiled up at her with love glowing in his gorgeous green eyes.

"Abigail Miller, no one would ever say our path was traditional. We started as friends—I think—and then I *really* fucked up, and you eventually came back to town to show me who was boss."

Snickering, Abby nodded. "You deserved it, buddy."

"I sure did. I never expected to fall for you, especially when you kicked my ass. But the more time I spent with you, the more I became enamored with your gorgeous smile and brilliant mind. After so many years apart, I was reminded of how caring and sweet and generous you were, and you also wore those fucking jeans that drove me insane."

Throwing her head back, she gave a joyous laugh.

"You were an exquisite warrior I knew I'd never deserve, but I still devised a master plan to win you over. By some miracle, you decided to give me a chance and, well, we'll know in about five seconds if I succeeded."

Abby's chin trembled as she waited for the question that would solidify her entire future.

"Abigail Miller, will you please make me the luckiest man on Earth and marry me? I love you so much, honey."

Overcome with joy, she nodded furiously and said, "Yes, of course, I'll marry you, Chad."

He removed the ring and slid it on her finger before rising and sliding the box back in his pocket. Pulling her into his arms, he gave her a blazing kiss, right there on Main Street for all to see. Cheers and whistles surrounded them, along with several shouts of, "Good for you, Mr. Mayor!" and "Go get 'em, Hanson!".

Drawing back, Abby laughed as she gazed into his eyes. "I had no idea you bought a ring."

"Scott and Peter helped me since they're already whipped," he joked. "I wanted it to be perfect."

"It's so perfect," she said, brushing a kiss on his lips. "Thank you."

"Good for you, Flabby Abby!" a voice called.

They both turned and yelled, "Shut up, Butch!" before facing each other and snickering.

"He's still such an ass," Chad muttered.

"*Such* an ass. I hope Cynthia's new nose collapses while they're banging."

"That's dark, babe, but I'd expect nothing less from you."

Drawing him in for another kiss, Abby drowned out the rest of the world, content to hold her fiancé for a while longer and bask in the glow of his perfect proposal.

The Kiwanis dinner that evening turned into an unofficial engagement party for Chad and Abby. Not only did they honor Nick for his years of community service and amazing food, but everyone in town seemed to be in attendance, and they voiced their congratulations.

When they arrived home, Chad walked Kitana while Abby prepped for bed, realizing she was in for several months of exhaustion if things continued as they had for the past several weeks.

"She's happy as a clam in the dog bed chewing on the new bone you got her last week," Chad said, walking into the bathroom and kissing her temple.

"Thank you for walking her," she said, smiling into his eyes in the mirror. "It's so thoughtful."

"Well, she's our first kid." Sliding his hand over her stomach, he rested his chin on her shoulder as he gazed at her in the mirror. "And we'll have another one soon."

"I was just contemplating whether the nausea and exhaustion are going to carry on during the entire pregnancy. They're really killing my vibe."

Chuckling, he slid his other arm around her waist and held her tight. "I'll help you, babe. We'll do this together."

Arching a brow, she muttered, "I mean, together is a stretch since I have to carry the little bugger."

"I'd carry the baby if I could. I think I'd look hot pregnant," he said, squinting.

"God, you're so weird. Okay, brush your teeth so we can bang. I have about five minutes left before I pass out."

"You really know how to turn a guy on, Abbs. Tell me more."

Palming his face, she playfully pushed him away and lay down in bed, not bothering to put on a shirt because she knew he'd tug it off as soon as he slid under the covers. Rolling to the side, she faced the wall and burrowed into the mattress.

"Wow, I guess five minutes was a stretch," he said, flipping off the lamp before spooning her.

Abby wriggled her butt into his cock, noting his arousal. "We can do it this way. I'll try not to fall asleep."

Chuckling, he slid his hand over her thigh and trailed his fingers to her mound. "I'll try to keep you awake," he murmured against her ear. "Relax those pretty legs, babe. I need to feel you."

Abby shivered, overcome with desire at the deep timbre of his voice. Following his directive, she released the tension from her muscles and he slid his finger between her folds.

"There you are," he whispered, finding her opening and circling it as she moaned. "Let's get you wet so I can fuck you." Rimming her core, he gathered some of the slickness and glided his fingers to her clit. He began stimulating the tiny nub as his hips undulated against her ass. The thick ridge of his cock pressed into her buttocks and she moaned as he caressed her.

"You looked so pretty tonight," he whispered in her ear as his fingers circled her clit. "All I kept thinking was, that's my wife. I get to marry that woman. You make me so happy, babe."

"Chad," she moaned, tossing her head back and straining further into his hand. "Oh, god, that feels good."

"I love touching your pussy," he said, trailing his finger back to her opening and sliding it inside her taut channel. "Are you ready?" he asked, gliding his finger back and forth against her slick walls. "I need to fuck you, honey."

She nodded, wriggling into him. Skimming his hand across her hip, he lifted her leg, drawing it to rest across his thigh. Aligning the head of his shaft with her wet core, he began to nudge inside.

"I like it this way," she said, pushing into his cock. "You feel so good and you can rub my clit while you're inside me."

Lifting his fingers to his mouth, he wet them before lowering them back to her clit. His hips moved in sure strokes, surging into her from behind as he stimulated the engorged nub. Whimpering, Abby turned her head on the pillow, arching toward him...craving connection as he loved her.

His lips covered hers, devouring her in a heated kiss as his cock and fingers took her higher. Breaking the kiss, he gazed at her, desire evident in his eyes even though the room was dim.

"I love you," she whispered, overcome with sentiment as he gazed at her so reverently. Unable to control the emotion, her eyes welled before a single tear slipped down her cheek.

"Don't cry, babe," he whispered, kissing the tear away. "You okay?"

Nodding, she cupped his cheek, his skin warm as their bodies melded together.

"Abby," he whispered, increasing the pace of his hips. "You feel so good, sweetheart. I love you so much."

Sparks of pleasure began to tingle in every cell of her skin, and she closed her eyes, concentrating on the ministrations of his fingers at her core. Her body began to tremble and she felt the orgasm on the horizon as she panted beneath him.

"Come with me, honey," he groaned, increasing the pressure on her clit while jutting into her. "I want to feel you let go...*fuck*..."

Her body snapped, back arching as he hammered deep within. A thousand shards of pleasure exploded from the nub beneath his fingers and she cried his name. Burying his face in her neck, he mumbled words of desire before emitting a deep groan. His body bucked and he began to come, shooting sticky jets of release inside her deepest place. Drowning in pleasure, she slid her fingers into the hair at his nape, holding him close as he shuddered against her.

Heavy breaths mingled as they slowly fell back to Earth, clutching each other's sweaty skin. Chad placed lazy kisses along her neck as they languished while their bodies cooled. Abby ran her nails over the back of his neck, and his resulting groan sent tremors through her sated body.

Lifting his head, he drew her hand to his lips and kissed her palm.

"Do you like the ring?" he asked, rubbing his thumb over it.

"I love it. Did you buy one with sapphires because of my hair?"

He nodded. "Is that cheesy?"

Smiling, she shook her head. "No, it's adorable. Loveable mayor Chad Hanson has done it again."

Resting his chin on her shoulder, he studied her in the moonlight that wafted through the window.

"What?" she asked.

"Let's do it soon."

"Get married?"

He nodded. "I mean, you're already knocked up so there's really no point in waiting."

"How romantic," she said, rolling her eyes.

Snickering, he nipped her. "Come on, hon. I'm ready. And I really want you to be sworn in as Abby Hanson and not Abby Miller. I mean, if that's what you want. Or, Abby Miller-Hanson. Any variation that includes Hanson will suffice."

Abby grinned. "I think I'm fine with just Hanson. It's a nice name, even though I kind of hated it for twenty years."

"I was terrified you weren't going to forgive me," he said, shaking his head. "I was so into you and you kept pretending you hated me."

"Was I pretending?" she teased, closing one eye.

"Yes," he said, playfully biting her shoulder. "You were mad for me the second you saw me at the pub. I mean, it was between me and Smitty, and although the old geezer is pretty hot, I knew I was the one who ultimately caught your eye."

"It was close for sure. Smitty's got something."

They lounged for a bit before Chad grabbed some tissues from the nightstand to tidy them up. After tossing them away, he snuggled back behind her, spooning her as he rested his palm over her stomach.

"Let's think of a date we can do it before the inauguration on January 2nd."

"Well, I have to win first. Let me do that and then we'll pick a date."

"Sounds like a plan. Let's finish this campaign and get you elected, babe."

Holding her close, Chad steeled himself for three more weeks of intense campaigning so his fiancée could cement her victory.

Chapter 26

A bby threw every ounce of energy she had into the last weeks of the campaign. Although the surrogates she'd recruited had all returned home at the end of September, she invited them back for the one debate she'd agreed to with Sterling Rydell. The four of them sat in the front row, while Chad and the Ardor Creek crew sat behind them. Abby was on her A-game during the debate and creamed Sterling on several issues. When the debate was over, Abby headed into the crowd and right into Chad's arms.

"I think I killed it," she said, pecking his lips.

"You fucking annihilated him, Abbs. Man, I'm so scared of you right now. It's hot. Let's go bang."

"Um, hi," Ashlyn said, raising her hand. "We can all hear you. I get that you're in that newly engaged honeymoon period but get a freaking room."

Abby just beamed and hugged everyone in the group, so thankful for their support. Eventually, the days grew shorter as October came to an end and, finally, the day of the election arrived.

Abby ended up winning the election with fifty-nine percent of the vote to Sterling Rydell's forty-one. It was a stunning victory and one that Abby relished. She'd set her sights on becoming the first female mayor of Ardor Creek years ago and had finally accomplished her goal. Of course, she worried about Chad, understanding he was struggling with leaving the job he held so dear.

"Don't be sad, sweetheart," she said, stroking his jaw as they lay on the couch one day in mid-November. "You're going to be such a great state senator and the mayor-elect of Ardor Creek can't wait to work with you."

He smiled as he caressed her cheek with his fingers. "I'm excited to try something new but I'm also a bit scared. Does that make me a pussy? All I've known for eight years is being mayor of Ardor Creek. You have so much faith in me. I hope I don't let you down."

"Fear is good," she said, placing her chin on her hand as her elbow rested on his chest. "That means it's important and you want to succeed. You have a lot of changes on the horizon. Husband, dad, running for state senator. It makes sense you'd be a bit scared. But you have me, and I know you're going to crush it."

"I thought about what we discussed regarding the wedding date. I think it's just weird and quirky enough to be perfect. Do you think everyone else will go along with it? Our friends and your family since they have to travel?"

"There's only one way to find out. Let's talk to my family first and then we'll talk to the crew at Thanksgiving."

"Sounds like a plan."

It turned out that Abby's family was one-hundred percent on board, which made her ecstatic. Armed with their consensus, she and Chad headed to Thanksgiving dinner at Scott and Ashlyn's home. Once they were all seated around the beautiful table Scott had fashioned a few years earlier, Abby decided to make the announcement.

"Okay, guys," she said, standing and holding her sparkling cider high. "This is going to be a bit out of the ordinary, but it's me and Chad, and we kind of dig being weird."

The group laughed as they sat around the table.

"No one is disagreeing so I guess you should continue, babe," Chad said, tugging her arm as he sat beside her.

Grinning, she made eye contact with everyone at the table: Carrie, Peter and their boys, Scott, Ashlyn and Grant, Teresa and Mark, Justine and Avery, and Terry and Brian. "It's really important to me and Chad that we're married by the time I'm sworn in on January 2nd. It's tough for my sister and her family to travel unless it's a holiday, and she wants to attend the wedding *and* my inauguration...so we've decided to have a New Year's Eve wedding!"

Everyone stared at her as the announcement sunk in.

"We've already spoken to my sister and parents, and they're on board. We want to have it at the bed and breakfast and we'd like everyone to stay over. We're thinking we'll have the ceremony at six o'clock, then have dinner afterward, and George and Lina have graciously offered to watch the younger kids and put them to bed while the rest of us party and ring in the New Year."

"We're going to be filling the place to the max, so George and Lina are happy to do it, believe me," Chad said.

"Mom said we could stay up until midnight this New Year's Eve," Sebastian said.

"Well, then, you're officially in the older kids category. Welcome to the party. You, me, and Charlie can all have sparkling cider together."

"And me," Ashlyn said, raising her hand. "Unless this baby pops out somewhere along the way."

"We'd love to have you in our cider drinking crew, Ashlyn," Abby said with a nod. "Kitana will be our ring bearer and we'd like to ask Sebastian to perform the very important job of Supervisor to the Ring Bearer. Kitana loves you so much and that means you can walk her down the aisle while she has the ring tied to her collar."

Sebastian beamed. "That will be cool."

"And we didn't forget you, Charlie. We'd like to ask you to be our official Sparkler Dispenser."

Charlie's brows drew together. "What's that?"

"We're going to go outside and have everyone light sparklers so we can get a really cool picture of me and Chad running under them when it's dark. We'd like to ask you to dispense the sparklers to everyone. It's a very important job and I hope you'll help us out."

"I can do it, Abby," he said, nodding.

"Perfect. Well, now that the jobs are assigned, we hope you all will agree to attend our New Year's Eve wedding. What do you say?"

Various looks were exchanged before everyone lifted their glass and toasted in agreement. Smiling down at Chad, she smoothed his hair as he grinned. The New Year was coming and they were ready to seize it with arms wide open.

Epilogue

New Year's Eve

C had Hanson had one true love...and she was walking down the aisle, giving him that shy, sweet smile he remembered from so long ago when he would talk to her by the lockers. Overcome with love, he swallowed thickly as she approached. She was a vision in white, with a long veil covering her multicolored hair, and he wondered what the hell he'd done to deserve her. It must've been pretty amazing because she was magnificent.

"Hey," she whispered, smiling up at him as she faced him in front of the altar Scott had built. His friend was getting pretty darn good at building altars since everyone in Ardor Creek seemed to be on a marriage binge.

Grasping her hands, he noticed they were shaking. "Hey," he whispered. "You look amazing. I can barely speak."

"That's a first," she said softly, winking.

"Are you nervous?" he asked, squeezing her hands.

She nodded. "I don't know why."

"Um, okay, this is really engaging but I think we should probably get to the ceremony, guys," Peter said, standing beside them. He'd offered to become an officiant for their wedding since Chad had performed his, and Abby and Chad had loved the idea. Plus, he was hilarious so they knew the ceremony wouldn't be boring.

"Go for it, man," Chad said, gazing into Abby's eyes.

They spoke words of love, vowing to honor each other for the rest of their days. Abby gave Sebastian a nod and he untied the rings from Kitana's collar, handing them to Peter.

"Great job, buddy," Peter said, taking them. "You can go sit with Mom now."

Sebastian scurried over to the empty seat beside Carrie and she kissed him on the head before placing her arm around his shoulders.

Abby and Chad exchanged rings and Peter proclaimed them husband and wife. Cupping her jaw, Chad kissed her before whispering against her lips, "Just imagine them all...*you know*. Then you won't be nervous."

Laughing, she shook her head. "I can't believe you remember that."

"I remember. You were so pretty that day as you smiled up at me. I might have been in love with you back then and not even known it."

"Okay, we can debate this later because there's no way that's true. Come on. Let's get this party started."

Facing their family and friends, they lifted their joined hands before jogging down the aisle. Everyone headed into the large reception room where the band was situated in the corner, ready to go. After dinner, the small kids left with George and Lina, and the rest of the group tore up the dance floor. Abby even danced, which made Chad extremely happy. He only made fun of her for stepping on his toes a few hundred times.

As midnight approached, they donned their coats and headed outside, lighting the sparklers that Charlie handed out. Chad and Abby got some great pictures, courtesy of Terry who'd offered to be the wedding photographer. Heading back inside, they counted down the seconds until the New Year started and the band broke into Auld Lang Syne. Pulling Abby close, Chad swayed with her as the band played.

"Happy New Year, Mrs. Hanson," he said as his forehead rested upon hers.

"Happy New Year, Mr. Hanson. This is fucking perfect."

"I know. Thank god our friends understand how weird we are."

"Is it really that weird to get married on New Year's Eve?"

"Yes, Abbs, it's super weird."

Snickering, she nodded. "Okay. You would know."

Donald and Claire approached them, and he patted Chad on the back. "This is a nice ceremony, son. I'm so happy for you two."

"Thanks, Dad. We're so glad you brought Mrs. C. as your plus-one."

"Me too, dear," Claire said.

Clearing his throat, his dad placed his arm around Claire's shoulders. "Now, I didn't want to give you your wedding present until things were solidified, but Claire and I have talked it over and we're ready."

"I thought the check you gave us to help pay for the band was your present, Dad," Chad said. "We don't need anything else."

"Son," he said, cupping Chad's shoulder. "Your mom made me promise to look out for you in the time I had left. She knew in her bones you'd have your own child one day and I'm so thrilled she was right."

"Me too, Dad," he said, pulling Abby close and kissing her temple.

"You two are going to need somewhere besides that tiny apartment to raise my grandbaby, so I'm giving you the house as a wedding present."

Chad felt his eyes grow wide. "No way, Dad. That's your and Mom's house. You built your life there. I won't let you do that."

"He's thought a lot about this decision, young man," Claire said, "and the thing is, the two of us don't each need a big house to live in. Donald is going to move into my home and give you his."

"Oh, Mrs. C., that's too much," Abby said. "We can't accept that."

"I won't take no for an answer, kids," Donald said. "I love you both very much and I know this is what Karen would want me to do. Now, I've spoken to Mark and Peter and they're going to help us with the deed transfer next week after Abby is sworn in."

Abby appeared stunned as tears welled in her eyes. Turning her head, those brown eyes searched Chad's, and he lifted his shoulders. "They seem pretty adamant."

"If you're sure, Donald," Abby said, shaking her head. "I just...this is more than I could've ever asked for. I love Ardor Creek and I love you too. I would be honored to raise your grandchild in the home where you and Karen raised Chad."

"Then, it's settled," Donald said with a firm nod.

Chad threw his arms around his dad, patting him on the back as he gave him a strong hug. "Thank you, Dad," he said, his throat raw with emotion. "I love you."

"I love you too, son," he said, pulling back. "Now, don't make your old man cry, okay? This is a happy day."

"Speaking of, Donald owes me a few more dances before the band stops playing. Come on, dear. Let's show these kids how it's done."

Chad watched Mrs. C. lead him away, floored by his dad's generous gift. Looking at Abby, he shook his head. "I don't know what to say. I had no idea he was going to do this."

"It's so generous. I see where loveable Chad Hanson gets it."

"He's the best. I hope I'm half as good a dad as he is."

"You're going to be great," she said, sliding her arms around his waist.

"Come on," he said, giving her a sweet kiss. "I finally got you to dance with me. Don't stop now. A little bit longer and then we can bang."

She scrunched her features. "It's like you're incapable of going more than a few minutes before mentioning sex. It's unbelievable."

Chuckling, he arched a brow. "Well, you're stuck with me now, babe, whether you like it or not."

Extending his hand, he clutched hers tight and led her onto the dance floor beside their beloved friends and family. After many more dances, he led her to the room, where he was absolutely, one-hundred-percent focused on sex. And, for once, his wife didn't even perform the nighttime ritual first. She just removed her dress and seduced him, which, to Chad, was the definition of a damn near perfect wedding night.

Before You Go

W ell, we finally made it to Chad's wedding! I hope you enjoyed your time in Ardor Creek. Are you ready to read Justine and Gary's story? I'm so excited to bring it to you. I think we all fell in love with them in **Desires Uncovered** and it's time they got their happy ending too! You can read their story, **Passions Fulfilled,** now!

P lease consider leaving a review on your retailer's site, Book-Bub, and/or Goodreads. Your reviews help spread the word for indie authors so we can keep writing smokin' hot books for you to devour. Thanks so much for reading!

About the Author

♥

Ayla Asher is the pen name for a USA Today bestselling author who writes steamy fantasy romance under a different pseudonym. However, she loves a spicy, fast-paced contemporary romance too! Therefore, she's decided to share some of her contemporary stories, hoping to spread a little joy one HEA at a time. She would love to connect with you on social media, where she enjoys making dorky TikToks, FB/IG posts and fun book trailers!

ALSO BY AYLA ASHER

Manhattan Holiday Loves Trilogy
Book 1: His Holiday Pact
Book 2: Her Valentine Surprise
Book 3: Her Patriotic Prince

Ardor Creek Series
Book 1: Hearts Reclaimed
Book 2: Illusions Unveiled
Book 3: Desires Uncovered
Book 4: Resolutions Embraced
Book 5: Passions Fulfilled
Book 6: Futures Entwined

Made in the USA
Middletown, DE
12 September 2024